Bunny Man's Bridge

A Short Story Collection

By Ted Neill

Dedicated to the other founding member of *Love Contusion*, because, oh my God does love hurt, but I'm still grateful for all the happy memories.

Table of Contents

^D*A story featuring Daniel*

^S *A story featuring Sidney*

Introduction

According to legend, on the outskirts of the town where I grew up, there was once an asylum for the mentally deranged. The shuttered ruins, crumbling and moss covered, could still be visited in a boggy dell deep in the woods. The asylum had been closed because of inhumane treatment of the patients, but one of the patients never really left. He still lived in the woods near the property. Nobody knew his real name. He had been abandoned there when he was a child. With no family to claim him, no home to return to, he simply lingered in the forest, close to the only home he had ever known.

The asylum had been built more like an eighteenth century prison than a hospital: all heavy, mortared stone, windows barred with iron, and bare cells—their floors strewn with straw like animal stalls. This one patient in particular kept to himself, eventually settling in an abandoned farmhouse where he managed to be self-sufficient, growing his own food. He eschewed human contact, preferring the quiet company of a few dozen wild rabbits, whom he domesticated, eventually breeding hundreds. The rabbits were his sole companions, and he knew every single one by name.

Years passed and people in town left "the Bunny Man" alone, writing him off as an eccentric hermit. He was undisturbed until some high school students snuck onto his property one night. They were three football players and three cheerleaders: letter jackets, cardigans, knee socks, and all. The girls thought the bunnies were cute and wanted to take some as pets. The football players wanted to prank the Bunny Man, with the old ring-and-run on the doorbell.

It was all innocent enough, at least until the girls tried to run away with some rabbits for pets. One of them tripped and fell on a stolen bunny, breaking its neck.

That was when the Bunny Man snapped. The long dormant madness erupted as the Bunny Man chased the teens through the midnight forest, a forest he knew well from years of wandering and foraging. They did not stand a chance. Lost, separated, and frightened, the teens were easy prey. All that was ever found of them were scraps of their bloody letter jackets and cardigans. And then there were the dismembered body parts found hanging from the nearby train trellis that dated back to the Civil War.

There was no real evidence for the Bunny Man story, of course, except the landmarks of the train trellis, an old graying farmhouse, and a crumbling stone building that many assumed had been the asylum, although some said it was instead a prison for the Union army, others for the Confederacy, maybe both. After all, the lands of Northern Virginia had changed hands numerous times throughout the war.

But evidence isn't as important as imagination when it comes to legends. The story of the Bunny Man was passed down from one generation of teenagers to the next as they took midnight trips down the dirt road to the sagging farmhouse or trekked through the woods with flashlights to the asylum—boys carrying six-packs and bags of weed, glancing furtively over their shoulders, hoping that the girls hanging onto their arms might let them cop a feel . . . or more.

Later iterations of the Bunny Man legend evolved to have the Bunny Man actually wearing a pink Easter Bunny costume in order to lure children to his farmhouse, where he would do unspeakable things before slaughtering them. The traffic tunnel that led to "Bunny Land," as the woods were called, even had a pink bunny spray-painted on its side, complete with murderous red eyes and a bloody mouth filled with overlapping fangs.

As preteens, we would hear whispers about the Bunny Man among our older siblings or babysitters, and we were, predictably, deeply jealous of our elders who would actually get to visit this midnight land of terror and adventure. In that way, a trip to Bunny Land became a rite of passage and, eventually, a fitting image I landed on when thinking up a title for this little collection of stories.

The stories are old and young at once. Old in that they were written almost twenty years ago, so long ago that I come across passages, characters, and snippets of dialogue that I have no recollection whatsoever of writing or even sketching. And to be frank, at risk of sounding immodest, I've been surprised, once and a while, by a twenty-year-old's level of craft and insight. But I ascribe this more to luck and having the great writers I was reading at the time to learn from than my own talent.

But these stories are young as well, written as they were by a young man, himself on the cusp of adulthood at the time, and influenced by more than a little bit by Raymond Carver (isn't everyone at some point?). I was looking back on a childhood that had come to a close, while trying to process the present and all its possible paths. As I wrote, I knew I was trying to prepare for this thing called "adulthood," which was stretching before me, a great unknown.

The characters are experiencing the typical things of that stage in life: coming of age, the sudden onset of insight, the stumbles of early relationships, the mystery of sex, the role of gender, and the wider question of what it meant to be a decent, successful human being. Some of the stories look back, others forward. Others are zany fantasies, tragi-comedies where I was trying to make sense of the confusion, to disarm the impending horror of growing up with humor.

A fair warning: when I submitted some of these stories to my university literary magazine my senior year in college, they were rejected. My friend Rasheed Newson, now a successful writer in his own right, was an editor that year and my mole on the selection committee. Although the editors had read the stories blind, he knew mine, and later shared with me that, in the opinion of the selection committee, my stories were the best submitted that year; however, they also concluded that whoever the author was, he or she was "clearly and deeply fucked up in the head." Despite Rasheed's own vote of confidence, he was unsuccessful in convincing them to publish a single one.

Certainly, there were short stories I wrote back then that don't deserve to see the light of day. They are not included here, although I don't know if the ones that remain in this collection will save me from the same judgment.

I can certainly see the stories' limitations today. The struggles and development of oblivious, sheltered, and privileged white kids in the suburbs are not exactly new territory in American literature. But on reflection, as I reexamined the settings, the characters, the plots, I saw elements that still resonate today: growing signs of diversity in traditionally white enclaves, reexaminations of views of sexual orientation, income disparity, a disappearing middle class, and a growing pathological obsession with celebrity and self-promotion. At least, I hope contemporary readers might find a few minutes of entertainment while they read this on their device, waiting in line at an airport or riding the bus or subway to work. At best, perhaps they will gain a flash of insight or a moment of identification.

That brings me back to the image of Bunny Man's Bridge, that train trellis traversing the dark unknown was a rite of passage, but it was also a sort of intersection where youthful exuberance, responsible adulthood, misplaced anxiety, and lurking insanity all met—suspended over some great abyss of loss and potential failure. Poised at that point in life, to a young man, they all felt like very real possibilities.

They still are.

I hope you enjoy reading.

—Ted Neill

1.

Vespers

Summer mornings, for me, were spent waking up over a bowl of cereal, followed by an hour or two of reading whatever "classic" novel my father had me reading at the time—usually one that he had been forced to read as a child, such as *Oliver Twist* or *Great Expectations*. Reading was followed by "homework" exercises, which could range from verb conjugations to algebra. All this was in some effort to keep my brain from "rotting" during the long, idle days when both my parents were away at work.

My afternoons were spent playing Nintendo, reading comic books, or splitting my attention between the comic books and the Nintendo while my Ethiopian friend, Masterwal, took his turn as player two. It was only when my older brother got home from his job as a lifeguard at the neighborhood pool and commandeered the television, or my parents got home from work and chivvied us away from it, that Masterwal and I would head outside to play in the woods or the creek behind the house.

The battles Masterwal and I fought together, whether through our comic books, video games, or just in our imagination while we passed hours in the woods, always teetered on the edge of the apocalypse. We were always cast as the heroes. We knew none of it was real, but it was all based on some assumption that when we came of age, those life and death struggles would, indeed, be our own. After all, that was what one story after another told us, whether in the plot of a book, movie, comic, or video game: young preteens were often called to an adventure that required saving the world.

At fifteen, my brother Rick seemed to be on the cusp of such adventures. He already had a driver's permit. And he would routinely get up early on Saturday mornings and disappear all day with my Uncle Gary in a quest for fish. They would come back in the evening, sunburned, smelly, and mosquito bitten, but usually with enough fish for dinner. At the table, we would hear of their exploits—about the one that got away, the one that pulled the boat at least twenty yards before they could reel it in, or the one Uncle Gary had to club to stun long enough so that it didn't flip the boat altogether.

What incredible adventures, and surely the sort of dress rehearsal one would need for the greater ones that lay in store.

I had seen the lake they fished at on a school field trip. Rick explained the size of the lake to me in terms of *thousands of acres.* There were islands in the lake on which no one was allowed to set foot because they were wildfowl refuges. But the real reason, Rick explained, was because the islands were burial grounds for First Nation peoples. Ghosts would follow any trespasser and haunt them forever. The most well-known island was Vesper Island. A few years before, a girl's body had been found there. I wondered if the murderer who had left her there was still haunted by the spirits of the Native American dead whom he had disturbed.

I never saw Vesper Island from the shore. Nevertheless, it loomed large in my imagination. I could picture the trees, with their cobwebbed branches disturbed by the occasional breeze, which carried the stench of carrion and the whispers of voices from beyond the veil. First Nation peoples did not actually bury their dead on Vesper. Instead they made high lofts in the trees where they would lay the bodies to rest. I imagined the canopy of Vesper Island was cluttered with such lofts, holding the decaying remains of noble chiefs and braves, while sentinels of ravens stood watch from the branches or rotated in slow circles in an overcast sky above.

9

So when it came, Rick's invitation for me to join them on my first fishing trip felt like a leap into manhood. The night before, I couldn't sleep. I woke every few hours, checked the clock, groaned when I realized it was too early, then rolled over. Finally, at 4 a.m. I couldn't go back to sleep, so I went down for breakfast and started to gather my tackle. Rick was slower and came down a bit later. The night sky was lightening, and the outside was noisy as birds sang out their morning calls. I practiced my cast on the driveway, letting the bobber click against the asphalt. I was still outside when my uncle's pickup truck rolled down the street and stopped in front of the house.

"Hey there, Daniel." He stepped out the driver's seat holding a 7-11 Styrofoam coffee cup. "You ready to catch some fish?"

I nodded. Behind the truck was a trailer with a sixteen-foot aluminum rowboat. I laid my rod in the bed of the truck and climbed onto the trailer. The boat boomed with artificial thunder when I stepped inside. I rocked the sides as if huge waves were threatening to tip us over.

"Can I ride back here?"

"Not until we get in the water. You can ride up front with us."

I sat in the middle seat. Gary and Rick talked about the weather, its consequence on the fish, and the best spot to start fishing.

"Looks like there's a front coming in. That will have them all screwed up," Rick said, looking out at the clouds on the horizon. I wondered what he read in their shapes and textures.

"Hard to get them to bite," Uncle Gary said, his fingers drawing down the turn indicator.

"Yeah."

"We'll still catch some, won't we?" I asked.

"Of course, we will," Gary said.

◆

The lake was an hour away. Rick helped me into the boat before he climbed aboard himself. He baited the lines and explained to me the different riggings—Texas rigging, Carolina rigging. Meanwhile, Gary dipped the motor into the water and pointed us across the lake.

The only sound not drowned out by the wind was that of the waves smacking like hand claps on the bottom of the boat. We stopped along a point and cast our spinner baits. I liked using the spinner bait. It made my rod feel like there was a fish on the end whenever I wound it.

After an hour or so without a bite, Gary finally said, "I can't believe we haven't caught anything yet."

He moved the boat along the shore and into the shallows, where a creek fed into the lake. Grassy banks closed in on either side of us. Gary told me to aim my line towards them. A faint odor lingered in the air. I had smelled it before in creeks but had never thought much on it.

"It smells fishy in there, but no one's biting," Rick said. If the fish close enough for us to smell were not biting I decided that I would have to make bolder casts for fish farther from the boat. I made a strong cast from the boat. My line traced a perfect arc from my rod towards the bank, a textbook effort . . . until it snagged in a tree. I shook it, but it was stuck fast.

"I'm sorry, Uncle Gary," I said, as he reeled his own line in then pointed the boat towards the trees.

"It's all right, that's fishing. It happens to everyone."

We floated under the branches, but neither Gary nor Rick could reach the feathery bait. Batting it with oars was not effective, and neither was shaking the line. Gary gave it a final fierce tug. The

11

hook broke free and shot between Rick and me, then landed in the water.

"Now why couldn't that land in the boat?" Gary wondered aloud while reversing the motor and bringing the bow to where the ripples were spreading in a circle. Rick reached into the water but, after a few seconds, shook his head and rolled his sleeve back down.

"Can't find it."

The spinner bait was lost.

"I'm sorry, guys."

"No problem, that happens." Rick said. "I'm going to rig his line with a rubber lizard, since we're not catching anything with the spinners. The fish may have moved out into deeper water." Rick replaced the lost hook on my line then skewered a purple rubber lizard with it. He showed me how to cast it and how to pull it in slowly so that I could feel it bumping along the bottom.

"If he actually catches anything with that kiddie rod, it's going to give him fits trying to pull it in," Gary laughed and sent out a cast.

"The more bumps, the better!" Rick said to me while tying my line. "Bass like to hang out under things, and when they see this guy bumping along, they'll grab him."

I did as Rick told me. It was more exciting than the spinner bait, because every tug and snag I felt through the line could be a fish. A few times, when my hook got caught, I would wind hard. The reel would make a squealing noise. Gary and Rick would look at my bent rod, but once they saw the end was stationary, they would know it was simply a snag. Rick would back the boat over the place where the line disappeared into the water, and it would come loose.

The morning wore on. I took off my flannel shirt and tied it around my waist. The air was warm and thick with humidity. Haze hung over the lake, and the day promised to be a hot one. I imagined Rick and Gary must be disappointed that we had not caught anything. Maybe I was bad luck. I was about to say so when I felt an unmistakable tug on my line.

"He's got a fish," Rick cried out, sliding across the thwart towards me.

I knew it too. The line danced back and forth in the water as I tried to reel. The rod was bent like a candy cane as I spun the handle of the spinner.

"What do I do?"

"Keep reeling," Uncle Gary said, his eyes bright. The fish flashed on the surface of the water. I could see its white underbelly, and then all I could see was the line slicing though the water and going under the boat. I heard the fish's tail slap the underside, and then it was alongside again. I went to grab the line.

"No, don't grab the line. I'll get it." Gary reached over the side and lifted out the two-pound bass by the lower lip. He dislodged the hook and held the fish out to me.

"You caught a fish, son!"

Rick slapped me a high five. My hands were shaking. Gary held the fish out to me. I knew he wanted to let me hold it, but I pretended not to realize it and kept both hands on my rod. I didn't want to touch it, much less stick my fingers in its mouth. I was disgusted by its gaping red gills and pungent odor. I felt a strong wave of sympathy for the fish, hanging there, its body trembling, its jaw stretched open.

"You want to keep it or throw it back."

I knew it was small for a bass, but it was the only catch of the day. We needed at least *one* fish.

"Keep it."

Gary put it in the back of the boat by the battery and took us away from the shore. The sun was a white ball in the hazy sky, its light diffuse, our shadows faint.

"Not biting much today," Rick said.

"I think it's because it's been so hot. They've probably moved into cooler water," Uncle Gary said. He stopped the boat in between two islands, where he thought the water would be cooler, then set us adrift. Rick decided to use the same bait as me. Gary switched to firetails. My fish was still on the bottom of the boat, its mouth rhythmically opening and closing. Once in a while it would flap around, making the same artificial thunder on the bottom of the boat that I had earlier that morning. Finally he was still, except for his fin, which would move pointlessly in the empty air.

"Is he dying now?" I asked.

"Ah, I'll take care of him in a minute," Uncle Gary said.

I had seen my brother stick a knife in a fish's head to kill it before cleaning it. I hoped that they would do something like that to my fish. It seemed humane. I turned my back and cast off to the side. I felt better if I could ignore him.

The brown end of a cigarette floated by in the water. I looked up to see Uncle Gary lighting another one. It surprised me that he would litter in the lake that he spent so much time fishing in. I hoped that Rick or Gary would catch a fish so that I wasn't the only one pulling them into the boat to die. Uncle Gary finally rigged a line and dragged my fish in the water. Gary's face was obscured by his sunglasses and hat. I could no longer recognize him.

"What are you doing?" I asked.

"Getting the water to go through his gills. It will revive him."

"Oh."

We had drifted into parts of the lake I had never seen before. I asked Rick how close we were to Vesper Island.

"It's farther down that way, past these little islands. We usually fish around there in the afternoon."

"There's fish there?"

"Oh yeah, there is."

"How close do we go?"

14

"Depends on how we drift. We can go real close if you want a look."

"No, it's okay."

I left my line alone while I fumbled in my jeans to make sure I had brought my pocketknife, although what use it would be against ghosts I was not sure. My rosary would have been better, and I regretted not bringing it. Gary was slowly bringing in his line. Rick was casting. Neither seemed too concerned about being close to Vesper.

"Here he is," Gary said as his rod twisted and bent. "He's big." Gary stopped reeling and adjusted the drag on his rod, hoping to tire the hooked fish out. His face fell, the rod going still and straight.

"Damn."

"Got away?" Rick asked.

"Yep, that was *my* fish. I should have just hooked him instead of playing with the drag."

"There'll be others."

"Not the way they're biting today," Uncle Gary said.

Rick said he was getting lots of nibbles where we had drifted. Gary heaved the cement anchor over. Only six feet of cord went out before it stopped.

"It's only that deep out here?" I asked.

"Yeah, it's only six or seven feet here."

"I can touch that deep in the pool."

"I bet you can."

"Want to try?" Rick laughed. I didn't answer.

◆

It was nearing noon, but it felt like it should be two. Gary reeled in his line and put his rod in the boat before settling next to the motor and revving it. Water bubbled at the stern as the propeller churned. "I'm taking us over to eat lunch."

"Sounds good." Rick pulled in his line and set it across the bow. Gary turned the motor on high and took us into the open center of the lake. The noise from the motor was becoming softer. The boat was slowing down. I looked back to Gary, who was leaning over the stern. We were now going half the speed as before.

"What's wrong?" Rick asked.

"I forgot to charge the battery yesterday," Gary said, gunning the sick motor.

"How much juice does it have left?" Rick asked.

"Enough to get us to the other side, I think. We'll have to use the oars to maneuver for the rest of the afternoon, otherwise there won't be any power to get us home."

He cut the motor, and we floated listlessly by a peninsula that ended in a small, mossy point. Gary opened the cooler and passed around the sandwiches my mother had packed for us. The sun had disappeared behind a bluish gray cloud cover that threatened rain. I was glad for the shade, hoping that we would call it a day soon. I had grown a bit bored. But Rick had other plans. He dropped his line and let the boat drag it along the bottom. Just a moment passed before the handle shifted and clanked against the side. Rick dropped his sandwich on the thwart and picked up the rod. The boat drifted backwards as the fish struggled to get away.

"That's it, you got him!" Gary said.

The fish didn't surface until Rick had brought it within Gary's grasp. When our uncle lifted it out of the water, its body looked smooth as polished silver. Its mouth could easily encompass my fist.

"That's a good six-pounder," Gary said while he proudly handed the bass to Rick.

"We'll have to get a picture when we get home," Rick said.

Lunch was eaten between casts afterwards. Gary caught two next, so he felt that he had made up for the one that had slipped away earlier. The air grew cooler with the sun hidden, and we rowed farther from shore, floating in between some quiet, wooded islands. The wind died down, and the water's surface grew calm and glassy. Mine was the smallest of the four fish we now dragged behind us.

"This is a good time of afternoon to catch fish," Gary said, his reel whistling as he cast. The boat floated among the islands, and Rick would row us away from the shores when we got too close. I saw the last small island glide by quickly as the wind picked up and moved us into open water. There was still one island ahead, larger than the rest, sitting alone in the dark water. ·

"Is that Vesper?"

"Yep, it is," Rick said, flicking his rod.

"Should we anchor and fish here for a while?" I asked, worried that we were drifting too close to Vesper.

"I'm not getting any nibbles here. How about you Gary?" Rick said, turning his head around to look at Gary.

Gary shook his capped head back and forth. "I think we'll just let the wind push us along. That bank over there goes out real far; we can fish all along it if the wind keeps up."

"Is there good fishing here, near Vesper?" I asked.

"Some days it is," Gary said.

I continued to cast. Gary and Rick were oblivious to the menacing island. Its trees were indeed overgrown. Their branches crowded each other so much that they hung out inches above the water. A hawk flew across the water and alighted on one of the highest boughs that crowned the top of the island. I imagined that from the hawk's perch he would be able to see the tops of the burial lofts and the skeletons adorned in their jewelry and headdresses.

I went back to my fishing pole, letting my gaze wander as I reeled my line. The lake had grown dark as it reflected a sky the color of charcoal. An imminence hung in the air. The water was calm, but on Vesper I could see green leaves spinning and twirling in the breeze. Finally, a rumble of thunder reached us.

"We need to clear the lake," Gary said, turning to the motor.

"If we use the motor now, we'll be rowing all the way back to the marina. We can row over to Vesper," Rick said.

I was alarmed by his calm.

"Isn't it haunted?" I asked. "By the First Nations people?"

"You mean Indians?" Uncle Gary asked, dipping an oar into the water and moving us towards Vesper. By the tone of his voice, I knew it was better not to correct him or even answer at all. Over his shoulder, sheets of rain had obscured the farthest shore. The boat was beginning to rock with the waves as the surface of the lake trembled in the wind.

Rick took a paddle to the bow. I turned my head to ask Gary if I there was anything thing I could do to help, only to see a lightning bolt sear a treetop on the shore. A violent clap of thunder followed, as if to convince me of what I had seen. The first large rain drops were plopping into the water and banging the bottom of the boat. I untied the flannel shirt from my waist and covered my head.

Rick paddled us towards a clear spot on Vesper then jumped into the shallows, landing with a splash, his feet sloshing through the water as he dragged us to shore to beach the boat. Gary tied the line of our fish to the cooler, which he deposited at the edge of the water.

"Come on, Danny, get out of the boat!" he said.

I set a foot out of the boat and into the water. With a reluctant step, I was on Vesper Island. A large wooden sign stood before me:

VESPER ISLAND
KEEP OFF
WILD FOWL REFUGE.

Rick pulled the oars and rods from the boat while Gary flipped it over. I was surprised to see the ground was bare of leaves. Instead, the earth had been packed down by the passage of geese, who'd left a scattering of guano and feathers. Gary pulled a blue tarp out from his day bag and ran inshore with it. Rick and I followed.

"We shouldn't be here, Rick," I whispered.

"Would you be quiet?" he said.

Gary ran a spool of line between two trees, tied it, then threw the tarp over, forming an A-frame tent. We slipped under, just as the rain began to pelt the outside. We pulled the ends of the tarp under us and sat on them to keep the wind from taking it.

"That came up fast." Uncle Gary was shaking out his hat.

"Is the boat safe? The water is really going to rise," Rick said.

"Yeah, I pulled it up far."

"And the cooler?"

"Even if the water gets that high, it's not going anywhere. I lodged it in between some roots."

"I bet those fish are scared," I said. "Being stuck in that choppy water."

"Well, Danny, if we're here long enough, I'm going to go out there and clean one of them for dinner," Uncle Gary said.

We sat for a while in silence, listening to the rain beat down and the thunder rumble overhead.

"Well, what do you think of your first fishing trip?" Rick asked.

I swallowed. The only thing on my mind was if we were in danger. "Should we be here?"

"Why not? You afraid of ghosts, little brother?"

When I said nothing in reply, Rick laughed. Uncle Gary spoke up and clapped me on the shoulder. "Don't worry, no Indian ghost is going to get you. People come here all the time." He parted the sides of the tarp and reached outside. When he pulled his hand back inside, he was holding a crushed beer can. "This a great drinking place. Come here, tell a few ghost stories. . .. always makes the girls scared. Then they want to cuddle."

There was another peal of thunder, and we heard branches breaking and falling through the canopy. There was a crash right outside the tarp. I screamed. Rick laughed and told me not to be such a "sissy." He started to lift the tarp. I pictured a broken burial loft fallen from the trees smashed onto the ground, just waiting on the other side, a ghastly moldering body sprawled out in pieces, a skull surrounded by a halo of broken beads and decaying feathers, grinning at us with a cursed smile.

Rick pulled his head back under the tarp. His expression was undisturbed.

"Big tree branch just fell, Uncle Gary. Did you set us up under a dead tree?"

"No, but that was close."

"There aren't First Na—Indians left on this island?" I asked, pulling my shirt off my head and putting it on properly.

"They're long gone, not a trace. You don't need to worry," Uncle Gary said, apparently finally feeling some sympathy for me.

I swallowed the lump that had formed in my throat. A new noise came from behind the tarp, but even I knew it was not supernatural: it was the grousing and honking of Canadian geese. Evidently they had come to the island to hide from the storm as well. The tarp was a bit of a curiosity to them: they would poke and peck at it with their bills. Rick would poke back, and the geese would scatter before returning again to repeat their investigation.

A half hour passed. There was little left to talk about. Dinnertime was nearing. My stomach ached. Gary decided to make a run to the cooler for what was left of our lunches. The thunder kept up for another few minutes. I grew more bored than scared. Finally the rain slackened, and the thunder eventually became less frequent. Gary pulled the tarp down to reveal a whole gaggle of geese milling about the place. They scattered as we emerged. It was not unlike visiting a petting zoo. I noticed a gosling dragging a tangle of fishing line with a lure in it from its leg. I bent to grab the gosling and free it, but it ran away. I had the sense that my uncle and brother would just grow impatient with me if I pursued it anyway.

The waterline was higher, the cooler nearly submerged. The fish, invigorated by their temporary respite, were pulling on their lines as they tried to swim out to the lake. With my shirt removed from my head, I took a better look around the island. The rain had stopped. The drops from the branches above now were from shake-down showers only, as squirrels danced from tree to tree. The clouds had brought with them an early evening, the crickets already beginning to chirp.

Crushed beer cans floated along the shore, picked up by the lifting water, their labels faded by the sun. I could count half a dozen black spots where other trespassers had built campfires. An empty, half-melted marshmallow bag hung snagged from the branches of a bush next to a crumpled page from a *Penthouse* magazine. The trunk of one of the larger birch trees was scarred with the initials of previous visitors. Someone by the initials of JT declared that he or she "WAS HERE" along with MJ, CC, BK, CF, JY, and TP. The woods were open; any underbrush had been trampled by geese, or the frequent trespassers, who had left cigarette butts and discarded airplane-sized bottles of liquor.

The trees were empty of any burial lofts.

The boat needed only a little bit of pushing since the water had risen. The lake was still choppy. Gary dragged up the cooler and set it in the bed of the boat. Rick picked up the lures and packages of bait that had spilled out when he flipped the boat. He left all of our trash and torn wrappers on the ground. When I tried to pick them up, he told me just to leave them. I still tried to leave them in a small pile—I'm not sure why—before I crawled into the boat. Uncle Gary gunned the motor.

"The battery seems like it's recovered some. With the wind at our backs we just may make it back without paddling."

Gary banked us away. We bounced hard on the lake's surface. Vesper Island receded. By the time the marina was in sight, all we could see were the lights on the pier. The night around us was dark and moonless, but for some reason, I was not scared. We stopped at a fast food drive-through for cheeseburgers with fries and chicken fingers on the way home. I fell asleep after.

◆

I was supposed to watch Gary clean the fish when we got back to the house. He used his electric knife. They were, to my surprise, still alive. He never stabbed them in the head before he started to saw their flesh off, head to tail. I was able to stand just so that Uncle Gary's body blocked the view of what he was doing. That way I watched without watching. My dad explained the real meaning of Vesper. It was a Latin word for "end of the day" or "evening." I didn't show much interest, I guess, because then he asked me if I was tired. I said I was and headed off to bed.

I took the steps one by one and put my dirty clothes in the laundry chute. I brushed my teeth and put on my pajamas. My comic books were waiting on the bedside table. On the top of a stack, a female superhero, who was at once sinewy and buxom, was winding up for a punch to send her adversary into an abyss. The glossy pages shimmered in the light of my lamp, but something about them seemed like a lie all of a sudden. I opened the drawer, shoved them into it, and knocked it shut. I tossed over and stared at the wall, waiting for sleep.

2.

Tree House

My father stared at his digital watch, its settings on "stopwatch" as it counted the seconds, and even the more rapid milliseconds. Whatever numbers he was waiting for appeared, and he lifted the top of the grill, releasing a pillar of smoke that cleared to reveal the drumsticks and chicken breasts he was cooking. I moved to throw the brown leaves that I had been collecting into the ash catcher. I watched, transfixed, as their edges glowed, and they turned to dust from one touch of the glowing red embers. It was dangerous, but dad wanted me to learn how to respect fire. I had managed, so far, not to be burned. When I ran out of brown leaves, I used green ones, which took longer to shrivel and gave off thicker smoke. But the transition from green to ash, then to nothing, still fascinated me.

The phone rang inside the kitchen. I was not old enough to answer, so it was nothing more than background noise to me, adding to the sound of bird chirps, lawn mowers, and HVAC units that hummed in our neighbor's, the Blumfields', backyard—they insisted on AC even on mild evenings like this one, when my parents would open the windows so that breezes could waft through the screens.

My mother came out onto the deck. "The Whitlocks just finished the tree house that Jim had built for Kent and Susan. Danny, why don't you go over and see it?"

My father cautioned me to be careful as I bounded down the steps of the deck. I was still small enough that I could have slipped and fallen through them, as they did not have backing like inside-steps, but I managed and ran around the corner of the house, looked in both directions, crossed the cul-de-sac, and made my way between two parked pickup trucks. I was too young to read the company lettering painted on their sides, but by the size of the tools and wood scraps in the truck beds, I knew the tree house had to be huge. The side yard was marked with piles of sawdust and trails of crushed grass, which I followed around back.

My eyes were fixed upwards as I rounded the house. Within the trees of the Whitlocks' backyard a huge tree house waited—more like a tree *palace* to me. Its shape was reminiscent of the pictures I had seen of the fire-watch towers that park rangers used to scan the forest canopy for signs of smoke. This was no ramshackle clubhouse like the other neighborhood tree houses. It was a true house, with a shingled roof, a hinged trapdoor, and shuttered windows.

"Look who's here," Linda Whitlock said, turning her attention from her children, Kent and Susan, who were looking down from the windows of the tree house. I was too distracted to be polite and acknowledge her. Instead I stared at Susan, who was waving at me.

I had one older brother, Rick, but Kent and Susan felt like siblings too. Their mother, Linda, was more of an aunt to me than neighbor. Once I had fallen face first from my bike onto my driveway. My nose was broken, and I was blinded by my own blood. Linda had been across the street. She was wearing a white dress and had been about to leave for a formal dinner with her husband Jim. She was watching Susan and Kent play HORSE at their new basketball hoop while she waited for Jim to finish a business call. After I fell, I groped around on the ground screaming, my disorientation and confusion only ending when Linda lifted me, pulled me to her chest, and carried me inside, whispering, "It will be okay. It's all okay."

I opened my eyes in the bathroom, where Linda and my mother were wiping the blood from my face and applying pressure to my nose. Once I could see, I noticed all the scarlet red tissues littering the floor. My Sesame Street shirt was wet with blood. I looked up to see Linda leaning close to me. The bodice of her dress was red and stuck to her frame the way material does when it is soaking wet. I started to hiccup with fresh cries, afraid I would be blamed for ruining the dress. Linda ran her hand through my hair and said, "It's okay, Danny. It doesn't matter."

But my mother paused. "Linda, I'm so sorry. We'll pay—"

"You will not."

"You'll be late for your dinner."

Linda scoffed. "We're already late. I'll be changed and ready to go before Jim even gets off the phone."

That was a year ago and hardly on my mind as I moved beneath the tree house to find the entrance. I stumbled over a plywood scrap as I walked, since all my attention was turned upward. The carpenters were collecting their tools. Jim Whitlock, his polished bald head reflecting the sunlight through the cloud of cigar smoke enveloping him, was talking to the foreman. Jim did not notice me. He usually didn't.

"Come on up, Danny," Susan said. She lowered a rope ladder down to me, but after one step I was too terrified to climb its wiggling struts. Linda lifted me up through the trapdoor instead, guiding me into Susan's waiting hands. I clutched at the sides until my feet were safely on the floor.

Susan and Kent competed to show me the best features of the tree house. Jim had arranged for a telescope, a zip line, skylights, and even secret compartments. As Susan lifted me up to a window I waved to Jim, but he still didn't wave back. I wondered if I had done something to make him angry.

◆

"Kent, my tummy hurts," I said, my arms folded across my stomach. I had spent the night at the Whitlocks' while my parents were at the hospital with Rick, who had fallen during basketball practice and broken his arm. For breakfast I had eaten my first bowl of Honeycombs. More accustomed to the low-sugar, organic cereals my mother insisted on serving, the Honeycombs were not sitting well with me.

Jim walked past carrying his briefcase. "Come on, Danny. Be a man," he said.

I tried. I wasn't. My stomach continued to hurt. I remember feeling inadequate. I looked to Kent for reassurance, but he had turned on the television. Once Jim was gone, I asked, "Kent, can we go to the tree house?"

"Sure." He said it so fast, I wondered if he had really been paying attention to the TV at all.

◆

"The Whitlocks found a possum in their downstairs closet," my mother said in the front seat of the car one night.

"How did it get there?" my father asked, his hands resting on the wheel.

"One of the interior decorators left the sliding glass door in the basement open."

"Mom, why don't we have our basement finished?"

"We don't need to. We have enough room."

"So do the Whitlocks," my father said. I didn't understand my father's tone. It sounded critical. Jim had told me that getting a basement finished was a good thing. He was going to have a pool table and a bar down there.

◆

After a soccer game, my family pulled into our cul-de-sac. A brand new red Jaguar waited in the Whitlocks' driveway. I walked over to take a closer look. I liked the silver cat on the hood and leaned in for a closer look, but Jim appeared from the garage with his bag of golf clubs slung over his shoulder. "Don't touch that, Danny boy." He was chomping on one of his unlit cigars. I noticed Linda at the doorway leading into the kitchen, but she said nothing to me and instead slammed the door after Jim.

The next week, a rival blue Mercedes appeared in the Whitlocks' driveway. My parents took furtive looks at it and spoke to one another in low voices, which always meant that something was upsetting them, something they did not think they needed to share with me. I had to eavesdrop to find the answers.

I knew "adult" subjects were always broached after I want to bed. So one night, I crept down the hallway, past my brother's bedroom where he was already asleep, and moved one step at a time down our staircase to listen to my parents talk. They sat in the living room, which was not far from the bottom of the steps. I listened, holding onto the banister, ready to bolt upstairs if one of them turned around.

"Jim bought that Jag without talking to Linda about it first," my mother said.

"So he bought the Mercedes to appease her?"

"No, Linda bought it to get even with him. He's making her take it back."

Silence followed. I pressed my face up against the banister to try to get a view of their expressions. The wood was cold and smooth against my face.

"It's probably pretty restless in that house tonight," Dad said.

◆

I was walking home from school alongside a neighbor's fence. It had been fashioned to mimic a rustic, split-rail fence you might find on a farm, miles away from the suburbs. I was pretending there were actually dairy cows and horses on the other side. The fence came to an end at the Whitlocks' yard. I heard voices in the back, behind the house. I put down my backpack on the front lawn and wandered around on the flagstone walkway. Kent and one of his new friends from junior high school, Greg, were in the woods at the base of the tree house.

"Hey, Danny." Kent acknowledged me then turned back to his work, pulling something through the underbrush. It was a twisted cable of some kind that snagged and ripped at the leaves of the saplings along the ground.

"What are you guys doing?" I asked, still standing on the outside of the woods, uninvited.

"Fortifying the tree house so no one can get to it," Kent's friend Greg said from the tree house. I didn't like his voice. It had just a hint of cruelty in it that I recognized from the bullies who teased the kids with learning disabilities, the ones in special classes, at school.

"What's that wire?" I asked, pointing to the cable Kent was stringing around the perimeter of the tree house.

"Barbed wire."

"That stuff is dangerous."

"Not for older people," Kent said.

"Can I help?"

"No, you're too little."

I stood quiet for a moment, watching Kent yank the wire to the height he wanted. When it was about level with my neck, I asked, "Kent, if it doesn't hurt older people, then how are you going to keep *them* out?"

Kent stopped and let out an exasperated sigh.

"I think I hear your mother calling, Danny."

She wasn't. She wasn't even home, but I left anyway.

◆

Susan was away at college, Kent was an upperclassman in high school, and I was a sixth grader when Jim finally asked Linda for a divorce. The phone rang during dinner, and my mother decided to take the call in the other room. Dad, Rick, and I ate quietly, trying to listen. The loudest sound among us was the breaking of rolls and the scratching of forks on our plates. Mom's food was cold by the time she returned.

"That was Linda," she said. "Jim just told her that he wants a divorce. They told Kent, and he locked himself in his room. They haven't told Susan yet. Linda thinks there is another woman, because Jim kept saying he was sure they both would meet 'other people' quickly."

My mother wasn't hungry after that. When Rick and I cleaned up, I wrapped her plate in foil in case she woke during the night hungry, but by then it did not look very appetizing. The fat on the chicken had hardened into white lumps and a film had formed on the gravy. I didn't know how she would ever be able to eat it. It looked less like dinner and more like a mess. I threw it away.

◆

Kent left for college the next year, leaving Linda to sell the house alone. I never saw Jim again. From my window I could see all the people that came to look at the house. I could also see Linda wiping her eyes as she closed the curtains in her room at night.

Eventually, a SOLD sign went up in the front yard. I kept the grass mowed for Linda, free of charge. We all waved good-bye as she drove away in her compact car, loaded with boxes and suitcases. She and my mother remained best friends, and we saw her regularly, but Kent and Susan did not come back into town from school very often.

◆

I quickly got used to the Whitlocks' house as the Durrands' house. They were one of the first black families in the neighborhood. I remember my mother saying something about hoping they felt welcome. The Durrands and my parents actually became pretty good friends. Their oldest son, Andre, became a good friend of mine as well. We were in some of the same classes at school, and both of us made the varsity soccer team. After our games, we would sit on his back porch with cold water and ice packs, resting our feet on soccer balls. The tree house loomed at us from the overgrown woods. Birds would not land on it, but occasionally a squirrel would climb up a tree, jump on the house, scamper across the shingles, maybe look inside, then—uninterested—continue up the trunk of the tree that ran floor-to-ceiling through the house. One Saturday, Andre's mother came outside after getting a phone call from one of the neighbors.

"Andre, the Hensons found a possum in their garage," she said laughing.

"That's what they get for keeping that door open all the time," Andre said.

"I know, that's what I told them," she said.

"The Whitlocks found a possum in their closet once," I said after she had gone back inside.

"No, really? Which one?"

"It was the one downstairs. It came in when they were having the basement finished."

"Did it die down there?"

"I actually don't know.'

Andre stretched his hamstring and rotated his foot. His shin pads sat, discarded and grass-stained, on the ground next to him. My shirt and shorts had similar stains, as well as a rust colored one where blood had dried. Andre looked up at the tree house.

"We have to take down the tree house, you know."

I sat up.

"No. Why?"

"It's falling apart. Half the roof is caved in, and the tree it was built around has grown so much that the floor is buckling and the shingles splitting."

"But it's cool. We could fix it up."

"Or die trying. I don't know if black people do tree houses, anyway."

I was not sure what to say to that, so I just stayed silent. Andre continued, "My mom will pay us to take it down. It will probably take a day or so. We can do it this summer, when school is out. You want to help?"

"I don't know."

♦

Andre and I were both sweating from working in the heat, but we did not dare remove our long-sleeved shirts or thick work trousers. They were our protection against the rusted nails and brown recluse spiders that were all over the tree house. Andre and I had succeeded in tearing most of the structure down; only the platform that had been the floor remained. The scraps made a jagged, termite-infested pile that both of us were afraid to touch unless at the end of a rake. We took turns knocking out the four diagonal supports that

31

held the platform up to the tree. When only one remained, Andre swung his sledgehammer at it. The beam shook but didn't give.

"Your turn," he said, leaning on the handle of his hammer.

I looked at the last support. The other three lay broken on the ground. A millipede crawled in and then out of a rotted hole in a plank of wood. I tapped a fungus-covered shingle on the ground with the end of my own sledgehammer. A rusty nail threatened my foot. I started to lift my hammer, but couldn't.

"I'm too tired. You do it."

"You sure?"

"Yeah, I'll just stand over here."

Andre gathered his strength and swung the sledge. I listened as the monstrosity fell but never lifted my eyes from my feet. Andre was standing over the wreckage, posing like John Henry.

"Dan and Andre, one. Tree house, zero," he declared.

"Yep, I guess."

"We'll pick up the scraps tomorrow. My little brother and his friends want to scrimmage before it gets too dark."

"I don't know if I can."

"We'll go easy on them."

"They would have to go easy on me. I'm pretty tired. I should just go home."

"Aw, man."

"Sorry."

"Well, come on, we'll take the tools in."

We picked up our weapons of demolition—hammers, saws, and crowbars—and carried them off to put away in the garage. I looked back at the ruins of the dark and moldy tree house one last time. It looked crumpled and expired, like a smashed jack-o-lantern.

3.

Quarry

There was a quarry down old Route 29 where Kurt and I would go to drink beers and talk. I loved that quarry; it was immense and beautiful. The far wall was so huge and far away it was usually obscured by haze. It was probably dust now that I think about it. The place reminded me a lot of the Grand Canyon. It was crazy to look at those walls and think about how much dirt they used to be buried under and how many millions of years it took for it all to form.

It was a good place to sit back and think, nice and peaceful in the evenings when all the trucks and machinery had been shut off for the night. It was our escape. After a tough day at school we'd go there. Kurt didn't have a lot of friends. I was respected at school, because I smoked and got in trouble a lot, but that didn't make you friends. Kurt was respected too, but that was because he was so fucking big. He was just a big kid. He could bench three hundred in his sophomore year. He was the only sophomore in the three hundred club. So he was respected, and I guess the guys in the weight room were his friends, but he always had to be tough around them. But he really wasn't like that.

So we were outsiders. We were each other's only good friend, but that was okay. We had the quarry. None else knew how to get in but us. Most people had seen it from the Route 29, which ran by its northern rim, but that was only a passing glance through the trees. Kurt and I figured there had to be a back entrance. So one day, we spent hours driving through the woods along these back roads, which we hoped would lead us to the southern side. The work paid off. We found an old entrance that looked like it hadn't been used since the forties. The gate was rusted and closed, but not locked.

33

Kurt nosed it open with the car. The road was hidden under grass that grew up to the windows of the car. The wheels kept falling into tire ruts that we couldn't see but that told us we were on the right path. We drove right up to the rim, and for the first time, we could just stand there soaking in the enormous size of the whole damn thing. That old entrance became our place. Fuck everyone else; we didn't need their parties. They would never see the quarry.

When we finished our beers, we'd fling the bottles over the side. It was so quiet there we could hear the eerie whistle they made as the air rushed over their openings. Then they'd land in the lake below us. The quarry was at least five hundred feet deep, maybe more at the center. But right below the southern rim, it was only about sixty feet down, and right below was a still quarry lake, the water navy blue.

One day when I was watching my beer bottle spiral down and plop into the lake, I had a crazy idea. I turned around and looked past Kurt. He was against his car, tilting his head back for a drink. There was an old road behind him that ran up a slope, which was treeless because it was just bulldozed slag from the quarry. Topsoil had been thrown on top of it, and this silky green grass grew all over it. I walked past Kurt and his car.

"What are you doing, Sidney?" he asked.

I ignored him; I was deep in thought. I walked up the hill. It was a good fifty feet high and fairly steep. I was catching my breath at the top when Kurt came up. We could see a little farther into the quarry from where we were. I could see cars flashing for a moment as they passed by the gap in the trees on the northern rim. I started running down the hill. It gave me huge momentum. I ran towards the edge. I was flying. The grass was passing by me in tall blur. The bottom of the quarry was opening up in front of me. I stopped abruptly at the edge and looked down. There was a shore of slag about five feet wide between the wall and the lake. I have one eye, so depth perception is a little hard for me. It made the bottom seem close and far at once. The vertigo was exhilarating.

We could clear it.

"What are you doing?" Kurt asked.

"Kurt, let's do something crazy."

"What?"

"Let's drive a car off this cliff."

"What?"

"Just like a movie. We'll get some beat up jalopy, back it up that hill," I was running back towards the hill now. "Ride that baby down and off the edge."

"And we'll be *inside* the car, as it goes over the edge and down?"

"Yep."

"Are you fucking nuts?"

"Nope."

"We'll get killed."

"No, we won't. It's not like we'll be some drunk driver going off into a river. We'll plan it. We'll be careful. Methodical, like stuntmen."

"We'll drown, Sid."

"We'll have scuba tanks in the car."

Kurt was quiet a minute. He looked down at the lake. It would be a frightful drop—and completely awesome. I don't know what went through his mind right then, but he looked down at the drop, back up to the hill, and then at the drop again.

"All right. Let's do it."

It was sunny that afternoon. The sun was on my face and I felt good, like anything was possible.

◆

We each bought notebooks to write down a list of things we would need. We were going to be organized and systematic about things. First, we thought about how we would keep from drowning and wrote down: *scuba tanks.* My brother Mitch and I were both certified divers and had our own equipment. If we would be swimming free of the car, it would probably be best not to wear shoes. So we wrote down, *aqua socks.* Of course, we would need goggles: *goggles.*

We carried the notebooks with us everywhere. I'd work on mine during class. I drew a diagram that I thought was pretty close to scale. I figured the forward motion of the car would get us over the shore, but how far would we make it? And how deep was the water? That was an important question. We went to the quarry that afternoon to figure it out. It was kind of strange to be there, on business. It seemed like we were violating the serenity of the quarry somehow, like conducting business in church or something. Kurt had brought a lead weight tied on some kite twine. I told him to throw it over so it landed just a few feet from the shore. The weight made a little silver splash, then the only indication of its existence was the string that it was pulling through Kurt's fingers. The line stopped.

"It's on the bottom," he said.

I looked down at the string. The white line of the string going down diagonally into the navy blue water made me dizzy; I think it was the angle. But it was also like a doorway into another world.

"Pull it up."

We pulled it up carefully. I took the point where the wet part of the twine began, and Kurt walked away towards the gate with the weight. This way we could tell how deep the water was. I watched Kurt walk to his car, then past his car, and he didn't stop anywhere near it. He was at the rusty gate when he looked back at me with the little weight in his hand.

"That's deep!" he yelled.

I looked at the string. It was definitely wet from my fingers onward.

"That *is* deep."

This was going to work. I knew it.

◆

The Stunt, as we called it, was all we talked about. It was all I could think about. I didn't pay attention in class, unless I thought it would help me plan for the stunt. Physics class helped with this. I was smart. I just didn't get good grades, because I was a slow reader. But all my teachers admitted that I was brilliant. I would walk by the honors classes and look in on all the "smart" kids. I'd have liked to see some of them put their noodles to work on our little project. Of course, they wouldn't; we were doing something they would never do. They'd be sitting at their preppy little parties, getting slightly buzzed and thinking they were the new rebels without causes. They'd grow up into their lives of banal suburban subdivisions, mundane minivans, and missionary positions, whereas Kurt and I would have this majestic vision of us plunging through air and into a rising blossom of parting water to look back on forever. And them? They would have nothing but a void or just boring memories of hours spent over books, calculators, or keyboards, studying for the next test, cranking out homework, or writing the next essay.

We would end up ahead. We'd live life to the fullest, without regrets. It didn't take a genius to see that.

Kurt came up with a few suggestions, but I was the real brains behind the operation. I realized that the impact on the water would be pretty fierce, so we would have to secure the scuba tanks so that they wouldn't hit us in the back of the head—an object in motion, you know. There would be a considerable impact too. *Helmets,* I wrote down. At the same time, we would have to be able to pull the tanks out of the car. They had to be secured, but we had to be able to get them free quickly. *Bungees,* I wrote down. Then I realized that Kurt had never gone scuba diving before. *Scuba lessons.*

◆

When the weather got warmer, Kurt and I climbed the fence into the neighborhood pool. It was Friday night. We had almost gone downtown, but we decided that we had work to do. I went over the basics with Kurt, about breathing slowly and evenly.

"Now, you're going to be pretty excited, so just remember: deep breaths."

"Yeah. Deep breaths," he said as he lifted the mouthpiece near his lips, bobbed his head up, then went down. He looked at me from underwater. He looked like a two-hundred-pound peach fly with his big pink goggles. He gave me the thumbs up sign and then surfaced.

"Sid, don't you think you should do this too?"

"I can do this in my sleep, man."

◆

We decided we would have to have a protocol, a routine, so we didn't panic when we went under. We sat at the top of the slag hill rehearsing what we would do. Land. Unbuckle. Mouthpiece. Un-bungee. Swim. L.U.M.U.S. We would launch with the windows down. That way, by the time we reached the un-bungee step, we figured the car would have filled with water, equalizing the pressure so that we could open the doors and swim out.

L.U.M.U.S. became our secret word. When we saw each other in the halls at school we would say: "Hey, what's up, L.U.M.U.S?"

"Not much, L.U.M.U.S."

People would try to figure out what we meant. I remember this girl in the lunchroom asking us if we were in a secret society or something.

"Something like that," I said.

One day when I was at my locker, Kurt came up to me.

"Sid, I just realized something," he said.

"What's that?"

"The windshield."

"What about it?"

"All that pressure when we dive. It—it may come inside and pin us."

Kurt had a good point. We would have to take the windshield out. But then the water would be slapping us in the face at fifty-some miles an hour. That was unacceptable. I was kind of sore at having to change something so fundamental, so late in the game. Maybe I was just angry at myself for not thinking of it. But Kurt was right. Then I realized the solution was not to take the windshield out, but to have the car land bottom first. The only way to guarantee this was by making the back as heavy as the front. We would have to put something very heavy back there. We decided that old car batteries would work. There were always a ton behind gas stations. My brother Mitch worked at the nearby Exxon, so we got fifteen from him. We kept them in the woods behind my house.

My parents were curious about what we were doing. I didn't tell them. They wouldn't approve or understand. But they didn't pry. They never did, as far as my life was concerned. Mitch was their favorite, even though he was the one who shot my eye out . . . but I digress. Anyway, Mom and Dad would say The Stunt was poor judgement, plain stupid, reckless, dangerous, and all that. But they were old, as old as that rusty gate that had originally barred our way into the quarry. I would tell them someday afterwards, when I was older, and they would be amazed. But they wouldn't understand now.

◆

We had everything set. All we needed now was the car. Between us, we scraped together 250 dollars from odd jobs and birthday money. We looked up the cheapest used car lots in the county. We wrote down the addresses from the smallest black and white ads in the yellow pages. The first place was Henry's Used Auto. The place was just what we were looking for: old cars, gravel lot with grass growing up through the stones. It was an overcast day. If it was a new car lot, it wouldn't seem appropriate, but since it was a used car lot, the dead sky and drops of rain on the hoods seemed to add to the cars' dilapidation. It was not like we wanted to drive a brand new car into the quarry. That would be crazy.

A guy in an orange rain coat and white cowboy hat came out of the office. I told Kurt to talk. He was big, so I reckoned the guy would think he was older, and strangers look at me funny because of my eye patch, like they are trying to figure out if it's real or if I'm just trying to look like a badass. I busied myself looking at a station wagon with wood paneling. It had rust all around the bottom. It couldn't have gone for more than two hundred, I was certain.

"How you all doing?" the salesman asked.

"Fine," Kurt said, trying to pitch his voice low. "Are you Henry?"

I pretended to be looking under the car, then I kicked the tires.

"Nope, Henry is my boss. He's not here on weekdays. I'm Jeb."

"Oh, well. I thought he would be, since it's his Auto World and all." Kurt laughed a little. He was trying to be funny. He always came off as an idiot when he tried to be funny.

"You boys interested in a car?"

"Yeah. Yeah, we are. Something basic, minimal."

"You have a certain model in mind?"

Kurt turned around and looked at me.

"Uh, no," I said.

"You *both* looking for a car?"

"Well. We're brothers. We have a farm, and we need something to carry around hay in," Kurt said. I couldn't believe Kurt was trying to lie.

"Then you need a truck."

"Uh, we have a truck. We need something smaller, that will fit into our barn," I said.

The guy was staring at us. He had sized us up and knew we were wasting his time.

"How much do you boys want to pay?"

I figured if he thought we had more money, he'd be a little more cordial.

"About five hundred."

I saw Kurt's eyes get big at my lie, but he tried not to look at me. Instead he rubbed his hands on his thighs.

"Well. Why don't you come into the office, and we can sit down and talk about financing, check your credit history, and I can give you an APR."

Now Kurt looked right at me, his mouth open.

"We were going to pay cash," I said, as cool as I could be.

"I'm sorry, but we don't do cash transactions. You can come inside to talk about financing if you like, otherwise I can't help you boys."

41

Kurt and I were both quiet for a second or two. I patted the fender of the car I was leaning on and stood up.

"Well, thanks for your time then," I said, all business-like.

"Have a good day," Jeb the salesman said before he turned his back on us and walked back to his office. Kurt and I got into his parent's car, which we had borrowed for the afternoon. He started the engine and the wipers. The rain pinging on top of the car and the gravel hitting the undercarriage sounded the same as we pulled off the lot. We had planned on going to more lots that day, but we went home instead. We never talked about The Stunt again. We never went back to the quarry.

4.

Michael's Story

I was happy because all my best friends were with me for the New Year's Eve holiday. Brent and Andre, along with my girlfriend Inez, had arrived at my parents' cabin in the mountains on the thirtieth of December. We were all excited. The four of us hadn't been together since August, when we all had left for our first year of college. After my parents went to bed, we stayed up telling stories from high school. Andre eventually fell asleep on the couch. Brent and I continued talking, with Inez listening on the couch beside me.

Eventually her body's presence next to mine became too much, and we went upstairs to bed. She was supposed to sleep in her own room, but with my parents already asleep, they would never know if I just . . . visited. We brushed our teeth, and she crawled into bed, sliding across the sheets to me. I liked the feel of her thighs around mine. We kissed. Her mouth was cool and tasted like peppermint toothpaste. I took off her pajama top, but not her bottom. She was from a good Catholic family and still didn't feel right about that. It was okay. I loved her, and it didn't matter. I rubbed her breasts, and we came from grinding on each other through our clothes.

Brent and Andre made fun of me, because Inez and I had been together for two years, and we still had not had sex. I told them it didn't matter. I knew we would be married someday.

It didn't matter.

◆

The next evening was New Year's Eve. My parents were taking part in a Progressive Dinner: each course was served at a different cabin. We would be serving dessert and toasting to the New Year at my parents' place. Brent, Andre, Inez, and I stayed at our place setting up decorations, dessert trays, and champagne glasses. At seven-thirty we went down the mountain to meet the roving party, which was at the Connors' cabin for the main course.

All the grownups were there and excited to see young people. I introduced Brent, Andre, and Inez. Everyone was excited to hear about how we liked college. People wanted to quiz Andre about what it was like to play soccer at a Division One school. Brent entertained folks with some magic tricks, while my parents looked on with approval.

But Inez was the star. She was all charm and eloquence. It didn't hurt that she looked amazing. When Mr. Conner sat down at the piano, she knew all the old songs he played then sang a few Bolivian Christmas songs in Spanish and even a few in Quechua, which impressed everyone. Everything was great. The grownups liked us. My friends were having fun. It was a successful New Year's, as far as I was concerned.

I was in line for the buffet when my mother came up to me.

"Danny, I need a favor."

"What's up?"

"There's a boy here; he's the Hachettes' son, and he doesn't know anyone, and there's no one here his age."

"How old is he?"

"Fourteen. He's handicapped and a bit . . . awkward. Can you guys let him hang out with you?"

"Sure thing."

"He really likes UVA. I think he'd like to go there. Maybe Inez could talk to him about it."

"Yeah, I'll get her."

Sure enough, Mr. and Mrs. Connor were chatting Inez up about Bolivian culture when I sidled up to them. It took a moment, but I was able to peel Inez away. She filled a Styrofoam plate with food, and we followed my mother downstairs.

The lower level opened out onto a deck where the furniture was covered in tarps for the winter. A TV was playing next to the fireplace. But otherwise the floor was quiet; everyone else was upstairs. The kid, Michael, was sitting on a footrest near the TV. He was a little fat and had bushy black hair. One of his wrists was bent downwards, and when he turned to us he had to use his feet to twist his torso around. They were motions he seemed to be used to. He spoke with a bit of a stutter, but I think that was because he was nervous about talking to college kids.

"Dan, Inez, this is Michael," my mother said.

I shook his hand. It was fleshy, and he had a weak grip. "My mom tells me you like UVA."

"Yes," he said, after a few attempts to get the word out. We were patient while he made the effort.

"I go there," Inez said.

Michael had a lot of questions to ask. Inez's answers were a bit vague. I had the sense she wanted to go back upstairs where she was the center of attention for a bigger, more sophisticated audience. She could be that way sometimes. The conversation stopped, and she looked at me.

"What kind of music do you like, Michael?"

I could tell by the angle of Inez's head that she was growing irritated with me. She just wanted to go. I tried to pretend as if I didn't notice. But I did.

"Temptations. Four Tops. I listen to the Oldies but Goodies station," Michael said.

I asked about movies next, and TV. He had not seen anything new or anything rated above PG. Inez was sitting next to me, her arms crossed and her foot bouncing. We had finished the food on our plates, but I kept talking to Michael. Inez was poking holes in her plate with her fork.

"I'm going to see what Brent and Andre are doing," she finally said, in the most chipper tone she could.

"Sure, okay," I said. Michael and I kept talking. Apparently he spent a lot of time on his computer. I wasn't familiar with any of the games he mentioned.

"I grew up with an 8-bit Nintendo. We were all excited when they upgraded to 16 bits."

Michael laughed, a little too loud. "Those graphics were Stone Aged."

"Yeah, well, it was better than playing Pong on an Atari."

◆

My mom came down and told us that the party was moving to the next cabin. Did I want to take Michael back to our place with us?

I said sure; it would have been mean to leave him now. I invited him, and he got excited, sort of giggling like a little kid. I helped him with his jacket. Brent, Andre, and Inez were waiting for us on the front porch, their breath curling about their heads in the cold air. Brent and Inez started for the car. Michael grabbed my arm while he negotiated the steps. It was just like my grandmother used to. Andre drove us back to the cabin. Michael sat in the front. I was in back with Brent and Inez.

When we got to the house, the dog jumped on Michael and he squealed. Andre sat down and started flipping through a case of old CDs. He asked Michael what kind of music he liked and read some of the bands we had brought up for the trip. Michael didn't know any of them.

"I listen to the Oldies but Goodies station. It's what my parents like," Michael said.

"Well, it's time we diversified your interests," Andre said, and slid an Outkast album into the stereo.

Michael eyes got big. He looked scared at first, but it didn't take long for him to start bobbing his head.

"I like this!"

Inez was sitting by the fireplace, warming her back. I was on the coffee table, facing her. Michael and Andre were on the floor in between while Brent practiced a few more card tricks before the rest of the partygoers arrived.

"So, what do you guys do at college?" Michael asked.

"Stress," Inez said.

"How about you, Andre?"

"Well, a lot of my time is taken up with soccer practice."

Michael got a bit quiet, as if he didn't know what to ask next, like he had hit the bottom of his list of questions. Then I realized, he had probably never been able to play sports. I cleared my throat and looked over to Brent.

"Brent, what do you do at college?" I knew I could count on Brent for a laugh.

"Eat, drink, and be merry!" Brent bellowed, and fell into his *Monty Python and the Holy Grail* imitation. Michael laughed, although he hadn't seen the movie or heard of Monty Python. Brent was funny anyway. He was always funny, and having an audience who had never heard any of his jokes before offered him new possibilities. He sort of took over from there, and we just listened and laughed.

Andre got up and went to the kitchen where he mixed a drink, occasionally responding when one was called for. He came out and sat with us. He had two mugs and handed one to Brent.

"What's that?" Michael asked.

"Baileys and cream," Brent said.

"Baileys . . . is that alcohol?" Michael asked. I saw Inez touch her forehead and look down at her knees.

"Ah, yes. Yes, it is, actually," Andre said, looking at me. I could read his expression. He was afraid he had made a mistake, that Michael would rat us out to our parents for taking some alcohol.

It didn't help when Michael asked, "Are you all twenty-one?"

Andre, Brent, and Inez just laughed. Inez got up to make her own drink.

"Do you want a drink, Mike?" Inez asked. I wasn't sure why she did that. It made Michael uncomfortable. He sort of curled into himself, his bent wrist pressing against his belly.

"No," he said. He shifted on his seat, his eyes moving towards the door. He probably wished he hadn't come.

"It's all right, Mike. I don't drink. We'll keep these guys in line," I said.

Brent was rapping along with Outkast. Brent is white as white can get, so Andre found this funny and started rolling on the floor with laughter.

"You know this song?" I asked Michael.

"Nope."

"Put on the next track," Inez said, sitting down with her own mug. "I'm sure he has heard it." I got up and got some water for me and Michael. When I came back, I hit "skip" to move to the next song.

"Why didn't you bring me something, honey?" Brent said, holding out his empty hands.

"Because you are a lazy fucker."

Michael thought this was really funny. I realized we all were showing off a little for him. The next song came on, and Inez got up and started to dance, holding her arms up over her head and moving

48

her hips in a slow orbit. Her breasts pressed against her shirt, and her mouth opened just a little before she bit her lip and looked at me.

I saw Michael's eyes look at her, move down to Inez's breasts and her thighs too. He wasn't discreet about it. He probably didn't know better. I got up and danced with Inez; she pressed her body against mine. I felt a little crazy for her just then. She had that effect on me and enjoyed it. When the song was over, we sat back down.

Michael's eyes were really big. He didn't seem too shy any longer and straight out asked, "Have any of you actually done the deed? You know, had sex?"

Inez's sat up, then took a long sip of her drink.

"Well, it depends on what you mean by 'sex,'" Brent said.

Michael didn't know what to do with this information.

"I'm waiting for marriage," Andre said.

"You fucking liar. We all know you are a total dog," Inez laughed with mock indignation. "Should I start listing them all?"

She didn't wait for him to answer, instead she followed with a litany of girls from high school onward. Andre interrupted her after she had begun to enumerate his partners on her second hand.

"Wait, we never had sex; it was only making out, you know, 'outercourse.'"

Michael seized on this. "What is that?"

Andre started to explain, but I stopped him, scenarios of being yelled at by my parents for "corrupting" poor Michael already running through my head. "Andre and Inez are just joking, Michael. *Right* guys?"

But I was too late. "So Andre *has* had sex?" Michael looked back and forth between us.

Everyone was giggling now. I realized I was just making things worse. I sighed, "Yeah, Andre has. But a lot of people wait,

Michael, and that's okay." I was proud that I had the opportunity to say this in front of Inez, to let her know that I was all right with this.

Michael turned to Andre. "What does sex feel like?"

Andre sipped his drink. I thought he would do a spit-take, but he was real composed and looked at the floor before turning back to Michael. He had that look a father might have before giving *the talk*.

"You really want to know?"

"Yeah," Michael said, as if it could be explained, sort of like you could explain getting a vaccination or a root canal.

Inez blurted out laughing so loudly and uncontrollably that she snorted. Then she ran into the kitchen with Brent. It pissed me off.

♦

The grownups started to arrive. Michael's parents were some of the first. His mom was pretty, and his dad was stocky and had bushy hair like his son. They sat down on the sofa flanking Michael. They looked worried. He talked to them for a half hour while the rest of the guests came in with champagne and cakes in their hands. I didn't know what Michael was saying and I was nervous.

I was setting out more desserts on the kitchen table, along with red and green napkins left over from Christmas, when Michael's dad came up and grabbed my shoulder.

"Michael said he really had a good time with you guys. Thanks for being so nice to him."

"Not a problem."

"He says he's a fan of some band named 'Out There' or something."

"That would be Outkast."

"Guess I'll have to look them up."

"Yeah, that's Outkast with a K."

"You mean instead of a C?"

"Yeah, it's sort of their . . . thing."

"All right, well, I'll remember that. Outkast with a K." He clapped me on the shoulder and smiled. "Thanks again. You all are good kids."

"Sure, anytime."

He grabbed a brownie and went and talked to my mother about her dessert dishes.

◆

Once the house was flooded with older people, Brent, Andre, and Inez went upstairs to the loft. Michael was listening to Mr. Connor's hunting stories, which would keep him busy a while. When I came up to the loft, Brent asked me,

"Dan, what does sex feel like?"

Inez leaned on my shoulder and said, "Dan, have you done the *deed?*"

They both broke down in giggles. I was glad that Andre spoke up. "Come on guys, weren't you curious at that age?"

"No," Inez said.

Of course, she wasn't.

◆

At midnight, we all danced and sang *Auld Lang Syne.* All the men lined up to give Inez kisses on both cheeks, like they all had suddenly become Latin. I hugged Brent and Andre.

"Happy New Year, lazy fucker."

"Happy holidays, you big douche."

When I saw Michael and his parents leaving, I went to the door and slipped Michael the Outkast CD and winked at him. He stuffed it in his pocket and smiled. I helped him out to the car. He was asking me about Outkast the whole time. He wanted to know where he could find their CDs in the stores, how many albums they had, and so on. He used me to steady himself again as we walked across the ice and snow. Andre and Inez ran by us; they had been throwing snowballs at Brent, who was now retaliating.

"Excuse us, Michael. Excuse us, Dan," Inez said, dodging Brent's attack. The three of them ran behind the house and disappeared. We could still hear them yelling. Michael was upset he wouldn't have a chance to say good-bye to them. I was pissed they hadn't said good-bye to him too. I told him I would tell them for him.

His dad came up to me again once Michael was in the car and said, "Thanks again for being so nice to him. He doesn't really have a lot of friends."

I felt a little bad just then, not just for Michael, but for his dad, who felt like he had to keep apologizing for his son. "Don't mention it. Bring him by the next time you're up here."

♦

Inside, Inez came up to me. There were snowflakes in her hair. I watched them turn to water droplets as she leaned into me. She kissed my mouth. She tasted like Baileys and was a little tipsy.

"Did you tell him what sex feels like?" she laughed.

I pulled back a little bit. I wanted to say something, but then thought better and just said, "No, he just wanted to know a bit more about Outkast."

"Sure, he did," Brent said, pouring himself another drink while my parents were not looking. "Inez, what was that word you called him, *el tarado*?"

"Shut up, shut up, shut up!" Inez said and chased Brent out of the kitchen, laughing.

Not long after that my parents went to bed. Brent, Andre and I finished off the champagne, but it was mostly me. I felt rotten. Inez was mad that I was drinking so much and went up to watch TV in the loft. She went to bed without saying goodnight. At two o'clock the guys and I were still up, talking about skiing accidents. Brent looked outside and could see the light from Inez's room on the trees.

"Her light is still on. She's still awake man. If I were you, I would have been up there two hours ago."

I stayed on the couch. I didn't move. I didn't go. I didn't want to be with her.

5.

Gunshot

I was getting out of Lee's jeep around ten at night when we heard the gunshot. Lee was the first guy I had dated seriously since I came to Tech. I had met him volunteering at the Boys and Girls Club. I remember when I first walked into the gym and saw him: a six-three white guy with a gaggle of black kids climbing on him. Even I was a little surprised that he asked me out, a black girl—a dark-skinned black girl with natural hair, at that—but I have to remind myself that it's the twenty-first century. I guess I have some of my own internalized stuff to work out.

Lee is tall, like I said. So my height was not an issue. He was not intimidated by a woman who is six-one and, well, I liked it. I could nuzzle in his arms and feel . . . girly.

And he never asked me if I play basketball. I sort of liked that too.

Lee was two years older than most college students our year. He had spent two years between high school and college as a student painter before he came to school. He had been real successful, eventually starting his own business. By then, it pretty much ran itself. He was studying history and economics. He talked about growing his business, or joining the Marines, or even about staying in school to be a professor, so he could write books and teach history. I knew that was an idea he was still getting his head around. He was the first in his family to go to college. He wasn't used to thinking of himself as a scholar. But he could be. He was that smart.

I called home and gushed to my mom about Lee. I called her a lot that first semester, nearly every day. She didn't seem to mind that Lee was white, just that I was happy and that he treated me right.

The shot had come from Lambeth, the grad student apartment complex next to mine. I stopped and froze when I heard it. Lee and I were both staring at one another, wondering, questioning ourselves if we had really heard what we just heard, and waiting—waiting for any sign or sound of another shot. Then somebody started screaming at the top of their lungs for help.

"You're an EMT," Lee said. I am, it's one of the ways I pay for school.

"Yeah,"

"Should we help?"

I knew it would be a few minutes before an ambulance arrived and those minutes could be critical. There were no more gunshots, so it didn't sound like an "active shooter" scenario.

"Let's go."

"Hold on, Melody. Let me get my gun out of the lock-box in back."

I stared him down. "Lee, you are so white sometimes."

"Really?" he asked. His confusion was sincere.

"Take it from an EMT, and a black woman at that, more guns never makes it safer. Leave it."

"Okay, but let me go first."

"Sure." I'd let him have that.

I started to run towards Lambeth. I knew he would catch up. It never occurred to me what I was actually doing. Lambeth had a large courtyard in the middle. There was a guy in the middle sitting on a flower box, crying.

"Did someone get shot?" I asked. He nodded his head. He was contorting his face as he rubbed his cheeks. I wondered if he was on something or just in shock.

"Where are they? I'm an EMT. I can help them."

"He shot himself. I can't fucking believe he shot himself."

He was drunk—at least. I could smell the beer on him. Lee touched my elbow and pointed to a door into a stairwell. A drunk girl in a tank top was hanging onto the railing while she tried to negotiate the steps. Just as we looked over, she started to weave, lost her balance, and tumbled face first with a flesh-on-cement slap. Her head hit the edge of the flower box, and her neck was at a sharp angle.

We didn't need more injuries.

"Lee, call 911."

Lee pulled out his phone while I ran up to the girl. She was panting and sobbing, but her neck was intact. She was like a three-year-old, grabbing my clothes and moaning.

"Mel, what's the address here?" Lee asked from his phone.

"It's either 15 or 19 Maxwell Road."

He repeated that into the phone.

"I'm going upstairs," I said.

"They say not to go inside," he said, this as I was already headed up the stairs. He followed me. "Mel, wait up!"

On the steps, people started staggering by me. They didn't say anything. Their faces looked like they were escaping from a burning building. I heard people cursing and crying. The floor was littered with crushed beer cans and empty beer bottles. I walked by a few apartments; the doors were open. Each room looked the same, furniture covered with broken potato chips, discarded clothes on the floor, lamps without shades, beer bottles and kegs on their sides. It must have been quite a party. There was one couple on a couch still making out, both naked from the waist up. Our presence didn't seem to disturb them. Most of the people were going in and out of one apartment at the end of the hall. I heard Lee relaying what he saw to the dispatcher on his phone.

A tall brown-skinned guy was leaning against the doorframe. His name was Rupesh. I had seen him in my statistics class. His shirt was spattered with a spray of fresh blood. He was pulling his hair with a clenched fist and staring at the opposite doorframe. I had seen him before but had never talked to him. I don't know if he had ever noticed me to recognize me.

"Hey, Rupesh, are you injured?" I asked.

He shook his head. Tears were running down his face.

"Has someone been shot here?"

He nodded his head. I was pretty sure he was on the verge of going into shock. He didn't seem to recognize me.

"I'm an EMT. I need to see him."

"You're an EMT!" he said, snapping out of his daze.

"Yeah."

"Is there an ambulance?"

"There's one coming. Where—"

"He's in the bathroom."

There was a crowd around the bathroom door. A lot of people were trying to call 911; the dispatcher was probably overwhelmed. One idiot was filming with his phone. Rupesh yelled out.

"Get out of the way! She's an EMT."

The people were not willing to move. They were like concert-goers defending their places in line. Lee muscled his way through with his elbow in the air, then pulled me behind him.

The floor was covered in blood, not even a movie would have had so much blood—critics would have said it was gratuitous and unrealistic, but that was how much there was. There is a lot of blood in the human head. Most of the spectators were standing in the spreading pool and didn't realize it.

The victim was a white guy. He looked older, probably a grad student. He was shaking and convulsing; his tongue was lapping behind his lips, flicking spit on his lips and face. The gunshot was to his head. His hair was wet and sticky. The gun was on the sink. It was a revolver. Lee picked it up and thumbed the cylinder release.

"He was playing Russian Roulette," Rupesh said.

"All the chambers were loaded . . ." Lee said, dropping the five bullets and one spent casing into his palm.

Two guys in baseball caps were trying to hold the victim down. He was splashing and rolling in the blood. The two guys had no idea what they were doing.

"Lee, get them out of here."

Lee grabbed them by the shirts and lead them to the door; they all were slipping on the floor. I watched Lee's boot rise off the tiles, red trails sticking to the treads. There was not a bit of white left on the floor.

"He's losing so much blood," some sorority girl said.

No shit, Sherlock, I thought.

I grabbed a towel from the rack next to the shower and wrapped it around his head.

"Lee, is the ambulance here yet?"

He went to the window and moved the curtains, which were splattered too.

"No."

"What's his name?"

"Lewis," Rupesh said from behind me.

"Lewis, can you hear me?" I looked in his eyes, but they were darting in random directions. He had a plaid shirt on and a white T-shirt underneath, which was—weirdly—still immaculate.

"Hold on, Lewis." I put his head in my lap. I held his hand with my left hand and checked his pulse with my right. On the other end of the bathroom his feet were squirming like he was trying to take off his shoes. I stared at them longer than I should have. Then they stopped. His hand was still twitching. I squeezed it back, but his pulse was gone.

"Lee, he has no pulse."

I set his head down and knelt beside him. My jeans soaked up the blood, and I could feel it, warm as bathwater on my skin.

So much for universal precautions.

"Lee, give me that other towel."

He gave me another towel from the back of the bathroom door. His lips were white and tight against each other, his brow furrowed, but he was still calm as he handed it to me. I was grateful for that. I put the towel under my knees. There were soon two red spots on it where my knees pushed it into the floor, but it was better than before. I told Lee to keep pressure on the head wound while I started compressions on Lewis's chest. His body shook from the force of my hands, but the rest of him stayed limp. His pulse didn't come back. The stream of blood from his head had slowed. I heard the ambulance. I kept up artificial respiration until the paramedics pushed their way through the crowd at the door.

♦

Lewis had died in my arms. The police wanted to talk to Lee and me, so we waited in the back of a squad car while they tried to get control of the scene. Lee held onto the revolver until he could turn it over to a cop. It soon looked just like the news: police tape around the courtyard, dozens of emergency vehicles with flashing lights, news vans with their antennas extended up to catch the satellite feed. The coroners brought Lewis out in a black bag on a gurney. I wiped the blood from my hand and held Lee's. I saw all the blood on me and started to kick the seat.

"I've got it all over me."

We were at the station until four in the morning. We sat at a desk while an officer took statements from us. All the desks around us were empty. The ceiling lights were turned off; the only light in the whole room was from the officer's desk lamp. The cop drank coffee from a Styrofoam cup. He refilled it three times while he asked us questions.

"Did you know the deceased?"

"Where were you when you first heard the shot?"

"Which direction did the shot seem to come from?"

I wished they would turn on more lights.

◆

Lee dropped me off at six a.m. It was Sunday morning; the horizon was pink. Some of the ROTC students were already outside warming up for PT. My roommate, Trisha, was still asleep when I let myself into our room. From the way her eyes were racing under her lids, I knew she was dreaming. I took my clothes off and threw them in the trash can. My shoes too. I noticed there was pink bubble gum on the top of my shoe. I was wondering how it got there and leaned closer. It wasn't gum. It was a piece of Lewis's brain. I felt ready to cry, but I was too tired. I took a long shower, scrubbed my knees and fingernails, then crawled into bed.

Trisha's clock radio clicked on thirty minutes later. We both lay there listening to the newsman. He said:

"A local university student died last night from a self-inflicted gunshot to the head. Police have ruled it an accidental suicide. No one, aside from the victim, was injured. According to reports, the victim had been playing Russian Roulette with his friend's revolver after they had been drinking. Services have not been announced yet . . . . The commerce secretary is predicting a robust quarter for local businesses in the coming months . . . ."

"I was there. Lewis died in my arms."

"What?" Trisha's voice was thick with sleep. Her hair was still wrapped in a silk scarf.

"The guy who shot himself. His name was Lewis."

"Melody, are you dreaming?"

"No. I haven't slept all night. Look at my clothes. They're in the trash."

She got out of bed, shuffled across the room, and walked to the trash can.

"Holy shit!" Trisha was Baptist. She never cursed.

"Don't touch them."

"Melody, are you all right? What happened?" She was standing next to the bed. Her nightgown was wrinkled, her eyes were big, and her mouth hung open. I could see her retainer wire across her teeth. I told her everything. Neither of us went to church that morning. We talked, but I never called home.

6.

Verities

When I think of my senior year in high school, I think of my court. It had three houses on it. The yellow house on the corner was the Campbell house; Mr. Campbell was a crotchety old man who came out and yelled at us if we made the intolerable transgression of stepping in his yard. He never said hello, or even acknowledged his neighbors' presence, unless it was to complain about some egregious violation of some minute HOA regulation, such as a non-approved paint color on the trim of a garage or a basketball hoop installed without a permit.

The other house on the court was the O'Reilly family's. Mr. Campbell I ignored, but the O'Reillys were like family, their house just being an extension of my own—a bright and lively extension as well. The O'Reillys had three children. Bryce O'Reilly was a senior in high school like me, his sister Emily was sixteen, and their little brother Toby was eleven. They had two dogs, a golden retriever and a black lab, as well as a rabbit, two birds, and a gerbil. Mr. O'Reilly was in the army, and we made great use of his retired fatigues and paintball guns. Mrs. O'Reilly taught preschool. In the basement, beside the pool table, her desk was littered with books like *Elmo goes to the Store* and *Everybody Poops.*

One Saturday afternoon, Bryce was sitting on the bumper of my car, tapping his feet and running his fingers through his hair. Bryce was always restless. There was a low grumble from the street as a red Camaro decelerated to pull into the court. Vanessa, our mutual friend from school, had come over to study with me for a chemistry test. She was a year behind us but was in advanced classes. Not too shabby. She parked under the plum tree at the edge of my yard. The Camaro had been an indulgence of her father, for himself, before he had settled down and had a family. Now Vanessa had inherited the oversized sports car and complained about how hard it was to park.

Bryce and I would have traded the ten-year-old sedans we were stuck with any time, but once Vanessa stepped out of the car, our minds shifted to things besides cars. She had stepped on some plums and bent forward to pick them out of her sandals. We both probably saw more of her cleavage than she intended. I walked over to help her with her books, trying not to betray the desire I felt.

Bryce knew me well enough to detect my interest in Vanessa, and perhaps her interest in me. That afternoon we had been playing paintball in the woods behind my house. She was early, and I had leaves and brambles in my hair.

"Justin, you're a mess. Why don't you take a shower? Vanessa, why don't you join him, to make sure he gets clean? I don't want you seen with a filthy guy."

I was nervous; so was Vanessa. Bryce laughed at both of us.

♦

Bryce and I grew up together. In our younger days, we had tromped through the woods behind my house, jumping over creeks and sliding down muddy embankments. On summer nights, we stretched out in the driveway, throwing balls of aluminum foil in the air so that bats would attack them, mistaking them for insects. We sneaked out at night and peeped into people's bedrooms from trees, hid from passing car lights in bushes, and considered all of this thrilling. Mr. Campbell wasted many a breath warning us not to go in his yard. During truth or dare games we would run around his house or ring his doorbell, causing him to call the police, or worse, our parents.

In junior high, Bryce and I discovered fire and all its wonderful properties: when coaxed onto a tennis ball with gasoline, it made a spectacular fireball for a thrilling game of street hockey. Fire could also be used to spell out expletives with flammable rubber cement, which Bryce eagerly demonstrated on Mr. Campbell's sidewalk.

In high school, we retired from tormenting Mr. Campbell. We let that torch be passed on to Bryce's brother, Toby, and his friends. Bryce and I would place bets as to how many times Mr. Campbell would come out to yell at children in a single afternoon, keeping track on three-by-five notecards like old folks at a bingo game. It *was* like a game: there were teams, underdogs, and star players—like Toby's friend Taylor, who always seemed to kick the soccer ball into Mr. Campbell's garage. When this happened, Bryce and I would stand on our chairs for a better view of the drama. After screaming at the kids and threatening to call their parents, Mr. Campbell would always look over at us, as if we had instigated the whole thing. We would smile and wave.

He never waved back.

♦

At Halloween our senior year in high school, Bryce and I were too old to trick-or-treat, so we decided to jump out of the bushes and scare kids coming up the court. Kids started coming to our court just to be scared. Later that night, Bryce and I even got our hands on some fake swords and put on a great show where we took turns killing each other—fake blood capsules and all.

One night early in November, before I was dating Vanessa, Karrie Rockford came over. It was a blustery night, and our old couch was sitting in the driveway. The Salvation Army was coming to pick it up in the morning. Karrie grabbed a blanket and we snuggled on the couch, watching the treetops and leaves dance in the wind against a backdrop of stars. The scene was a little surreal, sitting on a living room sofa in a driveway, the wind whipping Karrie's hair. I remember I liked the idea of having Karrie around, but I didn't necessarily like *her*. She was kind of dull. Very attractive, but she only talked about people at school and which football player was dating which cheerleader. I think she may have liked Bryce more than me anyway. That sometimes happened.

Bryce was the ultimate test of my girlfriends. If they liked him, they were acceptable. If they liked him too much, they were rejected. The best example of this system came from my sophomore year. I was getting to know a girl named Samantha. Bryce and I both noticed how she paid him more attention when he was around than she did to me. I wasn't exactly broken up about it. It was just that Samantha kept telling me that she was really into me.

Then one day she came over, and I wasn't home. So she just "dropped by" Bryce's place. One thing led to another, and she asked if she could blow him.

Bryce, who had inherited his father's brawn as well as his good looks, personally carried Samantha to the front steps, set her down outside, and slammed the door on her. He was very proud of himself that day. He recounted it all to me later, insisting that "no one lies to my best friend to get to me."

♦

Vanessa and I became a lot closer after our classmate Maria Lofton died. The funeral was mid-December. I remember standing outside in the courtyard of the church. Vanessa was beside me. She was wearing a gray sweater. Mine was navy blue and made my skin

65

itch. I didn't move to scratch, because that would force Vanessa to remove her hand from the crook of my elbow. She had put it there because she was upset.

The whole senior class was at the church. Vanessa was only a junior, but she was in a few senior courses with Maria and myself. We talked with Mrs. Hardy, my English teacher and a friend of my mother's. I kept looking down at my feet and the gray flagstones with black moss growing in between them. Maria would have been our valedictorian if she had not died. Junior year, she'd sat in front of me in chemistry class. I would play with her hair, which was so black that it was almost blue. The last time I had seen Maria was after school a few days before she died. I had helped her with her college admissions essay. She was a good writer on her own, but she was also thorough and wanted to get a second opinion on her essay. I remember thinking it was really good, better than all of mine. I kept going over that afternoon, replaying it in my mind for some sign of the depression Maria apparently suffered from. I had been too obtuse to see it. Almost all of us had. We thought she had been perfect. She would have had her pick of colleges.

Instead she killed herself with Prozac and a bottle of champagne. She was wearing her homecoming dress when they found her unresponsive in her bed. Her suicide note had read: *Isn't it obvious.*

After the funeral, Vanessa and I went to the International House of Pancakes for lunch. The place was all cheery with Christmas decorations, but we didn't feel very cheerful. We were in no rush to get back to school, but we were too spent to talk. That was when I realized we were comfortable enough just to sit with each other, not talking, just pouring syrup, eating pancakes, stirring coffee. She always put Sweet'N Low in her coffee, then tucked the wrapper beneath her mug. I could always tell how many cups she had drunk by the number of wrappers that stuck to the bottom of her mug. She always had at least three cups.

◆

In January, I was asked to speak at the National Honor Society induction. Vanessa was being inducted, so her family and I went out to dinner beforehand. I was too nervous to eat much. I had never given a speech to such a large crowd. While waiting backstage beforehand, I ran to the bathroom and vomited. I was sitting on the floor of the stall when I heard someone come inside.

"Justin, my man, where are you?"

"Bryce?"

The door to my stall opened, and Bryce stood looking down on me. Bryce wasn't in NHS, not by a longshot. His mother was always after him to raise his grades, but he didn't seem to worry about that too much. He was wearing slacks, a bright white shirt (just from the dry cleaners), and a leather vest. His tie was crooked and clashed with his vest. I felt embarrassed and weak, sitting there on the floor in my oversized suit and my dinner floating in the yellow water beside me. Bryce's face grimaced when he looked in the toilet.

"I'm a little nervous," I said.

"You got that right."

Bryce picked me up by the armpits and told me to stand up straight.

"There's a thousand people in there, including Vanessa and her family. I want to make a good impression," I said.

"You know, Samantha is in there too. Maybe I should sit by her."

I couldn't help laughing. Bryce moved us to the sink to help me clean up. I could see Bryce's reflection beside mine in the mirror. His skin, in comparison to mine, was more tanned, his shoulders broader, and his head higher. His face was dark with a manly five o'clock shadow. His lacrosse teammates would have laughed if they'd seen him so dressed up. But he had come to hear me give my speech, and his hands patting me through the shoulder pads of my blazer made me forget that I was nervous. He said he would cheer for me when I got up on stage.

"It's National Honor Society, dude. There is no cheering."

"I'll manage something."

I went and took my place on stage, dreading whatever Bryce was going to do when I stepped up to the podium. The stage was like limbo. It was completely dark ahead of me and completely dark behind me. The principal finished his introduction, and I got up with my speech in hand. My mouth tasted of bile and breath mints. My hands were shaking. I knew Vanessa was in the audience, although I couldn't even see the audience. Just as I stepped up behind the microphone, in that terrible moment before I had to utter my first words, I heard a man clearing his throat. Then he coughed and sniffed—finishing it up with a *hauking* sound, as if he were about to spit. Anyone else would have thought it was an old man, someone's grandpa with emphysema dragged out of the old folks home to the ceremony. But I knew it was Bryce's signal; no one else had such a unique sense of *discretion*. I wondered if he was sitting by Samantha. Then I thought of her offering to suck Bryce off and imagined her expression as he dropped her on her ass out his front door. I almost laughed.

My heart was bursting with for love for him.

Everyone loved my speech. I talked about hard work paying off, the value of scholarship, and its necessity for future success and ultimately changing the world. In retrospect, I realize I was just regurgitating the gospel of upward mobility, which we were being rewarded for having internalized with a little NHS pin that we could wear on our sweater vests and letter jackets, a pin that would remind us that we, indeed, were on the trajectory our upper-middle-class parents and teachers desired for us.

"It was the best one in all the thirty-four years that we've had the National Honor Society," the principal told me. He put his arm around my shoulders and said in a low voice that it was at this point in high school that he and the teachers could see which students were "pulling away from the pack." He said that I was on the right trajectory and not to veer off, even if I saw others diverging. That was just a fact of life, he said.

I wasn't sure what exactly he meant. I was glad to get away from him and pose for pictures with Vanessa and Bryce. To me, everything felt so perfect and solidified that night. Our lives just like the lives of those families we saw on TV. This was how the story was supposed to go.

♦

It was February that we knew something was wrong at the O'Reilly house. They always went to upstate New York to visit Mr. O'Reilly's brother. This time Mr. O'Reilly went alone; his family stayed behind. I went over to inquire. The house smelled of bread baking in the oven and Mrs. O'Reilly's scented candles, all the scents of a happy home life. Bryce and Toby watched cartoons on TV. At a commercial I asked if there was any reason they had not gone to New York with their father.

"Dad wanted to go alone." Bryce used the tone of voice that always meant our conversation on the present topic was at an end. I got the rest of the story from my mom. The O'Reillys were having fights. Mr. O'Reilly said he wasn't in love any more.

Shortly after that, Vanessa came over and I helped her with her history paper. We were still only friends, but later she said that was the first night she was tempted to kiss me. She got an A on the paper, so she took me out to dinner at this little rustic inn in historic Clifton, this little town that had barely changed since the Civil War. Vanessa wore a white blouse and a red pleated skirt. It was a great night. The restaurant was in a two-hundred-year-old building. The wood floors were slanted from the way the foundation had settled over time. Every step the waiters took elicited a creek or moan from the floor. The candles on our table were reflected on the inside of the windows while rain splashed the outside. I couldn't remember ever being so happy.

It was still raining when we drove home. The little country roads flooded. We drove through some standing water that splashed against her Camaro's fenders. Leaves floated by the tires. It was dangerous. The low-slung car could have sucked water in one of the intakes and seized up with vapor lock. But we laughed anyway. Vanessa rolled down the window and stuck out the ice scraper, as if she were rowing. We made it back to her place and watched a movie. Looking at her standing in front of the TV, I was fascinated by how her skirt hung so elegantly off the soft mounds that it concealed. The next week was Valentine's Day. I gave her roses. The following weekend we went on a ski trip. In the cabin, we kissed. We confessed that we loved each other.

After that, we were an item, as they say.

◆

There were awful days when I would go into my garage and look at Bryce's driveway. I was checking if his father had left yet. One day, it was spring and I remember the cherry blossoms gathered on the roof of Mr. O'Reilly's Honda Accord while it waited in the driveway, the trunk tied down with rope and filled past its capacity with cardboard boxes. A few lamps, golf clubs, and a small mahogany table were piled in the back seat. Mr. O'Reilly, a big man with fuzzy brown hair like Bryce's, caught me staring. He didn't say anything, just frowned as if to say: *it's a shame isn't it.* He flicked his keys out of his pocket, opened the door to the car, then drove away. No one else was on the court to see him leave. Bryce insisted that he didn't care if his father left. Bryce's mom now had three kids, two dogs, two birds, and two rodents to take care of by herself.

Shortly after that, I remember sitting in Bryce's sister Emily's room. I had come over to find Bryce, but he wasn't home. She had just gotten out of the shower and was in her bathrobe. Her hair was dripping, and she sat against the wall with her knees to her chest. She was naked beneath that robe. I had seen her breasts once during a game of truth or dare. She had wide pink nipples. Vanessa's nipples were smaller and redder. Emily was comfortable with me. She didn't mind if I was in her room while she was in her bathrobe. She just wanted to talk. She knew I would listen.

"My dad told my mom that he doesn't love her anymore," she said. "I don't think Bryce loves me either."

"That's not true," I said.

"How do you know, Justin? Bryce doesn't talk to anyone anymore."

I didn't have anything to say. She was right. It was late March and lacrosse season had started. Bryce was never home. He was always at practice, and his late nights were spent with his lacrosse teammates—mine, with Vanessa.

Emily's room was like a miniature universe, complete with moon and sun decorations on her sheets and stationery—old-style sun and moons like on medieval illuminations. There were also glow-in-the-dark stars above her bed. I was leaving for a journalism class trip the next day. I felt awful. Emily's eyes were shut tightly while she wiped them with the edge of her bathrobe. I couldn't leave her like that. I felt like my own family was breaking up. I had no brothers and sisters; the O'Reillys were my siblings.

But I left anyway.

♦

The journalism trip was to New York. I thought of the O'Reillys the whole way. I called Vanessa when I got to the hotel. My tears ran from my cheek onto the phone. She was so good to me. She promised me that things always work out for the best. She would run her fingers through my hair and make me tea when I got home. I missed her in New York and thought only of returning to her. I took special pride in the fact that I could go for a walk with her, sit her down on a park bench and kiss her, touch her. No one else was as lucky as I was.

♦

When I got the acceptance letter from Georgetown in April, my parents were not home. I ran over to the O'Reillys instead. It had just rained, and mud splashed on the letter as I sprinted through their yard. Mrs. O'Reilly opened the door and congratulated me. She said she had never doubted that I would be accepted. She looked tired and weary. She said she wished her Bryce had worked as hard for the past four years as I had. Now all Bryce did was stay out late and ignore his curfew. There were rings under her eyes. I realized that I couldn't remember the last time she didn't have rings there or when Bryce and I had last hung out. The dogs were trying to push through the door to me. She held them back with her leg. That was a Friday. That weekend Vanessa came over, and we made cupcakes with blue icing and white Gs on them (for Georgetown). I took them to school and celebrated, giving them to all the secretaries in the office, my teachers, and the students in my homeroom. Vanessa was happy for me, but I knew she would miss me. I assured her I would be home on weekends, since Georgetown was only an hour away by car.

Occasionally I went over to the O'Reillys' to see how things were. Bryce was never home; neither was Emily. Toby was the only one around, and he was always watching television. I had to compete with cartoons and MTV for his attention.

"Where are the birds?"

"Gave them away."

"Why?"

"Mom couldn't take care of them, I guess."

"How is she doing?"

"I don't know."

One Saturday night Vanessa and I were getting out of her Camaro in my driveway when Bryce pulled in across the street and parked at an angle in his driveway, one tire on the lawn. I ran over.

"Bryce, man, we need to hang out," I said, coming up to him and clapping him on the back. I noticed he smelled like weed.

"I'm just dropping off some of my pads and uniforms. I need to wash them. I'm headed over to Hartcher's place tonight. We're having a team party."

Hartcher was the captain of the lacrosse team. I followed Bryce into the garage, where he emptied one of his duffle bags into a pile on the floor.

"Bryce, have you decided on what you are doing next year?"

"Yep."

I waited for him to elaborate. The O'Reillys had a mud-room attached to the garage with a washer-dryer set. Bryce entered, turned the knobs on the washer, stuffed in his uniform and pads, and poured in detergent. Water sprayed into the barrel. He slammed down the lid. I finally asked, "Well, what are you doing?"

"Dad wants me to go to West Point."

"That's great," I said. I knew going to West Point required an appointment from a Senator. "Did you get appointed?"

Bryce unlatched a trunk on the floor of the garage and rummaged around inside, digging around spare lacrosse sticks, heads, pads, and balls until he found what he was looking for: a half-empty bottle of Jack Daniels. He pulled it out and closed the lid of the trunk. "Nope."

He walked back to the car. I followed. "Then what are you doing, Bryce?"

"Dad has me signed up to repeat senior year at some military school out in the Blue Ridge Mountains. He says if I do a year there, I might be able to get into West Point, like him."

"Oh." I stood there processing what he had said, sharing my thoughts aloud like some sort of idiot. "So, you're not going to college next year."

"Not all of us are that lucky."

He swung open the door to his car and tossed in the bottle of JD.

"Bryce, why don't you come over and hang with me and Vanessa tonight. we're going to watch a movie."

"Maybe another time."

♦

On April 17th, I got a ticket from school security because my parking pass had expired. It meant three detentions. On my lunch break I went over to the little Catholic chapel next door and asked the nun, who was the caretaker, if I could sit there a while—but I didn't finish my sentence; I began to cry. She came over and hugged me. It wasn't about the ticket. It was about Bryce and his family. I felt like *my* family, my life was coming apart. Everything that had always seemed so . . . permanent, wasn't. It was like I had counted on so many guarantees that had turned out to have never been there in the first place.

♦

Graduation was in early June, which is technically still spring, but it felt like summer beneath those black robes. Afterwards everyone gathered with their families to take pictures—pictures that would sit on their desks in their first-year dorms at college. My graduation party was on my back deck. Vanessa and my parents had tied blue and gray balloons along the railings. The cake had a picture of Georgetown on it. Gray smoke from the grill blew around everyone while they ate off paper plates. My relatives were there, and my neighbors, including the O'Reillys. Mrs. O'Reilly was wearing a dress that she said made her look fat. Emily and Toby came for a little while. They looked bored without anyone their age to talk to.

Bryce missed the party.

By evening, Vanessa and I were the only ones left. I should have felt happy, and I guess I did, but the fact that Bryce had not shown up bothered me. I heard him pull up into their driveway later that night, but he left shortly after. Vanessa and I cleaned up the wreckage of the party after my parents had gone to bed. It took two hours to deflate the balloons, clear all the plates, and wash the casserole dishes. I watched while Vanessa scraped some brown flaky debris from a pan. I just wanted to lose myself in her, in playfulness, in something light to escape from the cloud of thoughts and feelings I was trying to shove to the back of my mind. I flicked water on her. She spun around and hosed me down with the dish sprayer. I tickled her until she submitted, and then we spent another hour cleaning up the new mess we had made, whipping each other with dishtowels whenever one of us caught the other turning their back.

Everything will be just fine, I told myself.

It was around eleven when we finished. We spooned on the couch and watched TV. When the show was over, I turned off the television and dropped the remote control to the floor. While our eyes were adjusting to the dark, the only sound was the static from the cooling television. I pulled Vanessa closer. She had blue eyes, with streaks of brown along the edges of her pupils. I always told her they looked like eclipsed suns. She was wearing shorts that she would eventually unbutton and leave on the floor with her bra and my jeans. I ran my hands all over her skin, the friction making a soft sound, like an orange being peeled. I kissed her everywhere as we moved in cadence. After we had both come, I laid my head on her rising and falling breasts, and I told her I would always love her. She told me the same. We were forever. Nothing would change that. Our bodies were moist from one another and tired from our lovemaking, so we fell asleep, with our arms and legs intertwined.

Within a year we wouldn't even speak to each other.

7.

Oral Composition

NURSERY

DEIRDRE VOUSCH, late twenties, is breastfeeding her child,
BURT. The camera pans back to reveal HARLAND VOUSCH, early
thirties, painting a picture of his wife and child.

NARRATOR (VOICE OVER)

Burt was the first and last child born to Deirdre and Harland
Vousch. Harland was an accomplished painter of world renown. His
wife, Deirdre, was widely regarded as one of the most beautiful
women of her generation. She was Harland's inspiration. His
paintings of her hung in galleries from Long Beach to London,
Toulouse to Tokyo, Hong Kong to Havana. The birth of their first
child, a son, was an occasion of great excitement. The world waited
with expectation bordering on hysteria to see the Vousch child,
whose pedigree promised a great career as a model, an artist, or both.

For Harland, his wife's transition to motherhood opened an
entirely new universe of possibilities for his paintings, a new period
of his distinguished career to capture the essence, grace, and
enduring beauty of motherhood.

DEIRDRE, strokes BURT on his head while he continues to nurse. HARLAND adjusts the light.

NARRATOR (Continue VO)

When their son was born, everyone agreed that the child of Deirdre and Harland was beautiful: a work of art in human form. Burt was bright, precocious, and even at such a young age, one could see that he looked to his mother with the same love and adoration that his father did. It was a family full of love and mutual admiration. But then, one day, when the baby began teething, something went wrong.

DEIRDRE winces in pain and jerks the baby away from her breast. She puts her hand to her chest, and then raises her fingers—they are bloody. HARLAND races over and tends to her. She is more surprised than hurt.

NARRATOR

Burt, as it turned out, had been born with a prodigious set of teeth. Teeth that began to come in quite early.

CUT TO NURSERY, NEXT DAY
We see DEIRDRE pretending to breast-feed, holding her baby away from her chest while HARLAND tries to paint her. But somehow the

baby bites her anyway. HARLAND races over to tend to her, again.
He moves the baby away, placing BURT alone on a table. BURT
cries, distressed to be away from his mother.

NARRATOR

While Deirdre had been pregnant, she and Harland had
entertained using such names for the baby as Michelangelo, Sidneyo,
or Picasso, but now, Harland decided to name the baby, simply Burt.

CUT TO KITCHEN, A FEW YEARS LATER.
HARLAND, DEIRDRE, and BURT (three or four-years-old now) sit
at the table. BURT finishes his plate of food, then begins to chew on
the plate, taking a bite out of it.

NARRATOR

Burt had a teething period that lasted longer than most
children. This was an incredibly stressful time for his parents. If they
were not careful, he would eat his toys, his clothes, even his
furniture. But they learned that interfering with him was dangerous
for, sometimes, being young and not knowing better, his mouth
would stray.

CUT TO PLAYROOM
We see DEIRDRE reaching down to take a toy out of BURT'S
mouth. She jerks her hand away in pain. BURT looks up, in sorrow.

HARLAND comes into the room, and DEIRDRE hides her bleeding hand behind her back.

CUT TO HALLWAY, NIGHT

Light flashes as a thunderstorm rages outside. BURT runs, terrified, down a dark hallway to his parent's bedroom, where he wakes up DEIRDRE. She soothes him and pulls him into bed with her. They sleep soundly through the storm.

CUT TO MORNING

DEIRDRE jerks upward, clasping her shoulder. HARLAND also awakens. He looks down at BURT who is sleeping soundly. HARLAND tries to pry DEIRDRE'S hand away from her shoulder. She resists as long as she can, until he overpowers her and sees that there is blood on her shoulder. HARLAND turns to BURT, swings him out of the bed by his wrist, and carries him out of the bedroom. DEIRDRE tries to reach her son, but HARLAND keeps them apart. Mother and child scream and weep.

NARRATOR

It was the last straw. To Harland, Deirdre was his most prized and treasured work of art, made by God's own hands. He would let no one threaten that beauty. Not even his son.

CUT TO FRONT LAWN OF PRIVATE BOARDING SCHOOL.
BURT stands curbside in an oversized suit with a Dolce & Gabbana
suitcase. Under his arm are a few art books. He is wearing a
restraint on his jaw. HARLAND stands by their Alfa Romeo tapping
his feet, flicking his lighter, and chain smoking. DEIRDRE hugs her
son, wipes her eyes, and gives BURT bags of trail mix, caramel
squares, and saltwater taffy. HARLAND comes over to her and pulls
her away. BURT watches as they drive off.

NARRATOR

Harland arranged to send Burt away to school. The rest of his childhood was spent studying. During the summers his father signed Burt up for summer school, so he rarely could come home. During this time Harland was prolific. His best-selling works were always his portraits of Deirdre.

CUT TO STUDIO IN ART SCHOOL
ART STUDENTS stand in silence, watching HARLAND paint
another portrait of DEIRDRE, in which she is holding a different
baby. When the baby begins to cry and she is not able to soothe him,
the baby's MOTHER steps over, takes him, and calms him.
DEIRDRE watches the child move farther away with longing.
HARLAND steps in to turn her chin back to an angle he wants.

NARRATOR

For two weeks a year, Burt would come home. These were joyous times for him. He lived for those two weeks that he could see his mother. They sustained him for the rest of the lonely year.

CUT TO KITCHEN

BURT is at the kitchen table. He finishes his meal and begins nibbling at his fork. HARLAND does not notice. DEIRDRE shoots him a look, he stops, and they both smile.

CUT TO DORM ROOM

We see BURT studying at his desk. He is older now, in his early teens. He no longer wears a mouth restraint.

NARRATOR

Burt was growing up to be a normal and happy young man, if not for a few odd habits.

Beside BURT there are a few dozen pencils, chewed almost beyond recognition.

NARRATOR

He did well in school.

CUT TO CLASSROOM

BURT sits in class, chewing a pencil, and raises his hand.

NARRATOR

And he had many friends.

BURT sits on a lawn with a few other students, a teacher watching from nearby. BURT is chewing a huge wad of gum, laughing and joking with the other students.

CUT TO OUTSIDE THE VOUSCHS' HOUSE
BURT runs up his walk with his suitcase and finds a note on the door.

NARRATOR

One year, there were no summer classes due to renovations at the boarding school. Burt was overjoyed. He rushed home once sessions were dismissed. He could not wait to see his mother. But when he reached the house, he found that his parents were gone. His father had taken Deirdre to the Seychelles, thinking that being around Burt for the whole summer would be stressful for her. He said so in the note he left for Burt. Of course, he had not told Deirdre that their son would be left home alone.

CUT TO KITCHEN

We pan over a floor covered with discarded take-out containers and delivery menus from a variety of restaurants. BURT sits next to an open and empty refrigerator. There are empty bags and containers all about him. He chews on a Tupperware container, looking forlorn.

NARRATOR

His father had seen that the refrigerator was well-stocked, but in his loneliness Burt ate through the food and his remaining budget in one month. As he sat alone on the empty floor beside the empty refrigerator and empty cupboards, inside an empty house, he realized that without love, he too felt empty.

The world was a large and lonely place. All Burt had were these feelings, this pain, an insatiable desire to chomp, and an inexorable hunger to go along with it.

BURT stops chewing and looks upward. BURT goes upstairs and begins to kick at a locked door.

NARRATOR

It was his father that was behind all this, his father who had taken his mother away from him. And now Burt would get revenge.

BURT pries at the door, but he can't get it open. Finally, he drops to his knees and bites at the lock. The door opens. He enters. On the other side is his father's studio. There are paintings all over. BURT begins to take bites out of each one.

OUTSIDE THE VOUSCHS' HOUSE, DAY
HARLAND and DEIRDRE arrive home after their trip. They walk into the house and find it in complete disarray. DEIRDRE calls the police and reports a break in. HARLAND rushes upstairs to his studio. As he goes down the hallway, he sees that the paintings on either side of the wall have been chewed. Bite marks mar the frames and the canvasses. He bursts into his studio to find BURT, disheveled and dirty (he's been at this all summer), sitting amid a pile of ruined paintings. HARLAND loses control and beats BURT. DEIRDRE tries to intervene, but HARLAND slaps her in the face, then recoils in terror.

NARRATOR

When Harland arrived home and found all his works destroyed, he went mad with rage. He beat Burt senseless. When Deirdre rushed to help her son, he struck her too. Suddenly horrified that he, by his own actions, had harmed his beloved wife and risked damaging the appearance of his most important inspiration, Harland decided that the situation was simply unacceptable. Something drastic had to be done.

OUTSIDE THE VOUSCHS' HOUSE, NEXT MORNING
HARLAND carries BURT out and throws him to the curb. BURT lies there, stunned and shocked, sucking his thumb. As he lies there, his father comes in and out, tossing the ruined paintings down on top of him.

CUT TO THE VOUSCHS' BEDROOM
DEIRDRE is locked inside, pounding on the door to get out.

NARRATOR

Harland disowned his son. He threw Burt out of the house with the paintings he had ruined, along with the weekly trash and recycling. Then he took Deirdre and moved away, hoping never to see his curse of a son again.

OUTSIDE THE VOUSCHS' HOUSE
BURT is still on the curb, now sucking on the corner of a painting. HARLAND drags DEIRDRE out of the house. She tries to reach BURT, but HARLAND throws her into a waiting limo. They drive away.

OUTSIDE THE VOUSCHS' HOUSE, NEXT MORNING

NARRATOR

Burt waited outside his house all night, but his parents never returned.

Time lapse. BURT remains, unmoving, in the midst of the pedestrian traffic, weather, and passage of the season. Leaves begin to fall. Finally, three ART CRITICS walk by, stop, and stare at the paintings on the ground. For a long while they are silent, assessing.

ART CRITIC 1

This work, it is astonishing!

ART CRITIC 2

Breathtaking! Pure genius.

ART CRITIC 3 picks up one of the paintings and looks through a large bite hole in the canvas.

ART CRITIC 3

This is marvelous. Boy, who did this?

BURT

I did.

The ART CRITICS look at each other, aghast.

ART CRITIC 1

This is revolutionary.

ART CRITIC 2

How much do you want for these paintings?

BURT

Well, I don't know. I've never sold—

ART CRITIC 3

You've never sold a painting!

BURT

No. I've been in school and my parents—

ART CRITIC 1

He is undiscovered.

ART CRITIC 2

Well, of course he is. We have not heard of him, have we?

ART CRITIC 3

That means that we have discovered him! Imagine what this will do for our careers!

All three ART CRITICS reach into their pockets, pull out cash, and give it to BURT. He sits there watching as the bills fall down into his lap, landing there among the leaves and litter that have gathered there. The day passes and the ART CRITICS bring more and more people to the curb. until all the paintings have been bought, and BURT'S lap is filled with hundred-dollar bills. With all that money, BURT goes to an art store to buy more canvasses and paints, then he puts them on the doorstep with a bow and card that reads, "For Dad. I'm Sorry. Love, Burt." Then he waits. He sleeps on the doorstep beside the blank canvasses. Night comes, followed by morning, and still his parents have not returned. Crestfallen, he gets up and begins to wander down the street.

CITY PARK, DAY

BURT walks into a park. In the center of the park is a fountain with a stone statue. He climbs up on the statue and begins to bite down on it. A HOMELESS MAN gets up and stares. He continues to stare even after BURT has finished and climbed down. BURT walks through the city, wandering into parks, and eating at any and all sculptures. He walks by wall murals and gnaws at them. As he goes along, people begin to follow him and look at his work. He walks into a museum sculpture garden. It is later in the day now and POLICE OFFICERS follow him into the garden and begin to drag him away, but as they leave by the gates, they are surrounded by an ANGRY MOB OF ART CRITICS.

MOB

You can't arrest him. He is expressing himself! He is an artist.

MOB

This is artistic repression.

MOB

This is oppression!

MOB

Down with militarized police forces!

MOB

Down with repressive totalitarian regimes!

MOB

Freedom for expression! Freedom from artistic oppression!

MOB

Freedom now! Leave him alone, you fascist pigs!

CUT TO COURTROOM

A JUDGE reads over the notes of BURT'S case, as BURT stands before him.

JUDGE

Well, Mr. Vousch, you have pled guilty to defacing public property, and it is my job and duty to sentence you. But, since the public seems to feel that there is some . . . well, some merit in your . . . in these . . . these . . . Oral Compositions, your sentence will be one hundred hours of community service, and that service will be in the form of using your artistic . . . talents to improve upon this city's art work. Dismissed.

The JUDGE bangs his gavel, and the ART CRITICS in the room get up and cheer. They carry BURT out on their shoulders.

SCULPTURE GARDEN, NEXT DAY
BURT sits with his legs wrapped around a sculpture and chews idly at it while an enraptured audience watches.

NARRATOR

And so began Burt's career as an Oral Composer. He quickly acquired a loyal following. Members of art circles everywhere began to talk about the new young visionary:

ART CRITIC 1 *(reading aloud what he is writing on a note pad)*
. . . on the cutting edge of art. He is a criminal, and outcast, who from the fringes of society brings us a new definition, a whole new paradigm, in which our experience and interaction with what we call art has been transfigured.

ART CRITIC 2

(speaking into a recorder)

He is dangerous, and some would even say he is mad. To many he is an enigma, but what is certain is his art is astounding . . .

.

NARRATOR

Soon Burt's work hit the mainstream. There were knockoffs of his work, cheap imitations.

CUT TO ARTS' FAIR

CUSTOMERS examine paintings and sculptures with pieces apparently bitten out of them.

NARRATOR

There were even a few people who tried to imitate his methods.

CUT TO A SCULPTOR AT ARTS' FAIR

SCULPTOR holds up a piece of sculpture. He smiles and we see that his teeth are broken and chipped. A tooth falls out, and the SCULPTOR tries to catch it while keeping his composure.

NARRATOR

But no one had Burt's touch or his natural gifts.

CUT TO NEIGHBORHOOD STREET

BURT walks down the street wearing a beret and chewing a toothpick. A growing group of critics and fans follow a few steps behind. BURT walks by a house with a sculpture in the front yard. As he stops, the entourage stops. He walks into the yard.

CUT TO SAME YARD, A FEW MINUTES LATER

BURT walks away picking his teeth, the sculpture in the yard behind him, a bite taken out of its base, falls over. The entourage surrounds it and begins to take photographs and notes. BURT walks farther down the street and ducks into his own house—the same as his childhood home. The homeowner at the first house emerges, sees the crowd and the sculpture on its side, and immediately starts taking bids on the new "work."

OUTSIDE BURT'S HOUSE

A few devoted fans stand outside.

NARRATOR

As his fame spread, Burt became an international phenomenon. He received commissions to do work for corporate offices.

CUT TO TRAFFIC CIRCLE OUTSIDE OFFICE BUILDING
Men and women in suits cut a ribbon and clap at the dedication of
an office building. BURT is wrapped around the artwork in front
and is munching on it.

CUT TO EXT. BURT'S HOUSE
There are more devoted fans standing vigil outside his house.

NARRATOR

Soon he was asked to do an Oral Composition for the White House lawn. The Metropolitan Museum of Fine Arts gave him a grant to come to their galleries and chew upon anything he wanted, as did the National Gallery, and MOMA.

The public loved him. They said he had breathed new life into the art world. That there had not been such a revolution in art since the discovery of perspective drawing. He was the greatest genius since Sidneyo or Picasso.

CUT TO TELEVISION SCREEN PLAYING A TALKSHOW

ART CRITIC 1 *(speaking to a talkshow host)*

BURT is the biggest thing in *post*-post modernism. He gazes upon the artifices and edifices of a capitalist society in decline, where endless expansion into exurbs has led to a collapse in cultural centers, leaving them to decay and rot, in need of rejuvenation, or rather, revolution.

CUT TO GALLERY OPENING

ART CRITIC 2 *(speaking to reporters)*

Burt strips away the layers of hackneyed neo-classic tropes while permeating the boundaries of what is perceived as the conventional tableau, inviting the viewer on an inward journey, a quest for meaning, reexamining how we as consumers consume art, and how art consumes us, and consumption consumes the subject. This is the inevitable evolution that comes as subject, artist, and art become one, an ontogenesis from self-consciousness to meta-consciousness.

CUT TO NATIONAL PUBLIC RADIO STUDIO

ART CRITIC 3

While maintaining a subtext of visual and textual harmonies, Burt Vousch excogitates the contemporary and traditional into a pastiche of past, present, and future, leaving one with a feeling of sublime liminality *vis-à-vis* a deconstructionist point of view that is also, paradoxically, re-constructivist, posing the question of what is genuine versus what is contrived, what is authentic and what is façade.

FAN GIRL 1 *(buying a copy of* Seventeen *with BURT on the cover)*

He's so dreamy.

FAN GIRL 2

I want to have his babies.

CUT TO ART STUDIO

HARLAND, older now, snaps closed an issue of Time *magazine with a picture of BURT on the cover. HARLAND is surrounded by unfinished paintings of DEIRDRE, who looks forlorn. When he hears DEIRDRE coming, he shoves the* Time *magazine underneath a number of canvasses where he has hidden copies of* The New York Times *and* New Yorker, *each with cover stories profiling BURT. DEIRDRE enters, her clothes disheveled. She is carrying a bottle of whisky, and stumbles over to a seat under some lights where HARLAND is trying to paint her.*

NARRATOR

Harland did everything he could to keep news of their son from Deirdre. He took extraordinary measures, moving them out into the country, to an abandoned eighteenth-century manor, with no connections to the outside world. They lived off the grid, without modern conveniences. No electricity. No running water. Harland said it was for his art.

CUT TO INSIDE A DARK, DILAPIDATED BARN

The door opens and we see HARLAND carry in another painting
and set it atop a pile of paintings in an empty animal stall. The
camera pans, and we see one stall after another, each one filled with
more piles of unsold paintings.

NARRATOR

When, in truth, he had not sold a painting for years. He was
broke, and his creditors were looking for him.

OUTSIDE BURT'S HOUSE

More and more devoted fans gather outside BURT'S house.

FANS

We love you Burt!

NARRATOR

But in time, there was no art work left in the States for Burt.
So this young man, who had single-handedly reinvented art, was sent
to where he would have enough art for a lifetime: Europe.

CUT TO TARMAC AT EUROPEAN AIRPORT

Cheering fans await Burt.

HYSTERICAL FEMALE FAN

Burt! Eat Me!

NARRATOR

Europe welcomed him with open arms. Crowds of thousands greeted him on his tours. He set to work at a prodigious pace.

CUT TO OUTSIDE THE LOUVRE

We see more PEOPLE gathering outside while the camera zooms through a window and we see BURT working within. Women wave signs outside reading: "Je veux avoir les bébés de Burt" and "Mords moi."

NARRATOR

Burt snacked on Vermeer, he lightened up Rembrandt, he dined upon Sidneyo's Last Supper. He licked the Mona Lisa with a grain of salt. He peppered the Sistine Chapel with his mastication, and he bit off David's testicles with relish.

STREET IN FRONT OF BURT'S HOUSE

The street is completely filled with fans. Burt's limo is escorted by police vehicles. Helicopters hover above, and the crowds of fans jostle with the paparazzi and security

NARRATOR

But in time, even Europe grew boring to Burt and he came home.

A taxi pulls up to BURT's house and he gets out looking jetlagged. The crowd cheers and screams. He and his handlers push their way through to his front door and enter. The crowd begins to chant his name.

Time Lapse. We watch as people in the crowd come and go. Police motorcades and airport limos zoom in and out with BURT coming and going.

NARRATOR

The next year there was a tour of Asia, and a year after that, a tour of South America, then Africa, then Asia again. But after his last tour, Burt fell into a deep depression. Although his popularity remained high, and demand higher, he was tired of his Oral Compositions. After dining on the greatest works of the world, what was there left to do? He had money now, prestige, and fame. He had literally consumed the greatest works of art the world had to offer, but he felt empty, lonely. For a while he created no more Oral Compositions. Then of course, interest flagged, something, someone else new came along.

Time Lapse. The crowds outside Burt's house dwindle. The roadblocks are removed and regular pedestrian and then street traffic resume.

99

CUT INSIDE BURT'S BEDROOM

BURT looks outside his window. It is raining. A single girl remains.
She is holding a sign that says "Eat Me," the colors running from
the rain.

NARRATOR

But still BURT saw his own face everywhere.

CUT TO TOY AISLE AT TOY STORE

BURT walks down an aisle, incognito with sunglasses, fake
mustache, and a baseball cap. He looks at an action figure of himself
with a spring-action jaw.

NARRATOR

There were Burt action figures,

CUT TO GROCERY STORE, CEREAL AISLE

BURT walks down an aisle and sees his face on a box of Wheaties
on the clearance shelf. At the end of the aisle there are costumes of
him, including garish masks with oversized moving mouths, marked
for discount.

NARRATOR

Burt costumes,

BURT'S HOUSE, OUTSIDE
BURT walks up his steps with his groceries. There is still the GIRL
with the "Eat Me," sign. He motions for her to follow him inside.
She does.

NARRATOR

And yet, as long as he was not creating his compositions, the
public interest continued to diminish.

CUT TO BOOKSTORE
BURT walks by the Free-Books bin, now with his girlfriend, the EAT
ME GIRL. He looks down and sees the biographies about him in the
bin.

CUT TO GROCERY STORE
BURT walks by the Wheaties *boxes, but they all show someone else.*

NARRATOR

Burt was miserable. He felt like he was in a sea of people,
and yet, all alone. Yet, he had run out of ideas, out of inspiration.

BURT'S BEDROOM, EARLY MORNING
BURT lies in bed, as if he has not slept all night. Piles of self-help
books, including James Joyce's A Portrait of the Artist as a Young

Man *and Viktor Frankl's* Man's Search for Meaning, *sit on the bedside table, their spines marred with teeth marks. BURT'S GIRLFRIEND is sound asleep beside him. He gets up carefully, so as not to wake her, and walks down the hallway.*

NARRATOR

BURT stopped sleeping. He stopped eating. Life just held no more joy for him any longer.

As BURT goes down the hallway, he picks up packages of BURT figurines; there are dozens. The hallway is also filled with magazines and expired Wheaties *boxes with BURT'S face, as well as hardback and paperback biographies. There are even cartridges of BURT video games and racks of his clothing line—each piece of clothing with faux bite marks integrated into the distressed design.*

NARRATOR

But as he walked down the hallway to the bathroom, stepping over the dozens of Burt Vousch action figures, biographies, magazine articles, and Wheaties boxes that his girlfriend had bought—often before they were thrown away by retailers trying to clear inventory—it occurred to Burt that he had become quite a piece of work himself.

BURT goes into the closet and pulls out one of his most colorful outfits from his own clothing line. He dresses before the mirror. He puts on an outlandish pair of glasses, as well as his signature beret. He stares at himself a long time, a smile slowly forming on his face. His eyes brighten. Finally, he puts his fingers in his mouth.

NARRATOR

Standing before the mirror and gazing at himself, he thought he was more than a piece of work. He was a piece of *art*. He was artwork. Then an epiphany: the dark clouds of gloom parted and a ray of inspiration shone down on him. Burt suddenly knew what his last and greatest piece would be. It would revive his career, and as he contemplated it, all sadness, emptiness, and loneliness melted away. Even if he tried, he could not have even remembered what they were; it was as if he had not even the faintest memory of sadness, loneliness, or loss. He knew he must set to work right then and there, before the inspiration left him. It would be amazing. It would make his legacy a lasting one, one that would be hailed as bold, courageous, and of course, ingenious. So that morning, before his girlfriend awoke, Burt Vousch ate himself.

CUT TO INT. BURT'S ROOM, LATER

BURT'S GIRLFRIEND wakes up, rubs her eyes, and opens the shades. The camera follows her down the hallway to the bathroom, where we see her enter. Framed by the bathroom door, she makes the horrifying discovery of BURT'S body (OFF SCREEN) and

screams.

NARRATOR

But when the police and coroners found him, they decided to leave the body alone. For they knew it was not just a body at a suicide scene; it was *art*. They knew the inevitable art critics, the collectors, and the paparazzi would want to come and view Burt as he had left himself.

Time Lapse. The POLICE, the ART CRITICS, the COLLECTORS, the PAPARAZZI come and go, framed in the bathroom door taking photos of BURT (OFF SCREEN) in the bathroom. Camera pans back, moving down the hall, fixed on BURT'S GIRLFRIEND, who remains catatonic but shrinking in the growing screen, crowded with people.

NARRATOR

And when they did come, all agreed, that it was the greatest, most breathtaking, most marvelous, and most ingenious work of his entire life; his greatest and most lasting Oral Composition.

FADE TO BLACK

8.

When We Talk About Fights

My friend Sidney is a very handsome man. Women always smile at him when they walk by. When he is in downtown DC, if he is around the National Mall where all the tourists hang out, foreigners will ask to be in pictures with him, as if he is some strapping specimen of pure American virility.

The other notable thing about Sidney is that he wears an eye patch. It's custom made so that it fits snugly in his eye socket, not over it. His brother shot his eye out with a pellet gun in an argument. But Sidney doesn't talk about that; no one in his family does, except to joke that women love the patch. Sidney's brother Mitch calls it the "sex magnet." I had a friend, a psych major, who met Sidney. She said that women liked the patch because it made Sidney seem dangerous, but also wounded and vulnerable at the same time.

I don't know if he'd like the wounded and vulnerable bit. Dangerous, yes.

Sidney is seven years older than I am. He is like a big brother, and he even used to beat up my big brother, Rick, when he was too hard on me. I loved him for it. Sidney came to visit me while I was home from college at Christmastime. We went out to a Mexican restaurant for lunch. It used to be a pizza place. I'm comfortable in restaurants because I work in one, but that's only because Sidney got me my first job waiting tables. Sidney was practically born in a restaurant, and now works at his parents' café, which I guess he will be taking over someday.

The waiter sat us down at a booth beside a window. The curtains had green cacti and yellow sagebrush on them. Sidney arranged himself on his side behind his menu.

"Are sanchos like a soft taco?" I asked.

"Yeah, like a burrito really," Sidney said.

"Then I'm having the bean and cheese one. You think one will be enough?"

"I don't know man . . . so many choices."

The waiter came. I ordered the bean and cheese sancho with a side of nachos. Sidney ordered the same with an additional soft taco, as well as two waters and two lemonades. He said lunch was on him.

"Thanks," I said.

"Don't mention it."

Sidney looked around at the new décor and shook his head. It looked nothing like the old pizza place. The red-and-white-checkered tablecloths were gone, as well as the jukebox and Ms. Pac-Man machine—where they had been now stood a miniature covered wagon that rocked and swayed children on a journey along the "Oregon Trail" for seventy-five cents. "I remember the last time I was here, six—no, seven years ago. Man, that was a long time ago," Sidney said.

"The halcyon days of your youth."

"Halcyon. That sounds like a good word. What's it mean?"

"Calm. Peaceful. Untroubled. It's from a Latin word that, in turn, is derived from a Greek one for a type of bird. I was being ironic."

"Yeah. Actually, the last time I was here, I got into a fight."

"Really?"

"I was here with Kurt. It was stupid."

Sidney leaned forward with his elbows on the table. His right hand played aimlessly with his fork, standing it up, then letting it fall, then standing it up again. "We had just finished dinner and were walking along the sidewalk out there, and these two guys were coming right at us. It was one of those things where neither party really changed direction, so we just kind of stepped around each other at the last minute. The guy on my side was this muscle-bound guy with a shaved head and a bunch of earrings. I'm moving around him, and he just smacks me with his shoulder. He was bigger than me, so I kind of flew off to the side and had to catch myself. When they were gone, Kurt is standing there laughing at me and goes, 'Pussy.'

"Then I darted off, just like that, not thinking, right after the muscle-head with the earrings. I ran up behind him and punched him right here in the back of the neck." Sidney made a fist and put it to the base of his skull. The waiter brought us our drinks.

"That's right on the medulla," I said and stuck my straw in my mouth.

"Yeah. He fell flat on his face. He was stunned or something. He tried to get up but just waved his arms like a dying animal or something."

"Oh, man."

"His friend shoved me, and I took him by his arms and swung him around. We must've looked a little ridiculous, like square dancers or something. We spun twice before he tripped over his friend and fell between the curb and the tire of this parked car. I got in one punch on the side of his head before Kurt came and pulled me away. He couldn't talk he was laughing so hard."

"Did the guy get up?"

"Which one?"

"The one that was convulsing."

"Must have. No cops showed up at my door with a warrant for my arrest as a murderer."

"Lucky. Can you pass me the dessert menu?"

Sidney reached over to the napkin dispenser where the dessert menu was propped, then slid it to me. I looked at it: fried ice cream, Mucho Choco Brownie with ice cream, vanilla ice cream with caramel and nuts. I hated nuts.

"Can I see that when you're done?" Sidney asked.

I handed it to him. "Nothing good."

He studied it, his eyebrow over his good eye lowered. He flipped the menu over and set it flat on the table. "I remember this other time, when I was living in Charlottesville. It was that same year, but it was December. Anyway, there was snow on the ground, but it was old snow. It had hardened into that really gritty, crusty stuff. I was coming out of my house—"

"Your apartment or the house with the frat boys?"

"The frat boys. I've got stories about them too. But we were coming out of the house—this was when I was dating Corina. It was me, Corina, and my friend Mohamad. We were walking to the car, when these three guys pop up from behind this pile of snow and start pegging us with these ice balls. At first, it was funny and all. 'Oh no, we're being attacked, real funny.' Then one of them flings this flat piece of ice like a Frisbee." Sidney waved the menu as if he was about to demonstrate by flinging it across the restaurant. "And it hits Corina right in the face. She crumples. I look down and see she's bleeding."

"Did they mean to hit her in the face?"

"I don't know. I didn't care; it's not like they gave any thought to it. If they had, they would have realized 'hey this could really hurt someone.' Anyway, I flew, man. They had already started to run. There was this fat one, and he was trailing after the others. I think he was the one who hit her. It's always the fat ones; they're bitter cause they got made fun of when they were little."

"You think so?"

"I know so. I know a thing about being teased. Think about it. No one was probably sensitive to them when they were the little pudgy kids on the playground, so why should they be sensitive to others when they get older? They've got all sorts of resentments built up. Anyway, I couldn't catch up with him. Then again, I could have if I wanted—he was a lard ass—but instead I just threw my arms up and dove into his back. He fell down. Now, he still thought this whole thing was a joke, and he was laughing when I rolled him over. I was like, 'You think that's funny?' And I cocked my arm back, but Mohamad was behind me and held my arm, saying, 'No man, no man, chill, chill.' I tried getting my arm free, but couldn't, so with my other arm I just took a fistful of the fat guy's hair and started knocking his head against the pavement."

"Pretty ridiculous. Where'd you learn to fight like that?"

"I don't know if I would even call it fighting. It was scrapping. It's not like I learned; you just had to fight to survive in my house. Five brothers, you're going to have some rumbles, and I think my family was extra competitive, Mitch especially. Like he was always trying to test me." He paused for a moment, as if his thoughts had gone off into a different direction.

"Earth to Sidney."

"Sorry. Where was I?"

"Brothers?"

"Yeah. Anyway, that doesn't mean we didn't stick up for each other. I remember when Mitch got his ass whupped by these trailer-trash kids. Chris and Brent just got in the car, went right to their trailer park, and beat them up in front of their mother."

"Their mom?"

"Hey, it's the rules of engagement, man. You mess with someone, and they've got family, you better be ready for the retaliation. She understood that. It wasn't that bad anyway. They just gave the kids something to think about. Actually, they said the mother didn't even seem to care. Then again, I wouldn't have put up a fight if Chris and Brent had shown up at my door. Maybe if I had a baseball bat or a shotgun."

I took a deep drink of my lemonade through my straw. The waiter brought out my nachos. He was an old guy and had spoken with a Latino accent when he took our orders. He seemed friendly. Sidney thanked him.

"I got in a lot of fights in Charlottesville," Sidney said, reflective. "It was just a crazy atmosphere."

"College is a weird place."

"But I wasn't in college. I had transferred from community college and had deferred another year to earn some money for school. I was working. That made it worse. I was an outsider. So I was always being tested. After a while of that, you start to develop this mentality. You don't walk into a party looking for your friends. The first thing you look for is the biggest guy there. And if you go in like that, you give off this vibe, and the biggest guy ends up finding you."

"Frats are stupid. You're paying money so you can have friends."

"Yeah. Tell me about it. I remember one time my roommate Wells had three freshman pledges at the house vacuuming and doing dishes for us. See, Wells was a senior member of the frat, so for hazing week these guys had to be his maids."

"Did they have to dress in French maid outfits?"

"As a matter of fact, they did."

I laughed and so did Sidney.

"It was something, seeing this bunch of eighteen-year-old guys walking around in fishnets and lacy frills. I mean, it was not pretty, with their hairy legs and stuff."

"I can imagine, but I don't want to."

"Anyway, I came in from work and sat down with a beer to watch Star Trek. I was dead tired and these little pledges, in these maid outfits, were whining about how 'hard' hazing was on them. At a commercial, I turned to them and said 'I don't know why you subject yourself to that. If anyone tried to haze me, I'd come after them with a gun.' They got all flustered."

"Flabbergasted."

"Flabberwhat?"

"Flabbergasted means flustered, shocked. Like, gob-smacked."

"Flabbergasted. Gob-smacked."

"Or if you really want to up your nerd credentials, you could go with 'flummoxed.'"

"Flummoxed. I like that one. I'll learn something from you, if nothing else, Brainiac," Sidney laughed. He'd always called me Brainiac, but in a good way. He had always wanted me to do well in school. Always told me not to worry about the other, bigger, athletic kids who picked on me. He told me I'd do better in the long run because I liked to read, even when I didn't *have* to. He'd often ask to borrow my books, or ask me to tell him about them when he couldn't find time to read them. Sometimes, at the end of the day, his eye was just too tired. For Christmas I had bought him a bunch of books on tape.

He kept talking.

"Anyway, the pledges are all like, 'No man, you don't get a chance to fight back when your frat brothers haze you. They come in while you're sleeping, wrap you up in your own blankets, and carry you out.' I'm like, 'I don't care. I'd fight back, man.' They were silent a while. They obviously thought I was just full of myself. Then I said, 'No offense, but the whole thing is kind of stupid. All that inconvenience just so you can pay a certain amount of money each month, so you can point to a drunk undergrad in a bar and call him 'brother.' I've got four brothers, and they're my brothers because they came out between the same two legs as I did. Not because I pay them.' That was the nail in my coffin, I think."

"Why? Did they do something?"

"Not then. But that night there was a party at the frat house. They got together with some of their friends, had a few drinks, got their courage up, and thought, 'That guy Sidney is an asshole; let's haze him.' So I'm lying in bed, and I wake up as they're lifting me up to their shoulders. They were still in their French maid outfits, too. They were required to keep them on."

He shook his head. "Man, embarrassing. But I have to admit, they did a good job wrapping me in my blankets: I couldn't move. I was like, 'Okay. Really cool, I'm being hazed, yeah, this is really cool. Put me down.' Then one of them punched me right in my back, and then they started punching me all over. I guess it was part of the ritual or something. We were all on the steps now, there was about six of them—they had brought friends—and I started flailing my arms and going nuts. Then we all just tumbled down the steps. It was a mess. Legs, arms, feet everywhere. I started crawling my way back. All I had on were my boxer shorts, and someone grabs them. I didn't want to be naked on top of being hazed, so I turned around and decked the guy in the face. Then it was like king-of-the-hill meets Wrestlemania. It was a race to get to the top of the steps. I stepped on shoulders, heads, anything to get back up there. I was punching guys, boxing ears, scraping necks, grabbing them by their bra straps and fishnets. I got to the top and ran for my room. I could hear them tromping down the hall after me."

"They must have been pissed off by then."

"Yeah, the adrenaline and alcohol were not a good mix."

I took a nacho. The cheese made a string that stretched out between my hand and the plate, then fell down on the table. I tried getting it with my napkin. Sidney was animated, gesturing with his hands. He kept knocking the straw sticking out of his drink.

"I got to my room. They had unscrewed the knob to get in, so I couldn't lock it. I was in my underwear, for God's sake. I didn't feel like letting these guys manhandle me. I had this window in my room that never stayed open. So I had a two-by-four there to hold it up. I grabbed the two-by-four and spun around and whacked the first guy that had rushed in right behind me. It must have made a big old 'crack' sound, but I didn't hear it because the window slammed simultaneously. I went to town on them. The only advantage I had, 'cause I was still outnumbered, five to one—"

"I thought there were six."

"Not after I laid out that one with the two-by-four."

"Oh, okay."

"As I was saying, the only advantage I had was that the room was narrow and they couldn't outflank me.

"Sounds like the Battle of Thermopylae."

"Thermapole-what?"

"Thermopylae. Battle in 480 BC when a few hundred Greeks, led by the Spartans, held off over a hundred thousand Persians for seven days by positioning themselves in a narrow pass."

"Sounds pretty bad ass."

"Still didn't work out for the Greeks, at least not that day. They lost the battle but eventually won the war."

"Nice," Sidney said, nodding. "I should read about that one."

"But your story."

"Yeah. Anyway, they backed out the door, and I chased them down the hallway, whaling away at the last one with the board. They dove down the stairs like the house was on fire. I stood there at the top, holding the board like I was up at bat, screaming: 'Come on, motherfuckers, you want more?' But they didn't take me up on it. Then I heard a crash in my room. I went back. The first guy I had hit had been left in there. He had been trying to get out the window, and it had closed on his leg. He was sitting on the sill trying to lift the window back up, but he had no leverage. He was trapped. I came in and started whacking his shin. You should have seen him squirm."

"He was hanging out a second story window in fishnets. Show him some mercy."

"Did they show me any mercy? A few moments before, this same guy burst in my room and tried kicking the shit out of me. Eye for an eye."

I looked at the black-brown patch of leather fitting snug over his eye socket. He wasn't being ironic.

"Maybe Hammurabi had it right."

"Pause—who's Hammurabi?"

"Babylonian King who made up the earliest set of surviving laws, Hammurabi's Code. He was the one who said, 'Eye for an eye.'"

I said it, feeling a bit awkward, looking at his eye patch. He didn't seem to mind. I hadn't meant anything by it, but even if I had, I bet he would have been all right. I was one of the few people he let ask him about his patch. When I was little, I had asked him, sincerely, how he winked at people if he only had one eye. He had laughed, made an exaggerated wink with his good eye, winding up his mouth into this ridiculous grin, and had said, "Like this, Danny boy."

He nodded, looking out the restaurant window. "Well, Hammurabi was on to something. Someone fucks with you, you fuck them up back. Someone should carve *that* on a stone tablet."

"What happened to the guy?"

"He got his leg out after a while and pulled a Peter Pan down to the ground."

"He was okay?"

"Yeah. Bled all over my carpet though. But we weren't going to get that security deposit back anyway."

The waiter arrived with our sanchos. They were too hot to eat. We both cut a piece, then let it steam on the end of our forks.

"I expected immediate retaliation," Sidney said. "I pushed my desk up against my door and got back in bed with my two-by-four. When I woke up it was light outside, and someone was pounding on my door. It was Wells. I was like, 'Man, now I'm gonna have to whup him.' I opened the door, and he's standing there with his hand extended. 'I just want to shake your hand, man,' he says. I was like, 'Why's that?' He goes, 'We saw those pledges when you were done with them last night. You fucked them up. That's pretty impressive. Six to one, man. I want to shake your hand.' I realized I was still in my underwear, and wanted to get rid of him, so I shook and he promised me no one from the frat would ever bother me again. They didn't."

"What did Corina do when she found out?"

"Oh, she came over, said 'poor baby,' and then we fucked. That was the great thing about Corina, always ready to have sex. I'd come home from the gym some days, without even having a shower, and she'd be waiting at my place, and we would go right into it. It was great when I finally got my own apartment. I gave her a key. I'd get home. She'd have dinner cooking on the stove, then give me a back rub with her shirt off. She'd rub her breasts up against my back, because she knew I liked that. We'd usually end up having sex after that."

I started to eat my sancho.

"That's quite a girl," I said around the cheese and beans in my mouth.

"Yeah. She got me in my share of trouble though. She was always wearing these tight, *tight* pants and skirts. We'd go to a party, and some drunk frat boy would inevitably grope her. Remember the time I came to visit you and had scabs on both my knuckles?"

"Yeah."

"I had been at a party with her the night before, and this guy stuck his hand right in her crotch. Right in front of me. Then he saw me and laughed."

"He laughed?"

"Yeah. I head-butted him, then followed with two punches to this mouth. I think I knocked one of his teeth out."

"For groping your girlfriend."

"I had had a bad week, there was other shit going on too, and he just became a receptacle for all that." Sidney paused and took a bite of his sancho, his jaw moving slowly. Then he shook his head back and forth. He swallowed his food and took a drink. "But you're right. It was no way to handle stuff like that. On the upside, the amount of physical confrontations I've had with people has dropped considerably since I stopped dating that girl. She was nothing but trouble."

"I've never dated a girl like that."

"It's all right. You will one of these days. It's a rite of passage. Come on, you're what, in your second semester of college? It's about time you got your carrot wet."

The food in my mouth was too hot, and I took a drink of water. The plate underneath my sancho was damp, making the tortilla soggy. I didn't care. I tried not to think about what might have gone on in the kitchen while they were preparing it. Every waiter knew that the food served in a restaurant was never as immaculate as it was supposed to be. Eat, don't think.

I couldn't imagine being angry enough to hurt another person. Sidney had once told me that when he was really angry, he sometimes literally saw red flashes before his eyes. I was too repressed to have such feelings, but I remember seeing such flashes once when I was two or three while throwing a temper tantrum and tossing a broken toy at a window.

"I've never had to fight to get by," I said.

Sidney shrugged. "Count your blessings. Also, your Dad is a really laid-back guy. He grew up going to private schools and stuff. Lived in Europe."

"So?"

"My father grew up in downtown Austin. You didn't succeed there by being nice. He's kind of passed that on to us. It's that nature-nurture thing. I remember my father and my oldest brother Chris getting into it once. Dad just said, 'We'll take it outside.' Chris was like, 'Sure.' Chris wasn't out the door before he was knocked cold."

"Your dad hit your brother?"

"Yeah, he was still drinking then."

"What did you think about that?"

"It upset me. No one likes to see their family members beating each other, but on the other hand, it was good. Things were real calm for a while after that. It was like Chris had challenged the hierarchy, and it had stood up under pressure. Dad was still king, and we all knew it."

"That's not true now?"

"No. Dad's not confrontational like that now that he's sober. He's mellow and serene now. It's definitely for the best."

"What had your Dad and Chris been arguing about?"

"Nothing really. It was Chris and my mom. He had mouthed off to her, and my Dad wouldn't have it."

"Huh, that's interesting."

"My father taught us a few things to live by: always do your best, and then no one can say anything about you, and if they do, settle it honorably. But don't step out there if you don't plan on finishing it." He pointed his fork at me. "Never run from a fight, Daniel. You'll never stop running."

I nodded and had a nacho. We ate for a while. I finished my sancho and was still hungry, but didn't say anything. I'd have a sandwich when I got home. I ate all the nachos that had cheese on them, then picked at the olive and pepper slices that were left on the plate. Sidney started on his taco.

"All this talk about Corina is making me miss having a girlfriend."

"You miss Corina, or just having a girlfriend?"

"Coor-reeen--aaa. That girl—the only girl I have ever met who I had perfect sexual chemistry with. I was always changing those sheets on my bed."

Something inside me winced. I felt I'd never have sex like that. I'd never actually had sex-sex yet. I didn't say anything.

"There is this stripper that gave me her number the other night. I might give a call when I get home."

"How'd you meet her?"

"It was just last month. Jim's fiancée was out of town, so we were having a guys' night out. We were visiting all these strip joints down in Virginia Beach. Daniel, some of these girls were so fine. We got to this one place—Jim and I have this game. We try to get the ugliest strippers to do a lap dance for the other. Jim had this real fat, disgusting one picked out for me. He pointed at her and asked the manager to have her treat me to a private show in the back room. See, there are these private rooms you can go to and get a private show. The manager calls this girl over, but he points to the wrong girl. The girl that came over was so hot. Tight little body, brunette, huge boobs, and a great ass. Jim was about to shit himself. She took me by the edge of my jacket and led me to the back. I was like, 'Thanks, Jim!'

"We get to the room. There's two couches and a bouncer sitting there in the corner, but his chair is turned so that he can only see one of the couches. We sit down on the couch that was in bouncer's field of vision, and she does her thing on my lap. Now, I'm telling you, Dan, this girl was so beautiful, and I say to her, 'I know it's against the rules, but I was wondering if I could just put my hand right there.' I said this looking at her butt cheek. Then I said, really starry eyed, 'You are so beautiful.' Then she goes. 'You're not so bad yourself.' Then she grabs me by the collar and pulls me to the couch that the bouncer can't see. She takes my hands and runs them all over her body. Everywhere. I got her off a bit with my hand. She was going nuts. I went to kiss her, but she said no, she'd lose her job."

He stopped and looked out the window. Blew some air out between his lips, then took a drink of his lemonade until the straw made an empty sound.

"What happened?"

"We went back outside when she was done. But she slipped me her card with her phone number on it."

"Wow."

"I'll have to call her."

I took a drink of the water that had formed under the melting ice in my glass. I crunched some ice in my mouth.

"We didn't leave that place in good standing though."

"How so?"

"Well. After two in the morning, they start bringing out the second shift strippers. All the ugly ones that look better after you've been drinking. Anyway, this fat, disgusting woman is up there. We're talking two hundred and fifty pounds, maybe more. I don't know how she moved. She had really gross skin too. I think they just had her there for a joke. All the guys were cheering for her, but Jim and I were grossed out. I sort of felt bad for her. We went to the bar to get away and watch the topless bartender."

"After the fat woman finished her act, she came over to the bar where a bunch of guys were buying her drinks. She was so disgusting. She was *old,* man, and had all this hair on her chin too. I don't know why she was dancing. Sad. Anyway, she leans over the bar beside Jim, and he moves away. Then she puts her hand on his cheek and says, turning his head to face her, 'Hey, Honey, you scared of a real woman?' And Jim bats her hand away and says, 'I'm scared of the ugliest, fattest skank-ho I've ever seen.'"

"Now he shouldn't have done that. He shouldn't have knocked her hand, and he shouldn't have said what he said. It was just mean, and that was just the beginning of it all. Because she gasps, takes her drink, and throws it on Jim, then starts slapping him, then she starts hitting him with fists. All the other men were laughing while Jim was cowering. He was half the size of her. I try to get between them, and she punches me instead. That pissed me off. I was just trying to break it up. But at that point, I still felt bad for her. I just ignored her. Then another stripper comes up and claws my face. I get really protective when people start reaching for my face. You get that way with one eye. I sort of lost control then. I grabbed her by the throat and shoved her. Then the first one came up with a bottle. I looked at the bouncer, but he was laughing. What a fucked up joint. The fat woman didn't swing the bottle at me, but she did hit Jim with it. She didn't hit him hard but glanced his head. Still, she could have done some damage. Jim was dazed for a second. She had this feather boa around her shoulders that I grabbed and tugged. That threw her off balance, she was in heels after all, and she goes crashing onto this table. She was crying though. Actually, she was hysterical. I guess Jim had hit a nerve. It was mayhem."

"And the bouncers didn't intervene?"

"No. Looking back, I wonder if stuff like that was normal for that place. Crazy. Anyway, Jim still wasn't back on his feet, so I took him by the shoulders and pushed him through the crowd, like a battering ram. We made it out the door. The big woman was still following us with that bottle. We sprinted across the parking lot. It was gravel, so we were slipping because we couldn't get our footing.

She was throwing rocks at us now. We were laughing by now. The whole thing was kind of comedic."

"A farce."

"Yep, that. So we get in Jim's truck, and we hear this rock hit the back windshield. Jim flips. He is like, 'Fucking bitch.' He backs out and sits there waiting for her to get closer to the truck. He had this evil look in his eye. He let her get real close, then he spun the back tires and sprayed her with gravel. She was just wearing this skimpy outfit and the feather boa, so she was getting pelted right on bare skin. That stopped her dead. Last I saw of her, she was collapsed in that parking lot, rocks falling off her as she sobbed. Jim's a mean fucker." Sidney was quiet a moment after that, his mouth a thin line, the corners tugging downward. "He brings out the worst in me too. But she shouldn't have chased him."

Our plates were empty. Sidney paid the bill and the waiter brought us change with two mints. We unwrapped them and popped them in our mouths.

"These stories are crazy," Sidney said. "But if there's anything you learn from them, it's that you just got to stick up for yourself when the time comes, you know?"

He said it like he was trying to salvage the conversation, pull some moral out of it. I wondered if he was trying to convince himself, or me. The hard candy clicked against my teeth. I nodded. I guess I understood. We got up and walked towards the door. Sidney stopped, "Hold on, I need to piss."

He headed for the bathroom. I walked outside and waited by his jeep. I blew on my hands then dug them into the pockets of my jeans. Across the street, the Best Western sign was glowing pointlessly in the daylight. There was only one car in the hotel's parking lot. I wondered how much warmer it was in all those empty rooms with identical bedspreads, identical bedside tables, and identical glass ashtrays. Then I remembered Sidney never locked the doors of his Jeep. The door opened, and I stepped inside. I wasn't any warmer. The jeep's covering was just canvas and plastic, after all. The seats actually made me even colder. I stared at the still gauges with their sleeping orange needles. Sidney was still in the restaurant. I thought about what he had said, and I knew that if the situation ever arose, and my honor was questioned, if that test ever came, I'd never be able to stick up for myself. I would fail.

I sat in the cold and silence, trying to figure out what, exactly, that meant.

9.

Tyra's Story

In late May, Daniel went home from college for the summer. His friend Tyra stayed on campus, said she was going to look for a summer job. Daniel's parents lived in Fairfax, where his old high school girlfriend Inez lived. Inez was Daniel's first love. It was hard for him to drive by the Clifton Road Cineplex and the bookstore where they used to spend time together. Sundays were the worst, because then Daniel had to go to church at St. Mary's of the Sacred Heart. It was where he used to go with Inez. Now he would go, but all he could think about how she never visited him. How she never called. They were broken up, but they were supposed to have stayed friends.

But they didn't.

Tyra called, at least once a week. Tyra was the only person from school that remembered Daniel's birthday on June 29th. Daniel had met Tyra at school. Met her at Mass, actually. She was a Eucharistic Minister. She was impossibly beautiful, with auburn hair and curves that made Daniel hurt inside. She liked him too. She said he was sweet and smart, not like most of the guys that she knew. Daniel was sure he was in love again. They started to hang out regularly. Daniel would have said they were dating. But then one day, when he asked Tyra to be his steady girlfriend she said,

"Daniel, you're a really nice guy, but I have to be honest with you. If we were dating, I'd still be fucking other men."

It wasn't the response he expected.

Shortly after that, Daniel had started to figure things out. All the guys that said "Hi" to Tyra on campus, the men that would recognize her at bars when she came in with him: she had slept with most of them or their friends.

"I take my freedom very seriously," she said. "I knew I should tell you, but you were so nice and so good. I thought you'd stop being my friend."

They could be friends, Daniel decided. Not girlfriend and boyfriend, but friends. Then came the second blow. Tyra stopped going to church. She said she didn't believe in God anymore.

"We have to forgive people, even if they don't say sorry. God forgives us only if we *do* say sorry. Double standard," she said.

"But God loves us," Daniel said.

"Why create all these people just to love you? Just to worship you? God's an egoist."

"We have a choice."

"And we're punished if we don't choose him. We go to hell, right?"

Daniel couldn't argue with her. He couldn't ever date her now either; she was an atheist. He prayed for her. Every day, not just on Sundays, although on Sundays he would pray for Inez too.

The summer wore on. Daniel worked his job as a waiter during the day, saving money for tuition and school books. Most of his friends had not come home for the summer, so at night he read books that he picked up at the used book store, classics like *The Brothers Karamazov, Ulysses, Things Fall Apart,* and *The Bluest Eye.* One Sunday morning at Sacred Heart, he saw a girl that looked like Inez, sitting up front where he and Inez used to sit. He walked up behind her, but it was not Inez. It was some teenage girl—way too young—with braces. She smiled at him. He smiled back but sat on the other side of the church. One time, at the coffee and doughnuts reception after Mass, the priest saw Daniel sitting on a radiator, talking to some high school girls who wanted advice on college admissions essays.

When the girls had gone, the priest said, "Whatever happened to that lovely young lady from Bolivia I always used to see you with?"

"She dumped me." Daniel couldn't keep from adding, "She's dating someone else now."

Daniel felt an awkward pause coming. It arrived with all its eyes-to-the-floor, feet-shuffling glory. The priest stared out the window. Daniel got up and said he had to go to the men's room.

◆

Tyra called just as Daniel was dreading the approach of the Fourth of July, and all the picnics he would have to attend, alone. Tyra said that her dad still wasn't sober, had lost his job, and now there was no way to pay for school. She'd have to get a job. Actually, she had already got one. She was dancing.

"Dancing?" Daniel said into the phone.

"Exotic dancing," she said.

"Exotic dancing?"

"God, Daniel, you're so innocent. I'm a stripper."

"Oh."

"It's going to put me through school, Daniel."

"I guess you need to do that.'

"I went to church the other day."

"You serious?"

"I didn't burst into flames."

"That's great. It's really great, Tyra."

◆

It was September. Daniel was glad to be back at school. While he was headed to the cafeteria one evening, he saw Tyra

125

talking to a tall blond guy with big shoulders, a strong jaw, and a flat stomach. Whoever he was, he was wearing pleated khakis, an oxford shirt that showed off his biceps, and expensive sunglasses. Tyra was standing in pumps, blue skirt, and a pink fitted T-shirt. She had his attention. She had the attention of every male who walked by.

Daniel was going to keep walking. He didn't want to be introduced to the blond guy, but Tyra saw him.

"Daniel!"

Tyra jumped up and hugged him, hanging on his neck, her heels curled up so that her pumps touched her backside. He hugged her around the waist. The other guy was watching. She waved good-bye to him over Daniel's shoulder, and he left looking miffed.

"Daniel, it's so good to see you. I missed you," she said.

"I missed you too. Thanks for remembering my birthday. Everyone always forgets it, in the summer."

"No problem. Hey, we can celebrate it this weekend. Or we can do a half-birthday party in January."

"That would be nice," he said. His cheeks felt hot as they walked along the quad, and she put her hand in the crook of his arm. The trees were just starting to turn yellow, and a brisk breeze sent a rain of them down around them.

"When you going to come and see me dance?" A strand of hair swept into her lips.

"Jeez, I wouldn't know what to do in there, Tyra. What is strip bar etiquette?"

"You've never been to a titty bar?"

"Uh . . . ."

"Daniel, you are such a gentleman. You just come in. Sit down wherever you want. Ask the waitress to change a twenty into ones so you can tip the girls, then you watch."

"You make a lot of money?"

"Men are stupid. They'll fork it over."

He couldn't help but notice the note of derision in her voice.

◆

Daniel procrastinated. He dated other girls, but things never worked out. He took one girl out, but she only talked about her ex-boyfriend. Another girl deserted him at a restaurant when some of her friends came by and asked her to go clubbing with them. One girl, Tammy, whom he helped with her history paper, offered to take him out to a nice restaurant to thank him. She did. When the bill came, however, she claimed to have forgotten her purse and asked him if he would mind covering it.

One night he was home alone and the phone rang. It was Tyra.

"It's a slow night," she said. "You want to come up and keep me company?"

"Sure, okay."

Daniel rode his bike up Wisconsin Avenue to where Tyra worked. The club was next door to a Blockbuster Video store. Imagine that, he thought, mothers bringing their kids from soccer practice, T-ball games, and Christmas pageants, to pick up movies from the kiddy section and just a brick wall separates them from topless women.

He locked his bike up beneath a street lamp, just a block away from the club. The sidewalk was bordered by a stone wall with an iron gate. On the other side was the Episcopal cemetery; beyond that, the cathedral. Daniel contemplated the cathedral. The stone, hoisted up to impossible heights and mortared into permanence, was beautiful, breathtaking. He thought of grace, beauty, and transcendence. He thought of being with Inez. She could be breathtaking at times. But other times, she had been a pain, sort of full of herself, mean even. Maybe he was lucky to be rid of her.

127

Although a part of him wondered if any girl would ever love him again. Or even like him.

But Tyra liked him. It was good to have friends.

One time, Tyra had shown up at Daniel's dorm room after drinking at a party, and she had tried to kiss him. He'd turned his head away. He wanted to be special. Everyone made out with Tyra, and a lot of people fucked her. Daniel decided he would be the exception by not making out. He would be special. It was the opposite of Inez. She had had high standards. Even after dating all that time, they had never had sex. He was Inez's first kiss. Guys in high school had hated Daniel because he dated Inez. Because he "got somewhere" with her. Inez had tolerated him removing her bra, but never her panties, nor his boxers. Plus, they never touched each other *there* with their hands. Instead they would grind against one another until they climaxed. Never too many times in one night, or else Inez would become reticent and ashamed.

Daniel had loved her all the more for it. He was still a virgin and was happy for it. "Your virginity is a gift from God," she used to say to him. "Only to be shared with the one you commit yourself to for life."

He had agreed.

But the rumors that had reached him said that Inez was indeed fucking the new guy she was dating. It made Daniel wonder what had been wrong with him.

He walked up the hill and tried to focus on Tyra. The rules were different with her. He would stand out with Tyra by not "getting anywhere" with her on purpose. That would be how he would make sure their friendship was special.

He walked down the sidewalk, past empty office buildings, past a Chinese take-out joint. At the door to the strip club there was a cement rise, a step before the door. It wasn't quite high enough to be a real step, but it seemed to be trying. In its effort, it was more of a hazard than anything else, not high enough to be helpful, not low enough to be negligible, just *there* enough to warrant a red sign on the door with gold letters that read, "Watch Your Step."

Daniel went inside and saw another door, this one with a sign that said, "No Cover Charge." He pushed it open. A large bouncer dressed in black asked for his ID. Daniel gave it to him. He looked at it with a frown.

"This really you?"

"Yeah."

Of course, it was. Daniel didn't own a fake ID.

It was a profile shot. He asked Daniel to turn sideways. As Daniel did, he saw the length of the bar.

Three stages, three girls—dancing, twisting, topless, and bottomless. Men sat in chairs, across the aisle or at the foot of the stages, facing the girls, paying the girls.

Full nudity. Tyra hadn't said it was full nudity. *Titty bar.* Titty bar meant tits, but here were vulvas: shaved, pink, and stretched open for display. A man went up to the stage and dropped down a one dollar bill. The dancer raised her leg above her head, and her labia yawned open.

One dollar. Just one dollar, to see all that.

Daniel didn't know what stage Tyra used. She'd said they danced in fifteen-minute shifts. He sat in the second row, definitely not the first, in front of the center stage. There was a mirror behind each dancer, a mirror with letters that said, "Do Not Touch Dancers."

These were not good-looking guys. They were average guys, *very* average: a quiet, short one with a duffel bag; two chubby guys in college sweatshirts; a very fat man in a suit; a man in his forties, with spiked hair on top and hair down to the base of his neck in back, wearing a nylon jacket and sweat pants cut off at the knee; two men, brothers perhaps, with cardigan sweaters and cinnamon-frosty beards and thick professorial glasses. Daniel thought he saw one handsome young man with good build and good hair, but when he turned, Daniel realized he had buck teeth and a grotesque goatee.

Daniel was the most attractive guy there. A feeling he wasn't used to.

The others were men who would never see a beautiful girl naked, unless they paid.

And the women *were* beautiful, amazing really. All of them, but Daniel only picked out two he would consider "attractive." He had long ago realized the difference between attractive and beautiful: it was all about approachability. He had learned that Inez had been beautiful but over time realized she was not attractive. He wanted to consider himself a man of discriminating taste. Whereas he knew all the men there would take any one of the girls they could get. He knew, from hearing people talk about strip bars, that every man there wanted to leave with a dancer, go home with a dancer, have sex with a dancer.

He didn't. He told himself that this quality made him different. But the dancers didn't know that. He wanted them to. He wanted them to know that if he tipped them, it was because he knew they had rent to pay, and he wanted to help them pay it, not fuck them.

Then Tyra appeared. She walked down the aisle between the seating section and the stages. Every man turned to watch her go past. She was in black lingerie and a silver robe, a red Chinese dragon swirling around it. When she saw Daniel, she ran over and hugged him.

"Hey, sweetheart!" she said, sitting down next to him.

"Nice robe."

"Thank you. I got it at Commander Salamander."

"You have the nicest outfit here. It's really classy."

"Thank you."

A waitress asked them for drink orders. Tyra introduced Daniel as a "very special friend." He supposed it was their own code or something. The waitress winked at him and said his drinks would be free. He asked for a vodka tonic with two limes; it was what Daniel's older friend, Sidney, always ordered. Tyra had a Sprite. When the waitress left he said, "She seemed nice."

"She's the only one," Tyra said.

They talked about dancers, how they couldn't be trusted. How they let the guys think they had a chance, just to get tips. Tyra emphasized that none of the guys there had a chance.

"If the first time you met me, I was here—" Daniel said.

"We wouldn't be friends. But you wouldn't come here, Daniel. It's why I love you."

Daniel looked around at the girls. The reflections of the girls. The men, the men staring at the girls. Starring at Tyra. Staring at him.

"No. I probably wouldn't."

The men watched her, even with her clothes on. She was the best-looking dancer there. She had hugged him, kissed him. The men must have wanted to tear him apart with their envy, tear him apart and find out what he had done to warrant the affection a stripper. Tear him apart or lift him to their shoulders in triumph, because his victory was their victory.

She said that strippers were fucked up. They all had to be the center of attention. They had sexual dysfunctions. They had to have male approval. They had been molested when they were younger. It was like chaos theory, Daniel said, the theory that a butterfly's wings flailing in Africa could make it rain in San Francisco. An uncle or father's hand grazing a thigh at five landed them straddling a brass pole at eighteen.

"Daniel, are you a little tipsy?" Tyra asked, smiling.

"I don't know," he said. He'd never had a vodka tonic before. But he did notice he was talking a lot. "How many of these poor girls have been molested?"

"Most of them. All of them?"

"Not you."

"God, no. Dad's a drunk but not a pervert. I'm here to pay tuition. I was going to quit after the first month, but it's not like Pop is going to come through on my rent. It's up to me."

Tyra was wearing dark red lipstick. She looked dangerous. She lit a cigarette. A stream of gray from her mouth became a cloud of gray that touched the ceiling and the colored lights, and when it dissolved, there was a naked girl dancing in a mirror. Daniel stared at her for a while and lost track of the time.

"Earth to Daniel," Tyra said.

"Sorry. Hey, I'm glad you went to church the other day."

"Yeah, God pisses me off sometimes."

The statement made him cringe. He took a sip of his drink, the way people sip drinks when they're uncomfortable. He repositioned himself on his chair.

"Well, I'm sure we give him a real run for his money." He wasn't sure what he meant. Tyra didn't seem to care one way or another. She was looking at one of the girls.

"She does great pole work." Smoke came out with her words. "I don't know. There are some things about Jesus though that I find beautiful. I can't let go of those."

"So, you still . . . like Jesus?" Daniel said. His drink was empty. The waitress brought him another.

"I find him beautiful," Tyra said, sipping her Sprite. "That's why I wanted to be a Eucharistic Minister, so I could hold his body in my hands. He wouldn't care that I am a stripper. He hung out with prostitutes, adulterers, and tax collectors for God's sake."

It was something. Jesus was God. Did Tyra know that? Of course, she did; she was a good Catholic girl.

The bouncer walked by, a big guy with a bald head. He might have seemed friendly in any other situation, but now he was just ominous. Tyra reached out and touched him on his massive hand. He stopped.

"Rodney. This is my friend Daniel. He's a *very* good friend."

They shook hands, Rodney's enveloping Daniel's.

"Sorry I gave you a hard time at the door. Won't happen again," he said.

"No problem," Daniel said, trying to pitch his voice low to match Rodney's. It really was no problem. At least now it wasn't. He was just so relieved that Tyra still believed in Jesus.

◆

It was Tyra's turn to dance. The music never stopped; it was fed from somewhere else, not in tune with the comings and goings of acts. Not that the guys cared much. The dancer in center stage wound down her dance. She slipped on a dress that still showed her labia when she bent over. Tyra ascended. She pulled a roll of paper towels and a bottle of Windex from the side of the stage. She sprayed the mirror. Shots of Windex looked like giant gobs of spittle. She wiped the mirror. She wiped the poles with an up and down motion. She put the Windex and roll away, then spun around, her robe flaring out like an inverted flower.

She was dancing, with a vibrancy in her muscles and intimacy in her eyes that the other dancers lacked. The robe shimmered. It tantalized, it mesmerized. It was gone. Now she was a woman of dreams, in lacy black panties and with firm breasts. The perfect form from a lingerie ad. That was not real, that was a construction of a photography studio and air brushing; yet it *was* real, right there before all of them. Her skin was a perfect, unblemished amber under the red lights. Cigarette smoke was being blown her way by anxious lungs. The drinks the waitress had served Daniel had helped him to relax. He felt permeable. In a moment so removed from the present distractions that his thoughts were lucid, he realized this was why people went to hell.

But this was different. He had come for Tyra out of friendship. He knew he was special, because he wasn't trying to get anywhere. He wasn't objectifying; if anything, he was romanticizing. And after all, Tyra still believed in Jesus. She was just doing this to pay bills. That somehow made her more beautiful than all the other girls. Her skin was smooth, her hands running over it. Her hand moved over her panties, over her belly button, up her chest, and the bra snapped away. There were her breasts. They had always been there, but now he was finally *seeing* them. Then her panties fell down, and her six-inch heels stepped out of them. It wasn't that much of a shock to see her completely naked. Daniel had already seen the other naked dancers' vulvas—Tyra's wasn't that different. It was just anatomy after all.

She wrapped dollar bills around her fingers like rings. She raised her leg slowly, above a man's head, as if imitating a dog urinating, the man playing the role of a gratified fire hydrant.

He turned away happy.

Three men went up at once, placing tens, not ones, on the stage.

They turned away laughing, giggling.

The young man with the good build but ugly face went up. He turned away amazed, leaving three twenties behind.

Tyra would reach down for the money slowly. Looking at her patron and mouthing the word "thank you," accompanied by an intimate gaze, as if they were the only ones in on it.

The men loved it. They whooped, hollered, and cheered. Tyra looked at Daniel. He was looking in her eyes. She smiled. He knew everyone in the audience was now watching him, or aware of her eyes on him. She slid down the mirror, her hair collecting behind her, her knees bending, her thighs spreading into a wide V.

Then something unexpected.

She blushed.

It was all over her, in her face, the skin of her breasts, her lower back. Daniel shifted. They both were uncomfortable. He didn't want to hurt her feelings by looking away, or maybe she realized halfway down into her crouch that she didn't want him to look, but it was too late. She came up too quickly. Her movements were out of sync with the music.

♦

A man in a bruise-blue suit sat down beside Daniel. He had a cigarette smoldering in his mouth and a martini glass filled with brown liquid. He reached out his hand.

"Guido."

"Hi. Daniel."

"Nice to meet you," Guido said.

Tyra's Sprite was still beside Daniel's vodka tonic. Daniel was not sure how many he had drunk. Both drinks were sweating and turning the paper napkins beneath them into dark red pulp.

"Is she your friend?" Guido said, gesturing with his martini hand towards Tyra.

"Yes."

"She's very beautiful."

"I think so."

"You think so or you wouldn't be her friend, right?"

Daniel laughed, because he felt he should. But he knew he was Tyra's friend for reasons that were not as superficial as that. Guido was looking at him, waiting for him to say something. The stare was making Daniel nervous; maybe he needed another drink. Guido had one single eyebrow across the wide expanse of his forehead and a bristly mustache that was a smaller copy of the eyebrow. He would be a *hairy* old man, Daniel thought. Guido's eyes were slag gray. His hair close-cropped on the sides. On top it was longer; it looked gelled. It had to be gelled.

"It's more than that," Daniel said.

"Of course, that's why anyone has friends. It's more than that."

"Yes."

They looked at her, but now Daniel felt self-conscious. As if Guido was watching him watch her. Tyra's back was to them: a back nimble like an archer's bow, mounted on mounds of flesh, parted in a crescent moon.

"What's her name?" Guido said.

"Ambrosia," Daniel said. It was her stage name. Of course, Tyra never revealed her real name at work. He didn't like the name. It rolled off the tongue awkwardly. Of course, it did. It was Greek.

"Here's my card," Guido said. Daniel looked at the card without reading it, not understanding why he now had it.

"Maybe you can introduce us," Guido said.

"Uh. Yeah. You can introduce yourself. I'm sure she'll come around."

♦

But when Tyra came around after her set, she pointed towards some empty chairs in the back of the bar. She didn't want to sit around customers. Daniel shirked his shoulders at Guido as he got up.

From the back, Daniel and Tyra evaluated the strippers, picked out the fake breasts, talked about high heels. Tyra pointed out the girl who did the best "pole work" again. All the time, Guido kept looking back over his shoulder. Daniel noticed this because Guido's was the only head not turned towards the stage.

"That guy gives me the creeps," Tyra said.

"He gave me his card. His name is Guido."

"Figures."

Daniel stayed late. Guido stayed late—he kept ordering drinks. Guido had to. Daniel did not. The waitresses were friendly to him and didn't enforce the "you sit, you sip" rule on him. The other dancers walked by and smiled at him like he was an insider. At 2 a.m. Tyra was off. Another dancer would take her place in the schedule. She disappeared upstairs, then reappeared, her body concealed under a white turtle neck and black jeans. Daniel followed Tyra to the exit. The aisles got crowded with the shift change. Girls in robes were climbing up to the stages while others were leaving, their duffel bags slung over their shoulders. Daniel tried to stay close to Tyra. He saw Guido getting up out of the corner of his eye.

"Yo, Daniel," Guido said, leaning on the back of a chair.

Daniel walked. The music was loud. He pretended he didn't hear Guido. He was leaving with a dancer. Of course people wanted to call his name. Wanted to chant it. He couldn't help smiling at the thought. He hooked his finger through Tyra's belt loop. She looked back at him and smiled. It was just right, he thought.

Rodney wished them good night, shook hands with Daniel. Daniel felt like he was part of a club, almost felt like he was leaving a family reunion. The air outside was cold and refreshing after the hot clouds of cigarette smoke. They turned down the street. Daniel decided he would walk her to her car. Then he heard Rodney, in his voice of authority, his voice of confrontation,

"Hey. You can't go out with that."

Daniel turned to see Guido. He was coming out the door of the club. He had sideburns of sweat. He was drunk. In his hand was the object of incrimination: the martini glass, still filled with brown liquor. He felt Tyra squeeze his arm, press her body against the length of his. It thrilled him.

Rodney held Guido by the sleeve of the bruise-blue jacket. The padded shoulders lifted up and looked weird and unnatural. Guido was determined. They could see it in his face. Daniel and Tyra were frozen in place. They'd never turn their backs on a face like that. Guido pulled his arm out of the jacket; the shoulder pad deflated. Rodney lost his grip. Now there was something in Guido's hand. Now he was turning. Now, whatever it was, some weapon, some blunt object, perhaps just a garage door opener or a cell phone, or even a blackjack. Whatever it was, he was hammering it down on Rodney's face. Rodney fell back, his arms retracting to his nose, a fountain of blood the color of wine issuing forth.

Then the second calamity: Guido stepped. His foot landed half on the little non-negligible step, half off. Underneath Rodney's cries, there was a scuffing noise that was Guido's foot losing traction on the cement. The foot went, twisted clumsily, and his body tipped, suspended in a way that was beautiful and graceful and imminently painful.

"Oh, fuck," Guido said. He burped the words, saying them half-heartedly as he concentrated on swinging his arms. His hand reached up high. Daniel watched it fall, down, down, the cathedral appeared behind it, the stone lit blue and gray by ground lights. A plane flew behind one of the spires like a tracking star. The hand came down, towards a parking meter. The bruise-blue jacket was just touching the ground. The hand passed the parking meter, then the elbow.

Followed by the bang. Guido's head jerked back as it hit the meter, which didn't care if a living or inanimate thing collided with it. It stood fast regardless. The martini glass rolled out of his hand and broke in a spreading fan of glass.

The music was still playing. Rodney was holding his nose. A red and black crevasse yawned where the top of his nose had been opened. Someone inside felt a draft because the door was left ajar. When they came out, they saw the scene and called the police.

◆

Once they had made a statement to the police, Daniel and Tyra left. She drove them home. Daniel would come back and get his bike later. Tyra had her own studio apartment now. The couch was a foldout bed. Daniel told her to wash up. He would make the bed for her. She hugged him.

"Thank you, Danny. I don't know what I would do without you."

She closed the door to the bathroom. He pulled out the bed, fluffed the pillows, tucked the sheets under the mattress. Good and tight. He finished. She was still in the bathroom. Girls took a long time. He sat down on the bed since the couch was now gone. He wanted to watch TV, but she didn't have one. So he listened to her.

There were sounds of water running, drawers opening, closing, a bottle clinking on the sink top. She brushed her teeth. She spat. Water ran. The door opened. She walked over wearing a pink Winnie the Pooh onesie. Pooh was smiling on the front, oblivious to the breasts behind his ears. She laid down with her head on Daniel's lap.

"Going to get under the covers?" he asked.

139

"Okay."

He tucked the blankets around her and rubbed her feet to warm them. She squirmed.

"That tickles."

"Sorry."

He leaned on his elbow beside her. He ran his fingers through her hair and over her scalp, drawing the locks out on the pillow. That night she had come over to his dorm room drunk, the same night he would not kiss her, she had slept on his couch. She asked him that night, "If you won't sleep with me, Daniel, then just run your fingers through my hair, like my mom used to. It comforts me."

He did then. He did it again now. She smiled. Her lips were their natural color now, pink. He smelled of smoke. She turned on her side. She was a landscape to him: her hair on the pillow, a river delta; her shoulders, a precipice, leading down to the valley carved out at her waist, followed by the rise of her hip, then the gradual slope down her legs to the wasteland of the bed that was not her.

He realized he had not run his hands along a girl's body since Inez. He did so, letting his hand linger in the hollow of her waist before ascending the peak of her hip, riding in the air back to her hair to repeat the whole journey again.

He wanted her.

He wanted her close to him. Like she was when Guido first came towards them, when she had turned to him for safety, for protection. He wanted her body against him, that warm softness beneath him.

He was trembling.

"You cold, Daniel?"

"Yeah."

More minutes bred and died. Nothing happened. He ran his fingers though her hair again. It was straight now. All the tangles were gone. He curled it away from her ear, wrapping it under the lobe. He saw the little hole where her earring punctured her body. He kissed it. Then kissed her head right behind her ear. He felt her body shift. Her legs straightened out. It was her cheek that moved itself under his lips. He pressed his lips to her again, and it was her mouth. It tasted of toothpaste and cold water. She was soft, softer than him, but solid, full, and real. All he knew was Tyra. He heard the sound of the onesie unzipping. She unbuttoned his shirt and jeans. Her softness was bare and pressed close beneath him. Then it was rubbing against him. Then it was moving in cadence with him; it was all around him. He was inside her.

♦

Daniel was fucking Tyra. Blocks away, Rodney was bleeding underneath fluorescent ER lights. A needle was being forced under the skin of his face to inject lidocaine, another in his arm for a blood transfusion. Guido was on another floor, restrained as he was slid into an MRI machine to scan for a cerebral hemorrhage. Afterwards, he would be detained by the police. They would charge him with assault and battery and carrying a blackjack as a concealed weapon.

All this because Tyra still believed in Jesus.

10.

Milk Money

It's a milk chugging contest. A dozen or so competitors are gathered, and about twice that many stand watching. The competitors are sheepish—made sheepish, that is, by the presence of two football players among them, Doogs and Bill. Doogs with his stocky build, red face, and shifty eyes and Bill. Tall, solid Bill. As he lifts off his shirt before the competition, we see he has a forest of hair across his washboard stomach. Bill is calm and collected in front of the crowd, like Bogart, Grant, or Connery.

They commence the drinking. At first, one of the skinny guys keeps pace with the football players. Adam's apples are working hard, dancing in the competitors' necks. The skinny guys show their inexperience by sipping the bottle, then stopping to breathe. Sipping. Breathing. Sipping. Gasping. Bill is silent and persistent, slowly guzzling, not letting his lips move away from the bottle. He has performed this feat before, upside down in repeated keg stands at repeated parties. It is a skill he has honed with which the pencil-necks cannot hope to compete. The plastic jug contracts from the vacuum created. Doogs is faster, the vacuum in his jug seems slightly greater, but a skinny guy is still trying to keep up.

The first to break, to lean over the trash can in defeat, is a skinny guy with a goatee. Milk comes out of him in bubbly spurts, looking gray when it dribbles in his black facial hair. Two other skinny guys stop and put down their jugs simply from the sight. The crowd is cheering now.

This raises the stakes.

Doogs is ahead, and his football friends begin to cheer for him. Unlike others in the ring of spectators, they gesture, cheer, and jump; their limbs enter the circle. Doogs takes the jug from his mouth and waits. They cheer louder.

"Doogs, Doogs, Doogs!"

Bill still drinks. Slow. Steady. Unstopping. Doogs, smaller and stockier, smiles and shifts his eyes to his teammates. It's a contract, a deal between a clown and the audience that they all know. Doogs's face says it clearly enough: *if you cheer for me, I will drink.*

They do not cheer for Bill. Bill still drinks slowly and has yet to remove his lips from the bottle even once. He drinks because he chooses to.

Another skinny guy vomits. Two others drop out with him. Doogs waits, the cheers building, the pressure in his stomach growing. He drinks again. More cheers. The sight of white streams running down his neck sends the football players into full-throated ecstasy.

The goatee boy is still vomiting. Bill is still drinking, sucking slowly, his jug imploding from an imbalance of atmospheric pressure. Doogs pukes. First a cough that produces chunks, then a thick stream. His head dips. The crowd lets out a collective *Ewwwww.*

He drinks again.

There is a girl in the crowd. Her hair is dyed blue; Smurf blue she likes to call it. Smurfette is tattooed on her ankle. Her fingers are shaking. As she tongues the ring in her lip, she wonders if it is nicotine or caffeine she is jonesing for. Normally, she might be one to protest the injustice of such a wanton waste of milk. There are starving children in this city, she might say. But she doesn't. She decides it's nicotine she needs. She lights a cigarette and cheers for Bill. This is way too much fun.

143

Bill stops, leans over the can, and sticks his finger down his throat. There is method to his madness, an element of purpose in his gesture.

"Is he trying to make himself barf?" a girl asks.

"He's trying to make himself barf!" another girl says.

"Nice," the Smurf girl says.

♣

Bill knows he has to vomit before he drinks more. It is the only way he will catch up to Doogs. Experience has told him this. Doogs knows this too. He stops drinking. His teammates grumble.

"I have to barf again," he says.

Bill's finger in his throat didn't work. He pushes it farther, his hand disappearing to his knuckles. He chokes, coughs, but nothing except a few stringy drops are produced. A skinny guy lets out a gush of vomit. He collapses beside the trash can. He's out.

♣

Bill drinks. Doogs drinks. It was only ever between these two. Their faces grimace and their bodies contort with involuntary muscle contractions. These are reflexes that have served the human body for millions of years. Vomiting is an action like breathing, defecating, ejaculating. It is accompanied by a surge of stimuli to either encourage or discourage future repetition. In vomiting's case it is, of course, accompanied by unpleasantness—negative stimuli—a neurological reaction meant to remind the body of primeval man: next time, don't ingest that rotting wildebeest carcass, that berry, that mammoth gizzard.

They will never drink milk again.

♣

Bill needs no help from his finger now. He chugs. He bends. For some reason, the crowd does not *ewwww* as much when he does this. It is not funny. He is handsome and noble in his pursuit, and his vomiting is tragic. Doogs is the buffoon. We want to see him vomit. We relish it. When the milk is coming out his nose, and he puts his finger to his nostril and blows, we cherish it. Doogs blows out his other nostril. White shoots out at an angle. His teammates howl. So do we.

Bill drinks. Doogs drinks. The skinny boys watch in silent admiration, trying to smile, but their stomachs are constricted in knots with milk that they imagine curdling within them as they stand there under the hot sun. One of them looks at his own vomit. It reminds him of feta cheese: liquid, yet chunky. He will never touch cheese again.

"Put him in a body bag, Doogs!"

"Go Bill!"

Suddenly, Doogs's plastic jug is empty. He lifts it from his lips, and foamy bubbles drop down. The football players roar. The crowd gives a smattering of applause, drowned out in the immediate vicinity of Doogs by his own teammates. A man in a Bigcorp.com shirt approaches and hands Doogs a certificate. They, Bigcorp.com, organized this. They wanted this. They bought the fourteen jugs of milk when they were cold and sweating on the store shelf. They sat back watching while all this transpired. Why do they want to? Money, you suppose; it gets them publicity, customers, and applicants. Money makes money. Milk makes money. Milk money.

Doogs is still vomiting. The liquid he is expelling is darker, rosy colored. The effort exhausts him, and he leans heavily on the can. But he still looks up between spasms and smiles at his teammates. His teammates slap hands and turn to look at a girl.

Doogs cannot think about sex right now, only the white gathering on the bottom of the can engages his consciousness. The smell is overpowering.

Bill vomits long graceful streams, preceded by a tightening of his back and a slight lean downward, like a pushup atop the trash can. Even in sickness he is suave. He finishes, scratches his belly. There is no look of shame on his face, just cool Sean Connery panache. He squints his eyes and shakes his head—that's all the people get of his defeat dance. A shake of the head, a squint of the eye, as if to say, "Well, that's a shame."

♣

"That was great."

"Wow. That was amazing."

"Those guys are amazing."

"Was that for charity or something?"

"I don't know."

The great American college students say these words. Inspired, they go off to classes, paid for by distant suburban parents, and prepare to be recruited for ninety thousand dollars a year.

11.

A Favor

At four p.m. I got to the country club and walked in the employee entrance. Actually, it was probably a little after four, 'cause I have to walk kind of far. I park my car on the edge of the employee parking lot, but as close as possible to the members' lot. It's my attempt to be more sophisticated by parking near all the Jags, Mercs, and Beamers. But I have to walk farther for it. I said *Hola* to the dishwashers, who were on a smoke break behind the dumpster. I remember the golf course was looking good—I could see it for a second before I walked behind the dumpster and in through the employee entrance. I clocked in, then walked upstairs to the dining room. No one was there, so I checked the Presidential. It's the private dining room. Fabian was in there setting up tables.

Fabian is from Paraguay. He hates it when people confuse it with Uruguay. He's taught me most of my Spanish, which is useful for talking to the back-of-house staff. He's the stocky guy, square head. He has that birthmark on his face. It's a weird birthmark. It goes from his lip to his forehead, and his mustache and eyebrow are white where they cross it. He told me he was born with it. Anyway, he said that we were working a birthday party together, and now that I was there, we should go talk to Steve.

Steve is our boss. He was in the storage room smoking a cigarette. Steve is always mingling with the members, blending in with his expensive suits, or he's in the storage room smoking. He goes, "Rookie, you're working the Harmin Party with Fabe." Steve doesn't like calling anyone by their real names. Rookie was my nickname 'cause on my first day I had knocked over a tray of plates. It was fifty china plates, all smashed on the dance floor. It was so loud my ears rang for a half hour after. They started calling me "Rookie" from then on, and the name stuck.

I told Steve I already knew about the party, and he says, "Good, then what are you talking to me for—set up the goddamn tables."

I'm not exaggerating. That's just how he talks. Fabian and I rolled six tables into the Presidential. It was about five o'clock by the time we had them all in there. That was when we saw Mr. Ferguson arrive. He pulled his caddy into the handicapped space right outside the window.

Fabian says to me, "Looks like one of us is going to have drunk duty tonight."

"What's that mean?"

"You'll see," he says. Fabian has worked at the club for two years. I've been there just two months. He likes to gloat when he has knowledge I don't. "You've never heard about Mr. Ferguson?" he asks me.

"No. Should I?"

Fabian laughed and stayed silent again to keep me in suspense. Finally, he let up. "See, Mr. Ferguson is one of the oldest members. The guy is part of the institution. He made his money with a Men's Only club down in the city."

"Men's Only?"

"A strip joint, Sidney. A strip joint," he tells me.

"Just making sure."

"He made all sorts of money and even pimped a few of his dancers. He finally married one of his dancers who was way younger than him. Mrs. Ferguson? You haven't heard of her either?"

"No."

"Oh, man. Well," he got close to me, like he was telling a dirty joke. "Mr. Ferguson is too old to fuck her now."

"Too old?"

"He had a stroke a few years ago. Ever since that, his soldier can't salute. So Mrs. Ferguson sleeps around with all sorts of members here. She even slept with one of the waiters, Jesus. He was the guy you replaced."

"Did he get fired cause of that?"

"No. He got fired for being late too much," Fabian said while he was setting a centerpiece of flowers on a mirror in the center of the table. You see, we have to keep working while we do all this talking. But the talking makes it go faster. Fabian and I work well together that way. He kept talking and said, "Mrs. Ferguson comes here sometimes with Mr. Ferguson, but he doesn't like her to because he's afraid she'll pick up more waiters. Usually she's out with one of her boyfriends while he comes here and gets drunk. They have this agreement: he comes here while Mrs. Ferguson takes her boyfriends home."

"Get out."

"Yeah. He knows better than to go back before eleven o'clock."

"Does he have friends here?"

"Everybody hates him."

"What about Steve?"

"Steve hates everybody."

♠

I guess this next part is important. I asked Fabian if Mr. Ferguson can drive home after he's been drinking.

"He's wrecked a few times," he told me. "One time he drove up on the putting green, and all the golfers went ballistic, and then Steve went out there to settle things down and ended up cussing and yelling at everyone else. It was hilarious, man."

We set chairs up at all the tables, threw tablecloths on them, set up the buffet, and put the burgundy skirts on it. See, all those tables and stuff are just folding tables. With the right tablecloths and skirts, you can dress them up real nice. Anyway, so we set out the chafing dishes, which are sterling silver, four grand a pop. My Grandfather and I used to fish on Bull Run, the river that borders the golf course. I remember on some afternoons, if the sun was hitting the clubhouse just right, we could see all the silver forks and knives glinting on the tables from across the fairway. He always hoped I would make it big someday and could get the family a membership at the club. I told him I would. I was only five then, so things like that seemed possible. I ended up doing the next best thing: I work there and get to go in the club every day. I know lots of the members. We're even allowed to use the course once a month. I don't because I don't play golf, but I still have time to pick it up. I think of Grandpa when I'm setting up the chafers a lot. He'd be proud if he knew. He doesn't though, because he died when I was seven. It really broke me up; I couldn't go to school for a week. I haven't cast a reel since. I'm sorry, I guess that doesn't really matter right now.

♠

So we did all the candles; stocked the bar; sliced lemons, limes, and oranges; set the tables; and blew up balloons. We were lighting the flames under the chafing dishes just as the guests began to arrive. We ran downstairs and changed into our tuxedos. Then we came back and took drink orders.

It was a surprise birthday party for Mr. Harmin. He was fifty. The guy was pretty well preserved. Your typical country club stock, a little stocky, thinning hair, with a sunburned neck from being out on the course. His wife was pretty—most women there are; but she wore too much makeup—most women there do.

It took Mr. Harmin ten minutes to shake hands with everyone and thank them for coming. His wife stuck close to him. She was whispering the names of people in his ear when he forgot them. She thought the other people didn't notice what she was doing, but we all noticed. Mr. Harmin had squinty eyes when he smiled, and small hands. I got him a martini. The glass looked big in his little hand.

While the guests took their seats, the DJ arrived. He was late. Fabian and I were miffed and let him know, because it would be an inconvenience to bring in his stuff with all the people standing around. It's just not professional. I decided to seat people. I only brought six menus out at a time. That way I had to make a bunch of trips. This gave Fabian and the DJ ample time to carry in the speakers and set up a table for the CD player. We work well that way. Although the members probably thought it was because I'm some dumb community college graduate. Whatever.

Everyone was seated, everyone had a drink, and the DJ was playing music—finally. I went to Mr. Harmin's table to get orders. Mr. Harmin was talking really loudly. Everyone at his table was listening to him. I walked up with my pad out so that they would know I was ready to take their orders.

"We were coming into the seventh hole, and I was three strokes down . . . ." Mr. Harmin says.

"Honey, the waiter's here," Mrs. Harmin interrupts him.

"Hold on, he's not going anywhere."

"It's his birthday," she turns to me and says. "He wants to be spoiled."

"I don't want to be spoiled. I'm in the middle of a story for Christ's sake. Why don't you order?"

"I want to know what you're having first," she says.

"Don't worry about that. Just order. I'm down three strokes."

Quietly, she says to me, "Why don't you come back later."

I said "Sure," and walked towards the next table. Then I heard Mr. Harmin.

"Dammit June, now he'll never come back. Waiter! I'll have the filet, medium rare."

His wife got upset.

"Mick, you—"

"Shut up. It's my birthday—I'm sorry. I'm sorry, I didn't mean that."

"I did this all for you. The least you could do . . . ." Now the guests were all looking uncomfortable.

"I'm sorry. I'm sorry, Sweetcakes," he says. "I'm just excited, that's all. Waiter, can I please have a steak." Then he kissed her on her temple.

"Fine with me." She turned her face up to me and asked for the salmon.

♠

I walked by the bar with all the orders. Fabian waved me over and said he needed more Seagram's and a six-pack of Bud. I dropped the orders off at the kitchen, then went downstairs to the Mixed Grill. It's the casual restaurant in the club—guys can walk off the course in shorts and golf spikes and sit down for a dinner there. The main bar is in the Mixed Grill. Elias, the bartender, is in charge of the keys to the walk-in refrigerators. Elias wasn't there, probably in the john, which meant the keys were probably behind the bar. Mr. Ferguson was sitting at the bar alone in a blue blazer with a sailor insignia on the breast pocket. The second he saw me, he lifted his glass up and drained it. The ice was rattling in his glass all the way up to his mouth. I thought he was shaking it on purpose. to let me know he was out of liquor.

He slams, more like drops, the empty glass on the bar top and says, "Vodka tonic double."

"I'm not the bartender," I tell him.

"Congrats. You just got promoted."

I didn't understand. The Absolut bottle had been left within his reach, as was the soda gun. Most members help themselves when Elias isn't around. So I thought he was fucking with me.

"Bottle's there," I said, nodding at it.

"I see the fucking bottle, now pick it up and pour me one." He pushed the glass to me with the back of his hand. His hand started shaking the second he lifted it off the bar. I remembered what Fabian had said about the stroke and took his glass. I realized maybe he couldn't pour. I made him a vodka tonic, heavy on the tonic, then tried to get out from behind the bar.

"What's your name?" he says.

I lied and told him my name was Bob.

"Well Bob, get back here and make me a real drink before I complain to your boss."

I went back, took his drink, dumped it in the sink. I got out a big fat water glass, filled it halfway with Absolut—maybe it was a little more than that—then I topped it off with tonic all the way to the rim, stuck four olives on a toothpick, then slid it over to him. Biggest damn vodka tonic ever. It should keep him happy, if he can pick it up with those hands, I thought.

As if I had said something, he says, "Fuck you."

"Enjoy your drink, sir." As I left, I got to see him spilling half the drink as he tried lifting it up to his lips.

♠

Dinner went well. Mr. Harmin liked his steak. Mrs. Harmin told us we were doing a good job. She seemed like a nice woman. It always makes your night worth it when the people tell you they like the job you're doing. The room was loud as people loosened up from Fabian's drinks. Fabian is a good bartender. His black-and-white facial hair matches his tux. He's like a walking chessboard. But between him and my eye patch, we're pretty distinct looking. People either love it or hate it. It's like they think they are stuck with the freaky rejects or the unique and special snowflakes. Steve had pegged the Harmin's as the latter. He had been right, as usual. He may hate the members, but he sure knows them.

Anyway, people started setting their forks and knives at the top of their empty plates and leaning back in their chairs. We cleared the plates. They were ready for dessert. Dessert is my favorite part of the meal; people always insist they're full, but you bring out that cake, and they just can't help themselves.

I went to the kitchen to get the cake. We used two books of matches lighting all fifty candles. Fabian kept burning himself when his matches would burn down too close to his fingers. He kept saying we should steal one of Steve's lighters. We both found that really funny, mainly 'cause Steve has these expensive Zippo lighters with his initials engraved on them. We had to compose ourselves before we went back. We turned down the lights and brought out the cake. Mr. Harmin stood up and insisted on giving this long speech while the candles burned. He went on and on, thanking everyone there. Some people twice. Fabe's martinis had taken effect. Mr. Harmin was a little drunk. Finally, his wife, June, saw that the candles were about to burn into the cake. She stopped him short; she was obviously the brains of the family. He gave her this shitty look but then realized that the candles were melting over the cake and just blew them out. People clapped really loudly, probably because they didn't want him to start talking again.

Fabian says Mr. Harmin has three daughters. The two grown ones didn't make it to the party, but he also has an eight-year-old.

She's a little blond fatty. Fabian said she had probably been a mistake. We tripped over her all night. She was hiding under tables, hitting people with balloons, and trying to get behind the bar. Fabian had joked about spiking her Shirley Temples with vodka, hoping to get her tired. He says he does things like that sometimes; I don't know why, could get us in big trouble. I think he's mainly joking.

Anyway, the sugar in that drink makes kids bounce off the wall. She ran up to look at the cake and couldn't see it over the table, so she pulled the tablecloth towards her. Now, I had set the cake at an angle, with two empty candy dishes under one end, so people sitting down could see it. All it needed was a tug, and the whole thing—candles, icing, and all—rolled off the table and plopped onto the floor.

The whole crowd sort of gasped. Mickey Harmin walked over to his daughter, who was crying, and patted her on the back. He sent her over to her mom with some napkins to clean herself up, then he looks at me and says, "Well, I guess that comes out of your paycheck."

"Excuse me?"

"We're not paying for that," he says, pointing at his demolished birthday cake.

"Uh, I think your daughter knocked it over, sir."

"You think it's her fault? She's only eight. You don't set a cake up like that with a kid around."

He walked away, shaking his head at the guests, his hands out at his sides as if to say, *you just can't get good help these days, can you?* It was supposed to be my fault. All my fault. Fabian came over and picked up the cake. I was glad he was there. It took some of the heat off. He was all cool in front of the guests. I walked back to the kitchen. Fabian came in after me. Now that he wasn't in front of the members, he was all frantic.

"Come on, Sidney, we got to find some more cakes."

"Let him find his own fucking cake."

He kept telling me that the customer was always right, and that it wouldn't come out of our paychecks, but that we had to find some cakes—fast. We found some extra chocolate cakes in the downstairs kitchen, unwrapped them, and served them. I let Fabian serve Mr. Harmin's table. It was probably better if he just didn't see me. But when it came time to serve coffee, Fabian told me to take orders for regular or decaf. I didn't want to.

"Come on, you've got to go out there, or Harmin will think you're scared of him. You've got to kiss up now. Think tip."

I went up to his table. Mr. Harmin's face was red. He was drunk.

"Leopold Fitz is an asshole," he was saying.

Mrs. Harmin was the only woman left at the table. The other women were dancing. The men were smoking cigars. She touched old Mickey's arm and goes, "Honey." He ignored her. He kept saying, "He is an asshole." The other guys were laughing. "The biggest asshole I've ever met."

"Honey. Don't say that," she says.

"Relax, June."

"I'm just trying—"

"I know what you're trying to do. Don't. I'm having a good time. Sometimes you just—"

"Can I get you some coffee, Mr. Harmin?"

He looked at me with his mouth open, pointed back at his wife and goes, "Can't you see I'm having a conversation here? You mind holding on for just one goddamn minute?"

"He's just doing his job," Mrs. Harmin says.

"I know he's doing his job. He's doing it badly."

Their friends kept smoking the cigars. They were giving me dirty looks. Me, of all people. I could tell you who the real asshole was at that table, and it wasn't me. But what could I do? These people are our paychecks. Harmin asked for a Baileys and coffee.

His wife says to me, "He's had enough."

"That's it," Mr. Harmin goes. "That's it. Get up. Get up. Go over there and sit with your friends for a while. Just leave me over here in peace with my buddies." Mickey started pulling her chair out from under her. Her eyes were glistening. I watched the black line of mascara under them, waiting for it to break. She blinked, then got up and left the room.

I got Mr. Harmin his Baileys; he handed me a bunch of empty glasses from the table as if he couldn't wait for me to take them. But he was already ignoring me again, looking at one of his buddies' college-aged daughters with a D-cup out on the dance floor. The chairs were emptying out as people got up and danced. The DJ was the main attraction now. All we had to do was make sure the bar was stocked and tables cleared. Fabian needed rum. When I went downstairs to get it, I saw that Mr. Ferguson was still at the bar, talking to Elias. The two of them seemed to be real involved in some topic. I didn't see what Ferguson was drinking. He yelled out when he saw me and says, "Hey, there's Bob."

I acted like I didn't hear him. He goes, "I guess Bob is deaf and dumb."

That was what he said.

♠

Things went on uneventfully up in the Presidential the rest of the night. The Harmin guests danced. Other members strolled by as they left the Mixed Grill. Around eleven, things started winding down. The DJ was just doing slow stuff, and the floor was covered with deflated balloons. The Harmins' daughter was asleep on some chairs with her thumb in her mouth and someone's sports jacket over her. Fabian kept sliding drinks over the bar on little cocktail napkins, working on our tip. I loved him for it. Mr. Harmin was sitting in the corner, red faced, smoking a stogie with one of his buddies. Mrs. Harmin still hadn't come back, so I decided to check on her.

The only room that would still be open would be the lounge. Sure enough, she was there, sitting in one of the plush chairs, her fingers completely covering her face. She moved them away. Her mascara had run. Steve was sitting next to her with his elbows on his knees. I had not seen him all night, but that probably meant he had been busy with one of the wedding receptions upstairs. It was a busy night. Steve looked real concerned. He saw me, touched Mrs. Harmin's knee, then led me to the doorway. He put his hand on my shoulder.

"Rookie, I need you to do me a big favor."

"What's that?"

"Can you make sure Mr. Ferguson gets to his car all right?"

I thought of that big man and all the steps from the Mixed Grill to his car, and all the drinks that he had put in himself.

"Drunk duty," I said. Now I knew what Fabian had been talking about.

Steve's I-need-a-favor face melted away and he goes, "You're learning, Rookie. Go. I'm going to take care of Mrs. Harmin."

I'm sure he did. I remember one night a wedding reception got out of hand, and the bridal party ran naked through the sprinklers. I was looking for Steve. Someone told me he had gone out on the course to break up the streakers. I went out there, found him leaning against a tree, smoking a cigarette and watching the girls. He saw me and said, "Great view, huh, Rookie?"

♠

I went to the downstairs kitchen. The dishwashers were mopping the floor. I went out on the back patio and looked at the golf course. I sat on a folding chair that had been left outside from an earlier luncheon. It was a shit night, all humid and sticky. I couldn't even see Bull Run for all the haze. The course was empty, except for huge bugs flying in front of the floodlights. I decided I would go home after I got Mr. Ferguson to his car. Fabian could clean up. I'd let him get the whole tip. It just wasn't worth it to me. I was done with this type of work. I was thinking I'd get a job in an office somewhere. I know it sounds square, but at the moment, I never wanted to have to *serve* some asshole again.

I stared at some moths that had drowned in a puddle underneath one of the patio lights. I started thinking of my grandfather then. I spent about five minutes thinking of some of the times we went fishing. Those were good times. I had both eyes back then. Grandpa never knew me with the patch. Then I started thinking about when he died and going to his funeral. That was when I decided to go downstairs.

The Mixed Grill was dark. Elias was locking up the liquor in the wooden cabinets. Mr. Ferguson was slumped on the bar. I didn't think he was conscious. If that were the case, I'd never get him to his car, that's what I was thinking, but I guess he wouldn't exactly be able to drive if he was unconscious, and then getting him to his car would have been pointless. I started to reach into my pocket for my phone to call a cab. Just then, I noticed how ugly and old his sports coat was. It was frayed on the sleeves, and there was a hole burnt in the front from cigar or cigarette ash. You'd think a guy that rich would dress better. Then again, if he can't fuck, what's the point in trying to look nice?

Elias said to me over his shoulder, "Good luck, Sid."

Ferguson mumbled like Elias was talking to him. I tapped him on the back and told him it was time to go. He was pretty

159

responsive and pushed off the bar to get up. Then he began to fall over. Elias yelled at me.

"Come on, you've got to support him."

But it's not like he offered to help. I'm not small, but Mr. Ferguson is a big guy. I put my shoulder in his armpit. He turned towards the steps.

"Oh, no. We're taking the elevator," I said.

"What elevator? There's no fucking elevator, Bob." He still thought my name was Bob.

"Yeah, there is. It's for beer kegs."

I took him through the kitchen. The dishwashers were gone. The elevator is on the far side of the building; we use it for kegs and other things too heavy for the stairs. Ferguson was saying how he wasn't allowed back in the kitchen. It was for employees only, he told me. "For the help," he said.

I told him to fuck off, which was a mistake, 'cause then he turned around and tried walking back towards the steps, leaning on the counter for support. He was saying that he didn't need some kid insulting him. That was all I needed, him going off on his own, slipping and cracking his liver-spotted head open on one of the steel counters.

I said sorry about a million times and told him that I really respected him and how everyone respected him. I don't know if he believed it. I hoped he wouldn't remember my groveling. I got him to turn around and to walk onto the elevator. Once he was inside, the whole thing sank down about five inches. When I got on, he moved as far as he could from me, or maybe he was just falling against the wall. I hit the button.

The keg elevator is very slow and we were stuck in there a while together. He stared at the floor, his eyelids halfway down. I tried not staring at his ugly jacket; it just reminded me of how much I didn't want to be there. Then he looked up at me, stared me in the

160

face, like he was trying to focus or something. I knew what he was thinking. I know the look people get now when they are going to ask me about my eye patch and how I lost my eye. Maybe he thought because I had been such a suck up just before to get him in the elevator that we were friends now and that we were going to have a moment. But, thank God, he started, "How'd you . . ." but he didn't finish his sentence. Instead he coughed, and it just turned into a wheeze, and when he stopped he was just quiet, like he'd lost the thread or something, or just couldn't spare the breath.

He was breathing hard through his lips. I started thinking about his lips. They were all chapped and red, surrounded by whiskers he had missed shaving. But those lips had been all over his stripper wife's body, and now she was bedding down with some other man. There's been a few girls I've dated that I couldn't care less about. But others that, well, it still burns me if I think of some other guy boning down with them. It's probably worse with your wife.

No wonder he was such an asshole.

The elevator stopped. He leaned on me, and I led him out of the kitchen and through the lounge, which was empty. There were plenty of couches in there in case I had to drop him. Going that way, we also avoided the Harmin party. Ferguson never fell though. I guess I figured he was sobering up. My dad was like that. Heavy drinker, might stumble when he first got up, but sort of found his sea legs, so to speak, once he was moving.

I got Ferguson to the front door. He took the steps real slow. We didn't say anything. I led him to his Caddy. He pulled out his keys. They jingled in his hand like he was trying to shake out a tune—Jingle Bells, I thought. But everything sounds like Jingle Bells. I unlocked the door and started the ignition for him. Then he sat down. I wasn't out of the way yet, and he knocked my head, hard, against the frame of the door. I saw stars for a moment before my head cleared.

I was running my fingers through my hair to see if I was bleeding. One final injury to add to insult, I figured. I didn't know if he had done it on purpose or not. He reached for the seat belt but couldn't get it. It was just a few inches out of his reach. I was staring at that gap between the silver buckle and his fingers. Then I realized he was staring at me. His face was real still, like he was thinking real hard, trying to recognize me. But he didn't know me. Maybe he expected me to pull the buckle the two inches to his fingers for him. I don't know, but then he says to me: "What the fuck are you looking at, you dumb pirate motherfucker."

I slammed the door instead of helping him. He forgot about the belt, turned to the wheel, and backed out. He took a while to find the right gear, and then when he started forward, he made this big, wide turn. He came right at me. I had to jump out of the way. I hurt my wrist pushing off the hood.

Asshole.

That's it. I guess I was the last one to see him, if you don't count the people who would have seen him at stoplights he ran and stuff. I've probably told you more than you wanted to hear, but you said I can't be charged. My lawyer explained everything to me. It's a private club after all. So I took the liberty. I wanted you to know why I did that. You know—it was a whole combination of things that night. You see, it's fucked up, but I thought I was doing him a favor. I thought I was doing everyone a favor.

12.

Idolatry Soup

Soother was a peon working at the Megapolis Foods Inc. manufacturing, packaging, and shipping plant. He was a fairly handsome, if lean, young man with sandy hair and wire rim spectacles. When he was sitting at his job along the inspection line, one got the impression that Soother's mind was hard at work—on matters beyond his immediate task, for that required little thought. Soother was assigned to the soup department, where it was his job to ensure that all the labels on the soup cans were right-side up. If they were upside down, the can was pulled from the assembly line and disposed of.

Soother was a dynamic young man, bursting with ideas and creativity. He yearned for an opportunity to share them. He finally had his chance when Megapolis Foods Inc. was having problems selling one of its signature products: Megapolis Soup. As a result, the company's shares had seen a precipitous drop. Layoffs loomed. Worried for his own job, Soother decided he had little to lose. He walked upstairs to Mr. Megapolis's office and burst through the door. Mr. Megapolis was a tall, silver-haired man. His desk was at least the size of a nineteen-fifties Chevy. The back of his chair rose behind his head, much like a throne. Soother's palms were slick with sweat, but it was not fear that caused his hands to shake and his pulse to quicken, rather excitement. He got right to the point. He told Mr. Megapolis what the problem was and how to solve it.

"It's your marketing," Soother said. "The product is solid. It's the best out there, but the public needs to be reminded of that."

Mr. Megapolis was under considerable strain. The wrinkles in his forehead and around his eyes had deepened in just the past few days. He had a board of directors to answer to, as well as anxious stockholders, not to mention a lifestyle to maintain. He was ready to listen.

"How do we accomplish that, Mr.—"

"Soother, my name is Soother. And, well, we need a major change. We begin with the title of the soup. We don't call it Megapolis Soup, but rather: Idolatry Soup. Our slogan will go from 'Buy Megapolis Soup, It's Good' to simply 'Idolatry Soup: It's Better than GOD!'"

"I like it," Mr. Megapolis said, the lines around his mouth turning upwards in a smile for the first time in weeks.

The changes were immediate. Soon sales of Idolatry Soup were breaking all previous sales records. In short order, the entire name of the company was changed from Megapolis Foods Inc. to Idolatry Foods Inc. Soother was promoted to Senior Vice President and had an office next to Mr. Megapolis himself. Mr. Megapolis was profiled in business magazines. The public consumption of Idolatry Soup, per capita, was far beyond the government's daily recommended caloric intake. Obesity rates swelled. Sales of diet books increased, giving new life to a flagging publishing industry. At first, clothing retailers had to increase their orders of plus sizes, leading to improved sales for manufacturers, and those improvements moved all the way down the supply chain, to producers such as cotton farmers, who had to hire more workers and buy more machines to process more cotton. The farmers got to upgrade their beat up pickup trucks to luxury SUVs, which helped the auto industry and all those related. When the diets (and exercise) promoted by the diet books grew in popularity, sales of stylish workout clothes shot up, as well as sales of running shoes, gym memberships, and exercise machines. This was followed by another wave of purchases of new, stylish, slimmed-down outfits and stylish shoes and accessories to match. Single people joined dating websites. New couples went out on dates, allowing restaurants and coffee shops to expand. Young people got more jobs as servers and baristas. In time, couples had more babies, which meant sales of baby clothes and toys, and the virtuous cycle went on and on . . . .

Everyone in the world was satisfied, satiated, and fulfilled.

Except for one person . . . God. As one might have guessed, God was not a fan of Idolatry Soup. He was hoping that the name would just be a fad and would change in a few years as marketing trends tend to. But this did not happen. Quite the opposite in fact: Idolatry Foods Inc. became an institution of society. So, God decided to sue.

But this presented God with an immediate challenge: there were no lawyers in heaven. He thought of asking the Devil for one, but decided such a request would be inappropriate. He searched all about Heaven for a lawyer, but his search was fruitless. Finally, St. Paul, who had been a tireless advocate of the Church in life, volunteered to represent God. But first he had to apply to and attend law school. With his significant connections, St. Paul was accepted into a prestigious program and, by the grace of God, graduated in only one year.

They were ready to take on Soother.

Much time had elapsed though. By now, Soother was married to Mr. Megapolis's daughter. Together they had five children: Cain, Sodom, Jezebel, Salome, and Judas. Soother was also now President and CEO of Idolatry Foods Inc. As President and CEO, Soother had a deep bench of talented attorneys in stylish yet conservative charcoal-with-pinstripes suits.

God was suing Soother for slander and copyright infringement. But Soother brought his own countersuit against God. He said he was representing the 4.3 million people (the best estimate from archeologists and biblical scholars) killed by God in various floods, plagues, and tribal wars during the territorial expansion of his kingdom. There were also the various environmental protection laws that God had violated with his acts of turning the Nile into blood and burning a column of fire day and night for forty years without the proper permits or off-setting carbon emissions. Finally, the UN was even investigating alleged war crimes attributed to God. These included charges against God for the killing of non-combatants and even genocide for various acts during the Old Testament period. A team of investigators was sent to Jericho to gather evidence.

It was the trial of the millennium, albeit with a few initial technical difficulties. The court administrators would not accept "I am who I am" as a legal name. Then there was the problem that no one could actually *see* God, for his radiant presence blinded everyone in the courtroom. But this was sorted quickly, when it was pointed out that the glare was not from God at all, but rather the various lights from TV cameras. These were adjusted, and people could then see that God was actually a very fatherly-looking fellow with deep, sad eyes, white-as-snow hair, and a long beard. He was less like George Burns, Morgan Freeman, or Alanis Morissette for that matter, and resembled more of a vagrant-on-the-street picking through the trash for food. One older woman, who was a bit senile, asked him for his autograph, thinking he was Walt Whitman.

The trial began. St. Paul presented his case. Commentators agreed that he did a respectable job, considering it was his first appearance in court and that he was a legal team of one. But his reputation was called into question when opposing council brought up the unresolved issue of his participation in the stoning of the first Christian martyr, St. Stephen.

"That was two thousand years ago," St. Paul stammered. "I didn't even cast a stone. I was just holding the jackets of the guys who were doing the stone casting."

"Let he who is sinless hold the first jacket, or something to that effect," the judge said, a lapsed Catholic himself.

St. Paul could not help himself. "But Stephen and I are good friends now. We've patched things up. I mean, I did him a favor: if it weren't for me, he would not have been the first martyr."

The courtroom let out a collective gasp while the TV networks switched to various religious experts who began to debate whether or not John the Baptist had a more legitimate claim to being the first martyr. This led to a lively side discussion that kept viewers tuned in during the court's ensuing recess.

When the trial reconvened, God was asked to take the stand. Here another technical problem arose when God was sworn in. By who or what would God swear by? The line "so help me God" seemed quite self-serving and hardly impartial. Someone suggested that he swear by his mother's grave, but a quick explanation of his Prime Mover Proof from St. Augustine, who had come down from heaven to sit in the gallery and watch firsthand, ruled out the notion of God having parents. Opposing counsel then asked a famous physicist to explain how our understanding of the temporality of cause-and-effect did not apply in the beginning of the universe, since the laws of relativity and quantum mechanics were not relevant in the early universe due to its density and energy levels—and therefore St. Augustine's argument was fundamentally flawed.

Scout's honor was suggested and thrown out before the bailiff settled on pinky swearing.

The trial continued.

Pundits pointed out, after just a few minutes of cross-examination, that God was not a well-coached witness. He practically admitted to the murder of millions, the flouting of environmental protection laws, and inciting crimes against humanity. St. Paul raised objections to strike God's testimony from the record, but his requests were overruled. God tried to justify himself.

"You don't understand," he said. "I was a different God then. It was the Old Testament. You had to be firm; there were other gods to compete with."

Opposing counsel began to inquire about God's business strategies and whether or not some of his methods violated market regulations against unfair and uncompetitive practices during this period. They went so far as to suggest that Christianity may have been breaking laws regarding monopolies in modern times. St. Paul did his best to intervene and pointed out that Islam, Hinduism, and Buddhism also had large "market shares," at which point Soother's attorneys brought up the specter of an investigation of collusion among members of an oligopoly.

St. Paul requested a short recess and was finally able to convince his witness to plead the fifth. But they lost ground as soon as cross-examination resumed, and God characterized the Great Flood as population control.

Soother's lawyers were certain they had the case wrapped up. They had run circles around the plaintiffs and offered strong closing arguments. They portrayed Soother as a good citizen, an enterprising entrepreneur, the embodiment of the American dream. He was a job creator, and a family man who had become a victim of a murderous, racist, and misogynistic deity who also had a long track record of questionable environmental and business practices. The jury did not find God a sympathetic plaintiff. But once in deliberations, they were afraid to rule against God, fearing eternal punishment.

The judge declared a mistrial. Soother and his lawyers left the courthouse in triumph. God, St. Paul, and St. Augustine exited, their heads held low.

But God did not give up. He fell back on his former, Old Testament ways. First, he sent millions of frogs to Soother's Los Angeles home. But the pollution already present in the city adversely affected them, causing them to grow extra heads and limbs. They became a waste management problem. It was Soother who teamed up with local culinary schools to collect the frogs and prepare delicacies such as frog legs for various homeless shelters. This resulted in excellent PR for Soother, Idolatry Foods Inc., and its subsidiaries.

God tried locusts next, but Idolatry Foods Inc. was ready. Risk management experts had already predicted that God might try such a plague. The locusts were collected, sterilized, and processed into a cheap source of protein, and then converted into nonperishable porridge mix and energy biscuits to be sent to third world countries with food shortages.

Next, God turned thousands of cans of Idolatry Soup into blood. But Soother acted quickly, sending the cans in refrigerated trucks to Red Cross blood donation centers. The Red Cross and the City of Los Angeles presented him with a medal and the keys to the city. Not to be outdone, God resorted to killing Soother's first born, Cain. In response, while still heartbroken, Soother had Cain cryogenically frozen, investing millions into the technology, hoping that his son might be thawed when doctors discovered a cure for God—or someone else announced that he was dead.

God was discouraged. He swallowed his pride and took a trip down to Hell, where he asked the Devil if he could borrow a lawyer. The Devil, always a fashionable spirit, met God at the elevator door wearing the season's most in-demand double-breasted business suit with tailored vest, polished loafers (no socks, they were out that year), and chromed-out cuff links, tiepin, and watch chain. A gracious host, he invited God in for a drink. God reminded him that he was there on business purposes only. The Devil, disappointed, made himself a drink anyway. As he opened his cupboard, God saw that it was stocked top to bottom with Idolatry brand products. God turned to go.

"Where are you going off to? My God, you just got here."

"Never mind, I'll see you later," God said, stepping back onto the elevator.

God went back to his throne and slumped down with a sigh. He had lost the legal and PR battles. His only consolation was that he was immortal and Soother was not. The span of a lifetime to us, dear reader, is but a blink of an eye to an eternal being, and soon enough, Soother passed away after a full and happy life.

He went straight to Hell.

The Devil was hard-pressed for a justifiable reward for this mortal who had pleased him so much, but Satan is a creative sort. He decided to place Soother in a room with a screen playing reality television produced by Idolatry Production Company, while hoses pumped endless quantities of Soother's own Idolatry Soup into him through a high-pressure hose.

Soother's spirit was broken in a matter of hours, the taste of his own soup mixed with the rubber of the hose and the endless loops of fame-hungry contestants saying "I'm not here to make friends," was unbearable. His jaw ached from holding the hose, his throat from the flow of scalding soup, his stomach was distended beyond recognition, and his bowels were bloody from the volume of soup flushed through his system. His ears and nose bled soup, and his eyes cried it.

He repented for his sins.

God, being a forgiving and loving deity (despite what the lawyers had said), was moved. He came down to Hell and offered Soother a deal. Soother could start from scratch—provided he use a different slogan for his soup and company. Soother, as best he could with the hose in his mouth, signaled that he would accept God's offer. With a snap of God's fingers, Soother was whisked out of his eternal damnation, across time and space, and found himself again along the inspection line, a young man, a peon at the beginning of his life and career, watching conveyer belts of soup cans go by in a blur. It was like waking from a bad dream. He wept—real tears this time. He had his whole life ahead of him, children to be born, a woman to fall in love with and marry, a company, an economy, and a world to save.

Sure enough, as before, during Soother's time at Megapolis Foods, sales of their signature soup line were flagging. Soother, his mind only half occupied with the cognitive challenges of his position, brainstormed on solutions. Soon, he had an answer to all their problems. He rushed up the stairwell, burst into Mr. Megapolis's office and blurted out the slogan and rebrand that would save the struggling company: "Megapolis—it's a Hell of a Good Soup!"

"Brilliant. That is the best slogan I have ever heard!" Mr. Megapolis said before asking, "And who are you, young man?"

"I'm Soother!"

And so began a new lifetime of success that led to prosperity, fulfillment, and peace. Jobs were plentiful. Everyone in the world was happy, thanks to Soother. Soother (again) wooed and married Mr. Megapolis's daughter. Soother's new father-in-law promoted him to CEO and President. Sales grew. Hell of a Good Company Inc. branched into new sectors including technology, electronics, engineering, pharmaceuticals, finance, entertainment, and ecommerce. *Life is great!* Soother thought as he reclined in his corner office, looking out over the haze of downtown LA. Even the city itself looked bathed in a layer of Hell of a Good Soup as the brown haze thickened every day. Soother was happy. God was happy. Everything was gravy.

That is, until his executive assistant buzzed a bicycle courier into his office to deliver an envelope. The athletic young woman with tattoos and sunglasses walked in wearing spandex, a body-hugging satchel, and an aerodynamic helmet. She pinched her nose as she handed the envelope over to Soother. The odor of sulfur was overpowering. Soother opened it. Another subpoena slipped out onto his desk. The typeface was gothic and looked to have been printed in blood. The edges of the paper smoldered and were too hot to touch.

Soother was being sued again, and this plaintiff had no shortage of lawyers.

13.

Something We Had To Do

Emilia went to America and became a Christian. She was there for the summer as an *au pair* taking care of the Greski's triplets. The Greskis lived next door to the Hernandez family. Mrs. Hernandez, Elizabeth, became a substitute mother for Emilia; she was only seventeen, after all, and it was her first time away from her family. Elizabeth was a devout Catholic. She had been so shocked to learn that Emilia, from Italy, had not been raised with any faith whatsoever.

When Emilia went back to Italy, she told her doggedly secular family that she wanted to join a convent. It was the last thing her family expected, having prided themselves on their defiant atheism and all-out rejection of "superstitious" religions for so many years. The Catholics had ruined Italy, they often said. The Pope and Cardinals were sexist, homophobic hypocrites.

But after arguing, crying, and praying (on Emilia's part), her parents, while they did not approve, agreed not to stand in her way. But even then, Emilia had been certain that they were hoping that her entire interest in taking vows and becoming a nun was just a form of rebellion that would end up being a passing phase.

But Emilia knew it wasn't. She had grown up feeling as if she had been missing something her entire life. She remembered visiting historical sites throughout Italy on school field trips. Her favorites had always been the tombs, retreats, and chapels of saints—St. Francis of Assisi, St. Pudentiana, St. Margaret, St. Valentine, and St. Veronica. She remembered looking upon the nuns at the tombs and shrines, with their rosary beads and their devoutly bowed heads. Emilia saw in them the same mysticism as Tibetan monks. She read about these women, who had committed themselves to Christ, who would travel to the worst hellscapes in the world to provide service, love, and compassion to the poor and forgotten. They were unsung heroines, working in modesty, humility, and courage—of course, courage.

Emilia soon left for Our Lady of Sorrows Convent. She ministered to Albanian refugees in the former Yugoslavia. She read to blind pensioners. She journeyed to Rome to see the Holy Father himself. She even went on missions to Chad, Sudan, India, East Timor, and Madagascar.

Somehow, thirty-five years had passed, and she had lost touch with Elizabeth, whose devotion had initially inspired Emilia. They had written letters for many years, but it had been a long while since Emilia had received a response. She often thought of those great big American meals she'd had at the Hernandez home. Elizabeth would always prepare things that Emilia was less likely to have in Italy. Sometimes hot dogs, with a rainbow of green relish, red ketchup, and yellow mustard painted on them. But it was the Mexican food she liked the most: tacos with spicy, steaming beef, melted cheddar, fresh tomatoes, and peppers; enchiladas; and quesadillas. Even now, at the convent, on her night to cook, Emilia would often prepare an American-style meal for her sisters. They had come to call her their "little American," although she prepared Mexican-style meals as often as she did "American." But Emilia's English still had an American accent, so the name stuck.

Emilia had some time off for a sabbatical and had decided to visit her friends in the States. She had written letters to old friends and acquaintances alike. Most had answered, except Elizabeth. This upset Emilia, because Elizabeth was the type to write back promptly. In her last letter, Emilia had given Elizabeth explicit instructions: *Call me. I will be in my room between the hours of twelve and four, your time of course. I will do this every day until I hear from you.*

No call came on the first day, but Emilia was patient. On the third day, the phone rang.

"Is this Emilia Ragazzi?" It was a deep voice, a man's voice.

"Yes. Yes, it is."

"My name is Ronald Seroli. I'm Elizabeth Hernandez's brother."

"Oh, yes. Mr. Seroli, I am so thankful—"

"I'm calling because I got your letters, and I figured I should let you know that Elizabeth is now living in a home for people with Alzheimer's."

"Oh, no. How long—"

"She's been in assisted living for about six years now. I've been taking care of her affairs. It was just something we had to do. She had become confused and was wandering out at all hours of the night. She'd get lost and turn up in the strangest places. You wouldn't believe some of the places. We needed to put her somewhere she'd stay put."

"I had no idea."

"Well, you wouldn't, since you hadn't spoken in the last ten years—so I gathered from your letters."

"My letters?"

"I am her legal guardian. It's my responsibility to read all her mail."

"Oh." Emilia took a breath, feeling a bit exposed. She swallowed, trying to rally herself through her discomfort. "What about her daughters?"

"They're all up to their own things. They sometimes stop in and see her. Only one of them is not completely caught up in herself."

"Which one is that?"

"Lydia, the youngest. She lives alone still, not too far from where her mother is staying. We had Elizabeth in a place in

175

Weehawken, but it was too far from the rest of the family. Plus, she just wasn't happy there. 'Course she couldn't express that, she just jibber-jabbers now, but we could tell. So we moved her three years ago to this place by Lydia. We knew at least *she* would visit."

"What about Elizabeth's husband?"

"Carlos? Well, then it's been a little longer than ten years since you two talked, hasn't it?"

Emila was quiet.

"Carlos divorced her about fifteen years ago. She remarried after that, a guy named Frank. But he died of a heart attack. It was real tough on her. Real tough."

"Well, I didn't know. I was on mission."

"Of course, you were on mission. All sisters have to do that, I guess."

"Well, not really."

"Where were you?"

"A few places: Sudan, India, East Timor, and the last was Madagascar."

"Madagascar. Lot of titanium mines there. Could be a rich country someday. Titanium is used in everything from house siding to tennis shoes; it's the white coloring in them. Titanium is used for white dye. Isn't that something? I bet you didn't know that. But how do you know Elizabeth again. Wasn't she your godmother?"

"My Rite of Christian Initiation sponsor. She lived next door to the family I was staying with when I was an *au pair*."

"Oh, that's right. I remembered your name right away."

"I believe Sister Jerold introduced you and me once," she said.

"Oh right. I remember. Sister Jerold. I'd like to know what came of her."

"She's still living in Minnesota. I have received a few letters from her."

"She's still alive! Well, there's something. That's really something."

"Mr. Seroli, what is Elizabeth's condition now?"

"Oh, well, she doesn't remember her daughters. She remembers me for about half a phone conversation. She can still play the piano though. The doctors say she might retain that till the end. It's amazing, the human mind. What about Father Greenhall? I seem to remember . . . wasn't he a bit of a flaky guy? There's no way he's still alive."

"He's passed on. I received a letter from the last parish where he was a pastor, in Florida."

"That's too bad. Father Greenhall, that old son of a gun."

The line cracked with a hum of static.

"Is Elizabeth living in New Jersey? Is that what you said?" Emilia asked.

"Yes. Yes, she is. At least she *should* be there."

Emilia took a deep breath. "Well, I'm going to be in the States next month, and I was hoping to visit her."

"I was thinking of visiting Italy myself," Mr. Seroli said without answering her question. "It would be nice if I knew someone over there, though. Maybe I could sleep on your couch."

"It's a private convent, I'm afraid. But there are hostels nearby," she said, twisting her rosary beads in her hand. She didn't even remember picking them up.

"So much for Christian charity, Sister."

Emilia was not sure what to say. "No, Mr. Seroli, it's just the rules. I'm sure you understand."

"Don't worry. Don't mention it. I don't really have time for an Italy getaway. I'm too busy."

Emilia swallowed before she asked, "Do you think it would it be possible for me to visit Elizabeth when I come to the States?"

"Well, you can't do that."

"Why is that, sir?"

"Are you taking a tone with me, Sister? Wow, they don't make nuns like they used to, do they?"

"Mr. Seroni, I didn't mean to offend—"

"Seroli. My name is Seroli. It was Elizabeth's maiden name, you know. Or maybe you wouldn't."

"I didn't mean—"

"It would be inappropriate if you visited. I won't allow it."

"Now, Mr. Seroli, I appreciate your concern for your sister. I do, and I admire your devotion to her. Do you truly think my visit would upset her?"

"I am sure. I'm sorry. I shouldn't have made this phone call."

"Mr. Seroli, this may be the last time I'm in the States for some time."

"Well, I'm sorry. A visit would just confuse her. As her legal guardian, I have to look after Elizabeth's welfare."

"Well, maybe I could have her address and write to her."

"I'm sorry, no."

"Just a letter?"

"I'm the only one who gets her mail."

"Please, Mr. Seroli—"

"I can see this is not working."

"What is not working?"

"I'm sorry you don't understand. Good-bye."

"I'll keep her in my prayers."

"Keep us all there. It's a difficult job, keeping care of her and all. Hard on us all."

He hung up.

Emilia stood up, as if she had to go somewhere. But in her small quarters there was no room to pace. She went to the window. It was evening. The servers at the café below were rolling the kerosene heat lamps under the awning and chaining up the tables for the night—it would be too cold to let diners eat outside this evening. A group of children kicked a football in the piazza in front of the convent, sending the pigeons scattering into their air. They were children from all parts of the globe: Italy, Eastern Europe, refugees from North and West Africa. They played football with an abandon that she had seen in poor countries throughout the world. Not far away, Alberto, the homeless man who slept each night on the steps of the church, was taking up his place wrapped in his sleeping bag to beg the evening mass-goers for change. The football bounced from one child's foot to another's. Emilia felt like there was something she was supposed to be doing that she had forgotten. A wind picked up and turned over one of the tables in the cafés. Chairs skidded along the ground. The servers scrambled after them. Children shouted. Emilia buttoned her sweater tighter. She was cold. Winter was coming.

14.

Nazis

I couldn't believe it. Professor David Palmer of Weldon University, winner of the Noble Prize for Economics. The news didn't lie. It was that time of year when every day of the week the news announces the winners in another category. You know, they announce the names, you don't pay any attention. You just wait for the next story. Unless, that is, you *know* one of the names. Unless you used to sit next to the guy whose name they are announcing, his name called right after yours in roll each morning.

There was a small picture of him, Dr. David Palmer, beside the other winners. He looked older. We all do, but it was him. He had this big old smile. Dave always had a big smile, didn't always know where it came from, but it was to his credit. I smiled too, standing there in the kitchen drinking my coffee with a big helping of shock and disbelief. David had lived in this town, in the neighborhood by the grocery store where I still shopped. Now he was a world-famous figure.

And I had taught him how to throw a football.

I looked at his picture. It was definitely him. In the years since, he had gotten a little better at presenting himself. His hair was neatly parted, and he sported a scholarly beard. He had been ugly in junior high. With his stretched-out lips and rounded cheeks, at first glance he looked like he suffered from Downs syndrome. He also had bad dandruff and scaly red skin that was always breaking out in a rash, a reaction to something or other. The girls used to recoil at him and pinch their noses behind his back. His feet pointed outwards, so when he walked he bent over and breathed hard through his mouth. I wondered if he had used that same duck-walk when he'd crossed the stage to receive his prize.

He used to say things like "Top of the morning, Sidney" and "Good day, young chap" and called me "Laddie." He reminded me of my grandfather. Dave loved history and engineering. No one doubted that he was smart, but no one would ever have traded their looks for his smarts. He loved the history of warfare too, and was particularly fascinated by the German war machine. I had taken a few looks at my dad's artillery books while I was in our bathroom, so I could actually talk to Dave about these things.

"The bomb ended the war, Dave, but radar won it."

"That would be the one solitary example of the Brits getting the jump on the Krauts," I remember he had said.

"The Brits got the jump on a lot of things."

"The British did invent the first aircraft carrier, but the Germans invented the first jet plane, the Heinkel HE 178, predecessor to the Messerschmitt ME 262."

"Well, if the Germans hadn't had their gadgets, they would have lost the war in a month."

Dave had looked at me, aghast. His heels came together, and he poked at the air with his finger, which meant he was quoting someone important. "'The German's institutionalized military excellence. For every one excellent general on the Allies' side, the Germans had ten,' General Eisenhower, 1946."

"Well, I guess that settles it."

♠

I changed schools after sixth grade, so in seventh grade I was the new kid. My parents wanted me in a smaller, private school. They could still afford things like that then; Dad was still working his job in finance. It was a real small Catholic school—only two classes per grade. Real cliquish. The kids who had been there the longest were like the ruling class. They were the cool ones. I was a nerd because I was new. You could see the segregation between the cool group and nerds at recess. The cool guys played football on the back field; the nerds didn't. We just played catch near the school building. My friends were Pablo and Jeff. They were nerds too. Jeff, because he wore Metallica T-shirts, and Pablo, because he was poor and wore the same clothes every day. But Jeff and Pablo never considered themselves as nerdy as Dave. Even nerds have a strange kind of hierarchy, I guess. No one wanted to be associated with Dave. He was always raising his hand in class and providing these long-winded answers that even the teachers got tired of. But nothing could dampen Dave's enthusiasm for learning.

Yeah, big nerd, but no surprise about the Nobel, I guess.

♠

At recess, Dave would follow me around the playground. I acted like I didn't know he was there, but he was persistent as a shadow. When I would come up to Jeff and Pablo to toss the football, they'd inevitably look behind me and say, "Dave, you sit over there and watch."

So Dave would sit on the curb watching us throw. As we played, Jeff and Pablo would slowly move away, so that by the time recess was over, we'd be on the opposite side of the field from Dave. He'd sometimes still be sitting there, like we'd told him to.

One day, both Jeff and Pablo were absent from school. I had no one to throw with, so I turned around, facing Dave, and tossed the football. It hit him in the shoulder and fell to the ground at his feet, where it sat rocking. He stood staring at me through his watery glasses.

"You dropped your football, Laddie," he said.

"No. You dropped it. I threw it to you. I'm teaching you how to throw."

"Oh, splendid!"

Dave was not very coordinated or strong. His fingers were short and fat. Academic fingers, I suppose. I don't think he ever actually threw a tight spiral, but he could flub that ball pretty well. Pablo and Jeff were not thrilled when I said Dave could throw with us the next day. Dave couldn't catch to save his life. He'd close his eyes, and the ball would hit him in the chest, bounce past his fingers, and Jeff or Pablo would grab it. They begrudged me his presence. Every day they would run and hide from him behind the dumpster, but Dave would always find us, and we'd emerge to pass the ball. It was a weird little ritual they insisted on.

♠

It was over Christmas break that I lost my eye. I came back after an extra week out with a patch. Seventh grade is not a good time to be different. For a while it was like people felt sorry for me and didn't say anything. But it didn't take long for the teasing to begin. Mostly pirate jokes. I've heard so many stupid pirate jokes. It was Chris Solaris who was the first to start making jokes about it in the cafeteria. Started doing this loud pirate imitation. I ignored it, as if it wasn't happening. I wanted to believe it wasn't directed at me. If I pretended hard enough, I could almost convince myself it wasn't. I was still new to it. Later I would have throttled him, but then I just felt vulnerable and raw.

Jeff and Pablo were useless that day. They were not going to challenge Chris Solaris. He was a clown, but he had been at the school since kindergarten. Like I said, he was part of the ruling class.

I don't know what it was that Dave caught on to that day. Maybe it was because he was used to being teased, maybe it was because I had taught him to throw the football, but he piped up and said in his loud, nasal voice so the whole cafeteria could hear: "Chris Solaris, you should be ashamed of yourself! Some of the most famous people in history have had one eye, including Hannibal, who was one of the greatest military leaders of all time. Not to mention Samuel Johnson, who wrote the first dictionary of the English language. Theodore Roosevelt was blinded in one eye during a boxing match. Not to mention my personal favorite, Horatius Cocles, who single-handedly defended Rome on the bridge over the River Tiber when the Etruscans attacked—all with an arrow sticking in his eye socket. Mr. Solaris, you could only wish to be in such rarified company as that."

Dave's outburst effectively shifted the attention away from me, so I guess that was good. Still, to say I was mortified would be an understatement. I didn't want Dave coming to my rescue, and I didn't need people thinking we were best friends. I just got up and ran to the boys' bathroom, where I cried. It was weird. I could still cry out of both eye sockets but only see out of one. Had to pull off my patch so it wouldn't get ruined.

♠

Right before spring break, we were doing the yearbook's last will and testament section—you know, that part where you bequeath things to the lower classes. Jeff left all his gym socks to the kindergarten kids. Pablo wrote something obscene in Spanish. I wrote: *I leave all the phone numbers on the bathroom walls to anyone lonely enough to call them.* The editors wouldn't put mine in the yearbook, but they approved Pablo's and Jeff's. I don't think they spoke Spanish. Dave's also was accepted. He wrote: *I leave all my books to Sidney. Better get a bookcase, Laddie!* The class thought this was hilarious. Rick Davies left me a hammer and nails, so I could build a bookcase. Chris Solaris left me wood for the shelves. Brad Caveny, who was the coolest kid in school—he already had to shave in just seventh grade—started calling me "Laddie" whenever he saw me. This made my ears burn and my armpits itch with perspiration.

♠

I got in trouble for poking holes in my spelling book, breaking a red pen over them, and spreading the ink around so that it looked like blood. That, combined with the fact I finally punched Chris Solaris in the face, meant I lost recess privileges. But it was worse than that. I guess they were afraid I was homicidal or something. I had to sit in the counselor's office for observation during recess for a week. On the second day, Dave walked in. I realized he had come looking for me.

"Sidney, my good man, what ails you?"

"Nothing ails me."

"Why are you in the counselor's office?"

"Because I'm 'disturbed.'"

"Do I dare, disturb the universe? In a minute there is time. For decisions and revisions which a minute will reverse," he said with a grand sweep of his hand. He looked down at me. I knew he was quoting, but I had no idea what. He took pity on me. "T.S. Eliot, The Love Song of J. Alfred Prufrock."

"That's great, one of my favorites."

"Mine too. Mind if I join you, Laddie?"

"By all means," I said, copying his sweeping hand motion as I gestured at the chair across from me.

He snorted and smiled, then sat down. "Pablo and Jeff are off smoking behind the dumpster. They said they aren't going to throw the ball until you come back."

I figured they were likely throwing it now that he was gone.

"I'll be back next week."

"Oh, my." Dave looked around, his eyes landing on a box of checkers. When he opened it, we could see a bunch of chess pieces rolling around too.

"Fancy a game of chess?"

"Why not."

Dave decimated me, every game. But that was all right, I learned a lot of strategies and combinations from him. He was real patient with me too. I kept knocking over the pieces when I reached for them. I was still new to having one eye and had not recalibrated my sense of depth. Dave wasn't fazed. He knew what was up. He'd just keep talking, about Germans or the Greeks or British poetry, without missing a beat and set the pieces back in place.

One afternoon, a counselor who was also a nun walked by, stopped, and asked, "David, what are you doing here?"

"Greetings, Sister Camilla. I'm not in trouble. I'm just keeping my friend here company."

"Oh." She looked at me, likely surprised that Dave considered me a friend. We were an odd couple, I guess. She probably wanted some type of confirmation from me. I shrugged.

"I taught him how to throw a football. He's teaching me how to lose at chess."

Dave laughed uncontrollably. He came in every day that I had detention or observation, whatever it was. If he had been anyone else, the counselors wouldn't have allowed it, but it was Dave Palmer, and they probably thought he was a good influence on me. I was more comfortable talking to Dave in the counselor's office. None of our classmates could see us then. But I wondered if it meant he would follow me around even more. I made sure to walk ahead of him and not talk to him on the way back to the classroom each day, letting him duck-walk after me like a lost puppy or something.

♠

In April, Dave had his birthday. He invited Jeff, Pablo, and me. I called his house to say I couldn't go. His mom answered.

"Hi. This is Sidney. I'm Dave's friend."

"Hello, Sidney, how are you?" Her voice seemed really nice.

"I'm okay, but I can't make it to Dave's party. My mom says I have a fever."

"Oh, I'm sorry to hear that."

"Tell him I'm really sorry."

"I will. I hope you feel better."

I later found out that Jeff and Pablo didn't go either. I hoped someone had shown up, but I never asked Dave how his birthday went.

♠

One recess, Brad Caveny came up to us and watched me throw without saying anything. I was waiting for him to start making fun of me, but he goes, "Sidney, that's a good throw."

"Thanks."

"We need a quarterback. You want to fill in for Chris? He got suspended."

"Sure," I said.

"You can't take Sidney," Dave jumped in. "We were having a stimulating conversation on the Reich's use of the machine gun at the Battle of Somme."

"Reich?"

"It's, uh, German," I said, looking at my feet. My cheeks felt real hot, my armpits sweaty again.

"German," Brad said, turning. "Dave, are you a Nazi?"

I chuckled a little, mostly because I was nervous. But Brad took it as encouragement. Dave's voice rose a little bit, so it got real squealy. He always started to sound like a soprano when he was flustered, like an old woman, really.

"No, of course not. It's just that throughout history, the Germans have been some of the best engineers in the western world."

"Dave's a Nazi." Brad tapped me playfully on the shoulder. Dave's face turned red, and his big frog lips frowned.

"I am not a Nazi!"

"Dave, you always talk about German's. You have a swastika tattoo?" I said, joining in. I wanted Brad to like me. I wanted to be a cool kid, I guess.

"I am not a Nazi!" Dave stomped his foot and screamed.

"David is a Nazi. David is a Nazi," Brad was chanting.

Dave's face bunched up and he started whimpering. It quickly changed to crying. All-out bawling. He charged Brad and tried to stomp on his foot. That was as violent as Dave could get, stomping someone's foot. Brad jumped right out of the way, dancing and singing. I did this too, hopping away from Dave's stomping feet and bouncing on my toes in tune with Brad's singing. It was fun. The whole football crowd slowly came and joined the dance. Dave finally ran inside. I don't even think he could see us after a while, his face was so swollen, his eyes just pouring tears. We could hear his high-pitched whining all the way across the field. People did imitations of him for the rest of recess.

My team won that day. I threw two touchdown passes to Brad. After that, I sat with the football guys at lunch. I never said much there, but it was cool because the girls sat on the other end of the table, and we could flirt with them. At least Brad did. The rest of us watched and said nothing. Pablo and Jeff didn't move to our table; there was some silent understanding that they were not that cool, but they would hang out near us when we picked teams for football, and I always picked them so they could play with us.

Dave didn't come to school for a while. He finally came back when we had finals. He didn't come out for recess anymore.

♠

I turned the TV off. The anchor woman had moved on from the Nobel Prize announcements anyway. I poured my coffee into the sink and dumped my toast in the trash. I wasn't hungry. I stared out the window for a while. The sun wasn't up yet. I noticed our fence needed repairing before the neighbors complained. There were dishes in the sink. I set the coffee mug on top of them, and they settled with a slight clatter. There was a putrid smell of garbage coming up from the trash can. Coffee grounds, withered vegetables, and rancid milk cartons. I removed the lid and pulled up the bag to take it out. I pushed the backdoor open with my foot, and a blast of cold air hit me in the face.

Dammit, I was a stupid kid.

15.

Every Time I See You

Don stepped out of Phil's house. A black cat with a white face ran across his path. He started walking to the street, which was empty. Not a single car in sight. It was after midnight. When he reached the street, a boy called out to him.

"Excuse me, sir, do you have a phone on you?"

The boy was standing across the street, leaning on a bike. Don looked around for anyone hiding in the bushes. Phil had said the neighborhood was safe. Phil had been living there for ten years or so. Phil had been playing poker games with his buddies on Saturday nights all those years. This was the first one Don had been to. The men had smoked cigars and talked about sports and women. Don watched the TV that was on with no sound. A beautiful woman was the news anchor and when Don saw her in all her proper and stiff beauty he had said,

"I'd like to eat her hair pie."

Don knew the guys would have found it funnier if he had not laughed so hard at his own joke. He had never played cards with them before that night. That was because he had a beautiful wife, Felicity, whom he loved and he'd rather spend time with her. She was younger by a decade, but that just upped his status, he imagined. But even Felicity said Don should go out on Saturday nights. She said it was good for him to be alone or with guy friends. Felicity seemed happier when he went out. He usually would go to a movie, but tonight he'd tried going to Phil's.

Don had told the guys at the poker table about his arrangement with Felicity. They asked to see a picture of her. Then they asked what she did when he was gone. He said she read. Then they said she was cheating on him. Don said they didn't know her. He stuck around to play a few rounds, but the fun was gone after that, so he left. *So much for guy friends.* Don's friends Sidney and Daniel had said the same thing about Felicity. Sidney said he thought she was sleeping with a guy named Lance. Daniel had agreed. Daniel had been kind, circumspect about it. Sidney had not. He had been more direct. Don had not spoken to either of them since.

The men at the poker game had pressed Don too.

"Do you ever ask her what she does while you're gone?"

"No," Don said. They had all looked at each other.

Someone said, "You should."

That was when he left. That was when Don got up and left. Assholes.

"Do you have a phone?" The boy asked again, leaning on his bike.

"Do I have one or have I seen one?"

"Have one."

"No, why?" Don lied. He knew sometimes drug addicts would ask to borrow your phone and then run off with it. That was what you got for being kind, and Don knew he was often pegged as an easy mark. He figured it was better to lie to this kid.

"I had an operation on my knee, and I fell off my bike back there—a cat ran in front of it—and now my wound has reopened."

Don was in the middle of the street but not moving any closer. The boy lifted his pant leg, and Don saw that his sock was stained with blood. Blood had dribbled down the waffle soles of his running shoes and pooled on the cement of the sidewalk.

"That looks bad. You said the wound re-opened?"

The boy, he was around sixteen or maybe seventeen, started to lift his pant leg higher.

"No, I shouldn't, I don't want to gross you out."

Don was surprised by so much discretion in a kid.

"My friend's house is just back there, you can use his phone," Don said.

"No, I don't want to cause a fuss."

Don stood in the street. A car was coming. He crossed to the boy's side. The car passed. The boy sat atop his bike and used his right leg, his good leg, to start pushing down the sidewalk. He let the bad leg dangle off the side and bleed. He was going real slow. Don realized he would surely walk by him and pass him since they were going the same way on the same sidewalk. It would be awkward when he did—and Don couldn't think of any excuse to walk to the other side of the street—maybe if he saw a friend or something, but it was after ten, and that wouldn't be happening. So, Don slowed his pace when he came alongside the kid.

"What kind of operation was it?" he asked.

"I had a tumor they had to take out."

"When?"

"About three weeks ago. I just got the stitches out three days ago. This was only the second time my mom's let me go out since."

Don thought it must hurt.

"I was wondering if I could call my mom; maybe she could come pick me up. She's going to be angry, I bet."

"You saw a cat?"

"It jumped out in front of me. I swerved and fell. Actually, my right trouser leg is torn worse than the left, but the left is the one that's bleeding."

"Where are you coming from?"

"Work. You?"

"Poker game."

Don realized this made him sound very manly.

"You like poker?" the boy asked, still pushing himself down the sidewalk.

"It's good. You know, passes the time. It's kind of late to be coming home from work."

"Yeah, I've been there all day. Someone was sick and they asked me to stay for a double shift. I spent five hours there yesterday, just waiting to get a uniform. I was just sitting in the manager's office."

"Five hours, that's a long time to wait."

"They put me on the clock though, so I got paid."

"That's good. Where do you work?"

"Freddy's. I just started two days ago. I'm just learning how to grill hamburgers. Tomorrow I learn how to do the fries. Do you like Freddy's?"

"No."

"You a Wendy's man then?"

"No. I really don't eat fast food. I haven't been to Freddy's, McDonald's, or Wendy's in years. Actually, that's not true. A few years ago, my wife and I were travelling all over Europe, and one night we were in Zurich and we were broke, so we went to McDonald's." Don lied again. They went to McDonald's because Felicity had said she was craving "American" food. But he thought that made her sound like she didn't have much class. Saying they were broke, he realized, also might build some sort of solidarity between him and this young man, who obviously knew the value of a dollar and a hard day's work. "Previously I had been proud to say that I hadn't been to McDonalds in over five years, but I can't say that now."

Don kept walking along with the kid. They seemed to be going in the same general direction. Don figured the boy would be going towards Ridgewood, one of the less affluent neighborhoods. Don would walk along. His own lakeside townhouse wasn't too far away.

"Is that your uniform?" Don looked at the boy's pants.

"Yeah."

"I'm sure they'll replace it for you."

"Yesterday it was locked in a locker, and they had lost the key. That's why I had to wait so long."

"Have you ever read E.M. Forster, *A Passage to India*?" Don asked.

"No."

"I had to read it for a class in college. But there's this line in there that says something like, 'The English are always so calm in a crisis' and that kind of reminds me of you now. You're really calm, even though you're bleeding all over the fucking landscape."

Don wanted to sound cool, so he cussed, but the kid didn't laugh. Maybe he was raised not to cuss. He knew some working-class folks could be quite religious.

"Excuse my French." Don realized it was a bit of an awkward expression to use after talking about English literature. The boy didn't say anything. Don thought that maybe he had confused him. "Were you raised not to cuss?"

"Oh, cussing is all right," the boy said. "I was cussing a lot back there when I fell. I was cussing all over the place. Crying some too. Not so much from the pain, but from the frustration."

"It's been a bad day."

"Yeah. My basketball team lost. Not Duke, everyone around here cheers for the Duke, but UNC, they're my team. You follow college basketball?"

"Not really."

"Well, it's been a bad day since that happened." He was quiet as he looked down and briefly pulled the wet trouser leg from where it was sticking to his knee. "My mom is going to get all panicky when she sees my leg."

"At least the cat lived," Don said. "Animal lovers everywhere are indebted to you."

Don thought of talking about his bike wrecks from when he delivered newspapers, but he decided not to; it was better to keep the kid's mind off the pain. He had a nice bike. It was silver. Don bet the kid had bought it just so he could get to work at his new job. He was leaving little drops of blood along the side walk. There would be a whole trail to his house, like a trail of bread crumbs. Don yawned. It was late, but he would walk the kid all the way home. Maybe the boy would remember him; maybe he would remember that this stranger had done something nice for him. They walked along a while. No cars passed. Not one. At one point the boy said,

"See the hedgehog up there?"

"The what?"

"The hedgehog up there."

"No. Where?"

The boy pointed across the street. Don looked, but saw nothing. He was about to lie and say he saw something, when he saw a fat furry thing waddling near the curb.

"Yeah, I see it. It's big. I've never seen a hedgehog before."

"Yep. In two or three days it will probably ruin the garden, if there is one in the back of that house. You can't touch them; they've got little spikes."

"You mean it's a porcupine?'

"No. Wrong habitat for porcupines in this area. Hedgehogs just got little spikes."

"Oh. But you still wouldn't want to touch them?"

"No."

"Sounds like a porcupine to me."

The boy shrugged, steadying his handlebars. They had reached an intersection. The boy said, "That's my house down there, with the white car."

Don couldn't see the house. It was hidden by the hedge. The car was a jalopy.

"Okay, can you make it all right?"

"Yeah."

The wet pant leg was glistening in light from the street lamp.

"How long were you hobbling along before you saw me?" Don asked.

"What?"

"How long had it been between you crashing and seeing me.'

"I don't know, five minutes or so."

"Wow. You're tough. Hang in there."

"Goodnight."

"Goodnight."

Don decided not to wait and watch him walk all the way to his house—he might think Don was a pervert or something. Don walked home.

♠

Before he left Phil's house, Don had called Felicity. There had been no answer. She must have been asleep. Moths flew around the street lamps as he walked. When he arrived at his place, he took the stairs by twos and slid the key into his door. The lights were off inside. He made his way to the bedroom, guiding himself through the living room with his hand on the couch. He found Felicity in bed. She rolled over when she heard him come in.

"Hey, Honey, how was poker?"

"Fine. Good." He went to the bathroom and turned on the light. He could see her face. She still looked awake and alert. She must not have been sleeping long.

"Felicity, I met this amazing boy on the way back."

"On the way back from Phil's?"

"Yes."

"That's nice."

"Don't you want to know what made him amazing?"

"What made him amazing?"

He was not sure if she was just making conversation for the sake of it, or if she was really interested. "Never mind. I'll tell you in the morning."

"I'm just tired, Honey. What was it?"

Don hung up his shirt and pants.

"He was just real tough. Real tough, that's all. The boy was a man." He said the words again, slower as if they were new and intriguing. "The boy was a man."

"That's good," she said.

She rolled over. Don sat on the bed awhile in his boxers. He didn't want to get ready for bed, even though he was tired. Felicity was quiet beside him. She was probably falling back asleep. Don looked at her book on the night stand. It was a thick, hardback edition, with the shiny raised letters on the front. Very thick, very shiny. He stared at his shoes, which he had worn into the bedroom and set side-by-side in the closet.

"You didn't see Lance tonight, did you?" he asked.

"Hmmmmm?" she said, like she was just waking up, again.

"I said, 'You didn't see Lance tonight, did you?'"

"Lance Mulherin?"

"Yeah, Lance Mulherin."

"Why would Lance have been here?"

"I didn't ask if he had been here. Just if you had seen him."

"But why would you even ask?"

"I don't know. I just saw a car like his driving down the street on my way here."

"A lot of people drive cars like his, Don. What are you suggesting?" she said, sitting up in bed.

"So you didn't see him tonight."

"What are you saying?"

"I'm speaking English."

"No! Goddammit, Don, I did not see Lance tonight. How could you say that?" she said, slapping the mattress.

"Calm down. Calm down. I'm sorry. I just, well you didn't answer when I called. I thought maybe he dropped by."

"When did you call?"

"When I left. Check your phone."

"What time was that, Don?"

"Around 9:45 or so."

"I was in the bathroom, getting ready for bed. Then I was reading. I must not have heard the phone."

"Reading?"

"Yes."

He picked up the book from the bedside table. He flipped through it. The bookmark was on page one hundred. He took a breath before he spoke again. "The bookmark is in the same place as last night. I was just curious and had looked at what you were reading and noticed you were on page one hundred, that's the only reason I really recall."

"Just because the bookmark is there doesn't mean I'm on that page," she said. "Goddammit, Don."

She got up and closed her nightgown tightly, then went into the bathroom. Don sat in the darkness, the book in his hands. He heard the toilet flush, the water running, the tank refilling. She opened the door and looked at him, then turned out the light, and it was dark. Her nightgown made a slinky noise as she moved across the room. The bed groaned as she got back in it.

"I supposed you're going to quiz me on what I read." She was on her side, facing away from him.

"No."

"I'm on page a hundred and thirty. I left the bookmark on one hundred because it's a passage I really like. It flows nicely. It's written with the flowery language that I know you like in your books." She rolled over. "I'll see you in the morning."

Don sat on the bed. He didn't feel like sleeping. He sat a while. Felicity didn't say anything else, but he knew she wasn't sleeping. He got up, left the room, and headed downstairs, moving without thought through the living room to the kitchen where he sat down at the table. He heard the plunk of raindrops on the boards of the deck outside. Curtains of rain drew across the lake, blurring the surface and shattering the reflection of the lights of houses on the opposite shore. He loved the lake, all its moods, the textures of its surface, brought on by the interaction of seasons, the angle of light, and the weather of the moment. Thunder rumbled far away. It began to pour. *Good thing that kid has gotten home by now,* he thought. Don hoped his mother was not too hard on him.

He turned on the small television on the counter, the volume on low. But he wasn't listening or watching it. He realized that he was holding Felicity's book in his hand. He slid his hand along its side before he cracked open the pages to where the bookmark waited. Page one hundred. His hands were trembling. He closed the book, set it down on the table, and went to the liquor cabinet. He poured himself some gin. The ice rattled in the glass as he held it. He couldn't stop it and was afraid the noise would travel upstairs to their bedroom. He opened the cupboard and pulled out a stack of paper cups. He poured the drink into one. The ice still rattled, but it was just a soft tapping now. Felicity wouldn't hear. He drank it quickly then carried the cup and bottle over to the kitchen table.

He sat down again with the book. He opened it. On the TV, a dangerous looking man in a cowboy hat walked out of a saloon and scanned the street. Someone moved in the shadows, and the gunslinger pulled out his pistol and killed him. The volume was low, so Don didn't hear the shot, but he saw the smoke issue out of the barrel and cylinders. He saw the body of some faceless, sinister character fall to the ground with fake, Hollywood stillness, as if the bullet had paralyzed him, making him stiff as a board, as well as killing him.

Fake.

He read page one hundred:

Ms. Laurelhurst usually did not make exceptions to her rules for anyone, and this ruffian certainly did not resemble southern gentry. But something in his eyes made her reconsider. Maybe it was their hazel coloring, or the sound of his voice that sounded like something sweet she could almost recall but couldn't quite. If you asked her, this is what she would have said. She was being a good Christian lady and a proper hostess. She had convinced herself of it.

But it was those very "proper" sensibilities that would never let her admit that it was his glistening copper skin, callused hands, the shade of whiskers on his jaw, and the smooth, hard pectorals just peeking out of his shirt that had truly swayed her.

"Why don't you sit down here on the porch, Mr. Craig. I'll have the servants bring out some biscuits and tea."

"Much obliged, ma'am," he said.

Ms. Laurelhurst turned and raised her hand to her lips to call the serving girl when her movements were arrested. She heard a click-clack of hooves and turned to see a carriage pull up, its window frames and brass door latches gleaming in the afternoon sun.

"Oh, that must be the Inspector," she cried, her hand to her breast. "Dear me, he's early. That is just like him."

Inspector Collingwood stepped out of the carriage, one black leather boot at a time. His mustache was neatly trimmed, his doublet well-tailored, his bearing aristocratic. The horses, their coats iridescent, shifted their hooves. The trip from the school to the plantation was all too short for them. Their muscles invigorated, their blood flowing, they were eager to run farther, even to be free.

"Oh, Inspector, it is quite a delight to see you."

Inspector Collingwood took her hand and brought it to his lips.

"My, Lady, you become more angelic every time I see you. It is lovely—"

Don set down the book. He stood up and went to the back door. The rain was splashing on the deck outside, pooling on the boards, which were sealed with polyurethane finish. Drops were skidding down the glass of the door. He slid it open and stepped outside. He was standing in the rain, getting wet down to the skin. But he didn't want to go back inside. The lake was hidden from him, except for in the brief flashes of lightning. He realized the bottle was still in his hands. He knew what he would do now. He would stand out in the rain and get drunk. He would stand out in the rain and get roaring drunk. . . .

16.

Everyone Can See It

Sam was an even-tempered man. He knew all his customers, if not by name, then by face. No matter who you were, if you came into Sam's Italian restaurant, Angelo's, he would remember you the next time and even pick up where the last conversation left off.

"How's Ricky doing with the T-ball?" He'd say to the Bridges; or "How's your daughter doing at that new job," he'd ask the Murdochs; to Mr. Clemson, whose house had been flooded by faulty plumbing, "Did you get that fixture repaired yet? I know a guy."

There was no host or hostess at Angelo's. Sam greeted every guest, every night. Angelo's was a family place, not corporate, but owned by a family: Sam's family. Started by his parents, who had immigrated from Syria: Aaron and Rosarita Albaz. He was Jewish, and she was Muslim, but with their olive skin and her name, most people took them to be Italian. Funny that. Most people even thought "Angelo" was their family surname. People often called Sam and his brother, Roy, the cook, Sam and Roy Angelo.

America, the place of reinvention.

It was a Friday night in May. There were all kinds of graduations that night. Tables one, eight, and eleven were reserved for parties of fifteen, five, and seven, respectively. This, of course, would be in addition to the other regular customers that would be expected on a Friday night.

"Big parties tonight," Sam said to Feleketch, the waitress. Really the only waitress. It wasn't a big restaurant, and with Sam working the door, along with the runners, bussers, and bartender, they made it work, pooling tips.

They all made more, Sam noticed, ever since he had hired Feleketch. Maybe it was just the restaurant coming into its own.

But maybe it was her.

Sam had known he would hire her the moment she walked in the door, the very first day he had put an ad in the paper for new servers. She had stepped inside, the soft light filtering through the curtains like a white cloud at her back. She'd had on slacks and a collared shirt, but the scarf she had looped around her neck gave her all the grace of a woman moving in royal robes. *Grace,* that was what he thought of her when she had moved inside from the door, smooth as a brushstroke on a canvass, her shape curving and tapered all at once. Her bangles had rung sort of like chimes when she'd reached her hand out to shake his. She'd said her name and explained to him that it was Ethiopian.

"Who's coming in?" she asked, preparing the checks in her black server book. Sam's mind came back to the present. Feleketch was in the starched button-down shirt and long black skirt she wore when waiting tables. Her hair was pulled back, but she still wore her bangles. He was glad for that. Her eyes caught him in their pull over her book of checks. *Luminous,* that was what one of the customers had once called them.

"Jacksons on table eleven with a party of seven, Mr. and Mrs. Jackson, three grandparents, two children. Their son is graduating from Lake Forest High School tonight," Sam said, laconic. He pointed to their table with his head. "Table eight is the Colemans; they'll need a booster seat for the youngest kid. They're celebrating Sally's birthday. She's forty or something but don't ask."

"Of course not," Feleketch said in that way that let him know she'd had everything long worked out in her head already. Three years of working together did that. She could read his moods better than most, and he her tones, spoken in that melodic accent of hers that the customers so loved.

"And the big party of fifteen people is at table one, the Shroders. Big dinner. Their daughter's graduating from Robinson High, valedictorian."

"Vicky, she's valedictorian?" Feleketch said, clapping her hands. "That's wonderful, I will have to congratulate her."

"Yep. Impressive girl. Varsity swim team, all kinds of National Honor Society Awards. Next year she's going to Yale. Real go-getter."

Sam wondered if he would ever have children to make him so proud, but that had not been in the cards for him. In many ways, the restaurant was his child.

"Do we have a cake for them?" Feleketch asked. It was just like her to think of that. She would probably go buy one for them if he said no.

"I'm sure they will bring their own. Don't forget to charge them a cutting fee."

"A what?" Feleketch asked, her hands closing around the order book and stuffing it into the pocket of her apron.

"Cake cutting fee. People just can't bring their own food into a restaurant. You have to charge them. We'll take the cake in back, slice it up, and serve it. It's usually twenty-five dollars," Sam said.

"You are being serious."

"I am," Sam said.

"I refuse," Feleketch said in a tone that told him he had already lost the battle.

"Why is that? It's standard in every restaurant," Sam said, tilting his head to the side.

"I don't care if it is standard. The Shroders are good, regular customers. They tip generously. I am not going to charge them for slicing a cake."

"They will expect it."

"Well, then they can be pleasantly surprised," she said. She was being assertive and was on the edge of annoyance with him. "The Jacksons are here," she said, nodding at the door.

Sam took his cue and went to greet them. The Jacksons were walking in the front door, two grandparents leading the way. The grandmother was round, stooped, and leaning hard on a cane. Mrs. Jackson held her arm with all the familiarity of a daughter. Mrs. Jackson was followed by her son, stooping through the door in a royal blue graduation gown.

"Nice gown, Jake."

"My mom made me wear it in here," Jake said with a grimace.

"Hi, Sam," Jake's mother said.

"Hello, Mrs. Jackson," he said, kissing her on the cheek.

"This is my mother, Sophia," she said. "My father, Anthony."

"It's a pleasure." Sam shook hands with Anthony and kissed Sophia. The old lady flushed and giggled at the attention. Sam winked at her husband, who seemed happy that his wife was happy.

Mr. Jackson came in the door with his mother, who was a bit younger than Sophia and Anthony. Sam kissed her cheek and shook hands with him. The Jacksons' younger son lingered at the back. He was smaller than his brother Jake, and lanky. Britt was his name. Sam suspected he played soccer, but he wasn't sure enough to mention it. Sam showed the family to their seats and told them that Feleketch would be right with them.

"Oh, wait until you meet Feleketch," Mr. Jackson said to his in-laws as they took their seats. "She's Sam's wife."

Sam chuckled as he helped Sophia into her chair. "Well, that would be something. Don't go spreading rumors about my employees."

Mr. Jackson looked up, the surprise on his face sincere. "What? But I thought . . . all these years I just assumed . . . ."

"Doug," Mrs. Jackson said, waving her hand at him. "Look at his fingers. Sam doesn't have a wedding ring."

"Oh, I guess you're right," Doug Jackson said, scratching his head. Jake seemed relieved that someone was now more embarrassed than he was. His brother Britt snickered as Jake whispered something to him.

Sam didn't want his Mr. Jackson to feel uncomfortable, so he lightened the mood. "No, I'm a bachelor. You know me, a real party animal with my argyle sweaters and sensible loafers. I think I got this pair at a garage sale just last week."

They all laughed. The moment had been diffused. Jake, in fact, stood up for Sam. "But Sam, you're totally smooth, like all Mafioso."

"Mafioso?" Sam repeated.

Jake's father leaned close to Sam and elbowed him, speaking in a low voice. "Well Sam, if you had not considered Feleketch, maybe you should."

He followed with a wink.

A look from his wife silenced him.

"Good evening Doug, Debbie, Britt. How are you?" Feleketch said, appearing at the edge of the table with menus.

"Feleketch, we were just speaking to Sam about you," Mr. Jackson said.

"Oh?" she said, pivoting and handing the menus out to the grandparents, women first. "You must be Doug and Debbie's parents, it is nice to meet you." Feleketch never missed a beat. She turned to Jake. "Jake, congratulations on graduating."

"Thanks, Feleketch." Jake smiled.

Sam left to get a water pitcher. They were in good hands.

♦

Something was wrong. By the noise and flow of the crowd, Sam knew they were already into the evening rush. He checked his watch. It was 6:15. The Jacksons were supposed to arrive *after* the Shroders. The Shroders had been due at 6:00. Sam looked at the big table they had set for them. Fifteen glasses, fifteen plates, seventy-five pieces of silverware, not counting butter knives. The butter knives made ninety. All that space would be taken up, all those dishes would be filled. Big check. The Shroders weren't usually late; they were good customers. Maybe the reservation was taken down wrong. Maybe it was 6:15, not 6:00.

When Feleketch came alongside him to add up a bill from a four-top he said, "Please, when you get a chance, will you light the candles at the Shroders' table."

"Sure, Sam."

A young couple, college students, came in and stood at the front. First timers. Girl was lean like a track runner. The young man was athletic looking too, lacrosse, football, maybe both. Sam shook his hand and led them to their table with a large friendly swoop of his arm. Feleketch nodded her head to signal she had seen them seated. Sam made a sign with his fingers for her to card them. She winked. She had it covered.

After that, a man wearing slacks and a dress shirt with the tie loosened entered. He had a *Newsweek* under his arm.

"Table for one, please."

"Sure, this way," Sam said, ushering him to a two-top in the corner. "It's Edison, right?"

"Yes," Mr. Edison said. "I'm surprised you remembered."

"I try to remember everyone who comes in. You were here a while back with your wife, right?"

"Yes," Mr. Edison said, sitting down as Sam took away the extra place setting and poured him some water. "She's out of town, and I didn't feel like cooking tonight."

"That's fine. That's fine, sir. Let us do the cooking for you."

"It's funny," he said as Sam laid the napkin over his lap. "All these years being married, I don't really know what to do with myself in the evenings when she's not around. I guess it's not like working with your wife."

Sam paused.

"Working with my wife?"

Mr. Edison nodded towards Feleketch. "That lovely woman who is waitressing, isn't she—"

"No, no, no. She's an employee."

"Oh, sorry. I guess it's just the family vibe this place has."

"I'm sure that's it," Sam said.

♦

After that, Harold arrived. Harold was a regular. He took a seat at the bar and ordered his usual Crown and Seven-Up. The bartender, Daniel, was new, just graduated from college with a degree in English. He had grown up in the subdivision across the road and had been coming in for years with his parents. To Sam, Daniel was something of a hybrid: half employee, half nephew. Now he was trying to decide on grad school or the Peace Corps, neither of which seemed like a good use of a college education to Sam. Daniel slid Harold his drink. Sam noticed how his eyes continued to follow Feleketch as she passed by, mouthing her order of one sauvignon blanc and one pinot grigio for table fourteen.

"Hey, eyes up here," Sam said, snapping his fingers.

"Sorry, she's just sort of spellbinding, you know."

"She's more than ten years older than you."

Daniel shrugged. "It was Herodotus who said that the most beautiful women in the world were from Ethiopia."

Sam had not gone to college, a secret he rarely revealed to his employees. "Herodo-what?"

"Herodotus, he was a Greek historian. He wrote that 4,000 years ago. Can you imagine, people have been raving about the beauty of Ethiopians since *then.*"

"Huh," Sam said. He remembered what Jake Jackson had called him. "Daniel, what does Mafioso mean?"

"It's like the mafia. You know, a cool character: smooth, generous, powerful. Like the Godfather. Why?"

"Jake Jackson said I was Mafioso."

"Oh, he's totally right, Sam. It's why everyone loves coming in here and being greeted by you. They feel special, like you are taking good care of them. You're the cool guy."

Sam looked at him to see if he was being sarcastic, but Daniel seemed sincere. Sam would have to think about that.

"Just keep pouring drinks, college boy. And keep your eyes on the customers, not our waitress. I don't need some romantic drama in here."

Daniel smiled. "A bit worried I'll move in on your game, Sam?"

Sam felt his hands tighten around the edge of the bar. "What do you mean?"

Daniel shrugged. "Don't ask me, I just pour drinks."

◆

The older couple in the corner still didn't have menus. Sam made an opening and closing motion with his palms and pointed at them. Jose, the busboy, saw him and took them some menus. It was 6:30.

"Did the Shroders call and say they would be late?" Feleketch asked, coming out of the swinging door of the kitchen after dropping off an order to Roy in the back.

"No, but we'll hold the table a little longer. They're good customers, like you said."

The candles on the Shroders' table were still burning. Sam wanted them burning when the Shroders came in, but if they were lit any longer they would burn down too low. The O'Hares were leaving. They always came early, 5:30ish, to avoid the big crowds. Sam waved them out. Mr. O'Hare took some peppermints from the basket by the door.

A middle-aged couple entered the front. They were very well dressed, must have come directly from work. The woman in a red suit had red lipstick, red nails, and brown hair. The red dress, matching her lips and nails, looked strange. Sam couldn't decide if it was attractive or not—just strange. Her husband was tall, with dishwater blond hair and a yellow tie. Sam sat them at table thirteen and carried menus over, because he knew everyone else was already busy.

A couple was sitting at the bar chatting with Daniel, who was listening with a big smile. The kid had good teeth, Sam noted. It was the benefit of having parents who could afford orthodontics. People liked Daniel, found him easy to talk to. Sam heard the man at the bar order his fourth Coors Light. Feleketch passed with a basket of rolls and tapped Sam's arm, directing his attention to the front door. The Colemans had arrived.

Rodger Coleman was the pastor at the local Baptist church. It was traditionally an African-American church, but Rodger's sermons had been drawing in crowds of all colors. Pastor Rodger had invited Sam more than once for service, but Sam usually attended the Coptic service on Sundays. Sam was not particularly religious, his parents having fled the religious strife of the Middle East, and the schisms of own families, to where they could choose to be anything. They had chosen, well, nothing. Sam and Roy had grown up thinking Americans believed in The Force, after seeing the popularity of Star Wars. Roy had married a Catholic woman, so they went to Mass. Sam had been attending the Coptic one ever since Feleketch had invited him.

"Sam, good to see you man," Rodger said, hugging him.

"You too," Sam said. He hugged Mrs. Coleman. "Happy Birthday, Sally," he said.

"Oh, Sam. How did you remember?"

He kissed Sally Coleman, patted the youngest children, Teresa and Jonathan, on their heads. He asked them if they were going to be good tonight and handed them boxes of crayons and paper placemats to color on. He liked the Coleman kids. They were always well behaved: they didn't make too much noise or run between the tables; they had never spilled anything. Sam shook hands with Dave Coleman, their teenaged son, and put his arm around him on the way to their table. Feleketch was waiting there and had already had set out the booster chair for Teresa. She and Sally exchanged hugs and kissed on both cheeks.

"How's life, Sam?" Dave asked. Sam had noted that *how's life,* was the cool greeting these days among teenagers.

"Can't complain."

"Looks busy."

"Yeah."

"Got a big party coming in?" Dave was looking at the Shroders' empty table.

"Yes, Vicky Shroder. She's at your high school, right."

"Yeah, valedictorian. Looks like they're a little late," Dave said. He must have noticed the candle's burning down low. *Perceptive kid*, Sam thought.

"Yeah, almost forty-five minutes, now that I think about it."

"Traffic is pretty bad out there. There's a big accident on route fifty," Dave said.

"Well that must have them delayed. Enjoy your dinner, young man."

◆

There were more people at the door, but all the tables were filled. Feleketch came up alongside Sam.

"Should we take the Shroders' tables apart?" She was holding the server book with both hands. She had long elegant fingers. He knew if she was asking, it was probably all right to break the tables up. She wouldn't have asked unless they had waited more than enough time. But Sam, for once, was not sure.

"Not yet. Dave Coleman said traffic is bad on fifty. We should blow the candles out though."

"Got it," she said and made a swift turn back onto the floor.

Sam told a new set of customers that came in that it would be a twenty-minute wait. They looked at the full restaurant, then their eyes landed on the empty table for fifteen. They said they'd be back another time. Other customers came in; some waited, some did not. Sam looked outside. Maybe he would see the Shroders. They'd probably be in a big hurry by now, crossing the parking lot in a big crowd of relatives, members from every generation.

He didn't see them.

The rush was in full swing. Sam brought out a basket of rolls, because Jose was too busy running food. The tray of food resting on his palm formed a big T with his forearm. Sam poured water to help Fatima, the busgirl, because she was clearing tables. Sam checked on the young athletic couple, the college students on the two-top. They were both drinking soda. So Feleketch had carded them. *Good.* Sam poured some water for them, made some easy small talk, got them

212

laughing, then noticed his brother Roy peering at him through the swinging door of the kitchen. Sam excused himself and floated over to him.

"What's up?" Sam asked.

"We're almost out of peppercorn vinaigrette."

"None in the fridge?"

"Nope."

"All right. I'll get some from the catering van. It's too busy to send anyone."

On the way to the door, Sam saw that Mr. Sanders was signing his credit card receipt.

"Mr. Sanders, thanks for coming tonight. And thanks for bringing your lovely wife."

"Oh, we're not leaving yet. We're still nursing some coffee."

"I have to run to our van to get some dressing. By the time I get back you'll probably be long gone, off to bigger and better things."

"Aw, Sam. *Angelo's* is the bigger and better thing," Mrs. Sanders said.

Sam could have hugged her right then. Her words kept his mood buoyed as he stepped off the curb into the lane outside the restaurant. The van was on the far side of the parking lot, close to the main road and the parkway. Sam had done this on purpose. With *Angelo's Italian Restaurant & Catering Services* plastered on the side, it was free advertising. A billboard he didn't even need to pay for.

The parking lot was packed. Angelo's and the other restaurants, the Thai place, the pizza parlor, the ice cream shop, were doing good business. Two ambulances went past on the highway, their sirens blaring. Sam turned his body sideways so he could walk between two cars' side-view mirrors. Such passages were becoming slightly more narrow for him these days. He checked the front of his shirt and brushed off some greenish-yellow pollen. This time of year, it stuck to everything.

He got to the van. He climbed in on the passenger side because the driver's side door was parked too close to the shrubs planted near the curb. He found a bottle of vinaigrette in the back. He also grabbed some extra bread baskets. He sat down on the passenger seat, just for a moment. He felt a drop of sweat run down his cheek. It itched, but he did nothing. It picked up speed as it went around his chin and down his neck. He stopped feeling it when it hit his collar. He imagined the moisture spreading out into the fibers of the shirt.

Something was on his mind, but he had pushed it away in the flow of customers and the turning of tables. It hid just at the edge of his consciousness for a moment before he remembered it with a start.

Feleketch.

Why was it that three people that night alone had said something about . . . them? But there wasn't a *them*. They were colleagues. He was her boss, of all things. He'd never use that position for something untoward, especially not for Feleketch. He'd have words with any man or boss of hers who would try something like that. He felt a rush of protectiveness for her, followed quickly by a sense of affection that he tried to ignore.

He did know he looked forward, each day, to coming into work because she would be there. Sundays, her days off, he had always liked least. But by attending the Coptic service, he had found a way of seeing her. It felt strange to go a day without seeing her. They'd meet after the Coptic service for the lunch with other members of the church. Sam had met Feleketch's family, her mother, her brothers. The two of them often were the last to leave the church hall. But he had always just stayed to help clean up the tables. That was what he was used to doing. He worked in a restaurant after all.

But she had stayed all those times too.

He wondered why.

A helicopter passed low overhead. A news chopper, or maybe a medivac? Going to that accident on fifty. He realized he had been daydreaming for too long. He had to get back to the restaurant. Personal thoughts were for personal time. He slammed the van door and began walking at a clip. On the way, he expected to see the Shroders, finally, arriving with their guests in a long procession. He pictured their daughter Vicky in a white graduation gown, rushing in with armfuls of presents and flowers.

Maybe they had meant to come in at seven o'clock?

Sam passed between two cars. A family of five was walking into the restaurant. Sam switched the baskets and bottles around in his hands. He wouldn't reach them in time to greet them. Feleketch would do it for him, maybe even better than he could. What was the word that customer had used? *Luminous.* Daniel had called her what? *Spellbinding.*

Sam would have to go over to the table and make small talk with the family of five when he got back to make up for not greeting them. Funny, what Jake Jackson and Daniel had said about him being cool, of all things. Was that how people saw him? He didn't mind, just had never taken something like that for granted.

Sam entered, the fifteen-top for the Shroders waiting still. The candles were blown out. It was already a $1,500 loss for the night, easy.

"What happened to the Shroders?" Daniel asked when Sam got behind the bar.

"Stood us up, I guess."

"They never called?"

"Never."

"That's not like them."

Daniel turned to make Harold another Crown and Seven-Up. Sam didn't say a thing. He couldn't speak. Feleketch and Fatima were bringing out Mrs. Coleman's birthday cake, Feleketch's face lit in the warm glow of the candles.

Spellbinding.

Sam walked over to the light dimmer and turned down the lights. Feleketch turned in place, waving her arms, and soon the whole restaurant clapped and sang along to Happy Birthday.

It was like a family, he thought.

Or maybe like a symphony, Feleketch the conductor.

Sam noticed that while he was out the Stevensons had arrived. They were a retired, silver-haired couple. They were very good friends of Sam's, some of his oldest customers. He brought them a plate of bruschetta, on the house.

"Have some no shows?" Mr. Stevenson said. He pointed to the Shroder table.

"Apparently. Apparently, they thought no one else would want those seats," Sam said, bitter.

"Wow, Sam. You, angry? I've never seen you angry. You're always so cool and laid-back."

"Yeah, that's what people have been saying," he chuckled as he shook the folds out of the napkins and set them across the Stevensons' laps. "It's just a rotten thing to do. Ends up costing us." he said, looking at the Shroder table.

"Some places would charge them, you know," Mr. Stevenson said. "They take your credit card number when you call now, and if you don't come in, they charge you for a meal anyway."

"That's a good idea. A very good idea. I should have thought of it."

Sam went to the bar and took two menus, handing them to the Stevensons. They thanked him and ordered half a carafe of Chianti. Sam gave the order to Daniel. Then he and Jose pulled apart

216

the Shroders' tables and reset them. The candles had burned too long. They would not be able to use them again. *A waste.*

Sam walked over to the bar, threw away the candles, and retrieved the carafe for the Stevensons. He stared across the room at the three empty tables they had pulled apart, with five settings each, five plates, five glasses, seventy-five pieces of silverware, ninety with the butter knives. It wasn't one big table now, but it was unlikely they would turn them all before they closed.

He really could charge them. Maybe he had an old receipt in the back.

Of course, he did.

"I can't believe they didn't show up for a reservation of fifteen people. You think everything is all right?" Daniel said, changing the coffee filters.

"They're just rich. They think they can walk all over anyone," Sam said, squeezing a wine cork in his hand. "People are just lousy," Sam said. "Just lousy."

The Jacksons were leaving. Sam waved good-bye to them. He hadn't the energy to walk over and say "good luck" to Jake. Poor Jake had finally taken off his graduation robe. Then Sam thought better of it and walked over. He shook Jake's hand. The rest of the Jacksons were leaving. He walked out with them.

"Mafioso, you say?" Sam said, ribbing Jake.

"Totally, man." Jake slapped his shoulder. Sam laughed and turned to his parents.

"Try to avoid route fifty. Apparently, there's a big accident there."

"Thanks, Sam," Mr. Jackson said.

Sam went back inside. The tables were messy, with sticky plates, half-drunk drinks, empty butter wrappers, and crumpled napkins. But all of the disorder meant money flowing into the register. All the tables had been used, all except for the three by the windows. Fifteen seats' worth. Not even a single turn on them for the rush. Sam's face felt hot. He tugged at his collar.

He would charge the Shroders, Sam decided. He would charge them right now. It would help him feel less angry. He walked back to his office, opened the door, and switched on the light. He rolled open the drawer of the filing cabinet and looked through the credit card receipts for the past six months. He found that the Shroders had been there twice just last month. They were good customers. But not tonight. He copied down their credit card number. Their phone number was there too. He could call them, but he decided he didn't want to talk to them. He would just charge them. This would be Angelo's new policy.

He took a spare menu he kept by his desk for phone orders and found the most expensive dish, fourteen dollars, then the least expensive, at seven. He averaged them, then included the price of salad. He was sure everyone would have ordered a salad. He multiplied by fifteen—for every person that would have been there. He decided not to include appetizers. He thought this was very generous on his part. Then he calculated soft drinks and then wine. They probably would have had red wine; everyone drank red wine now that doctors said it was healthy. They would have had champagne, of course they would, it was graduation, their daughter was valedictorian. But she was also underaged, so they would have had non-alcoholic sparkling apple cider too.

Couldn't forget the cake cutting charge. Twenty-five dollars.

He calculated the tip. Feleketch averaged around twenty-two percent. Not bad, but for a fifteen-top she would have deserved twenty-five.

"Sam."

Feleketch was at the door of his office, as if his very thoughts had conjured her. The house phone was in her hands. They were trembling.

"Feleketch, are you all right?"

"No. Sam, it's the Shroders."

"Oh, did they finally call? Don't tell me they were nasty to you?" he said, ready to include appetizers for every setting if that were the case.

"No, Sam. Vicky, Mr. and Mrs. Shroder, they're all dead. They died in the car accident. The one on route fifty."

He dropped the check he had been holding, as if it had burned his fingertips. But it refused to disappear. Instead it remained on the center of his desk, an accusation.

"Dead . . . but I just spoke to them this morning."

"Sam, I'm sorry," Feleketch said.

Sam stood up. He didn't want her to be worried for him. He didn't deserve that. But he was worried for her. He knew her, her nature. He knew she was hurting. He went around his desk but stopped short of her. As a boss, as the owner of the restaurant, he wasn't sure what he was supposed to do next.

She stood, staring at him, her hands clasped over her heart. Her elbows were pulled into her sides. She looked up into his face, small and vulnerable.

Roy burst through the kitchen door, stopping beside Feleketch. "Fele, you going to run these orders?"

"Cool it, Roy," Sam said. "The Shroders are dead."

"What?"

"That was why they didn't call," he said, one hand on his hip, the other pinching his forehead, the pads of his thumb and index finger pressing on his temples.

Feleketch wiped away a tear. Roy put an arm around her. She sniffed and put her head on Roy's shoulder. Sam wondered why he had not just done that. Why had he hesitated?

"I was just talking to them this morning," Sam said as the noise of the kitchen, the bar, the dining room seemed to recede.

Roy shook his head, stepping back to the kitchen. The entrees would not wait. "Just sort of reminds you," Roy said. "Cherish the people you love while you have them." He stopped in the doorway of the kitchen, his fingers splayed on the swinging door just below the window. "Love you, brother."

"Yeah, you too."

Roy's eyes darted from Sam to Feleketch, then back to Sam again. Feleketch was not looking at Roy; she was looking at Sam. Sam swallowed, standing close to her in the doorway. Feleketch wiped her eyes and started to turn. "I'll get those entrees for Roy."

"Wait," Sam finally said. "Wait, Feleketch. There is something I need to say to you . . . ."

17.

The Houseguest

"Society's improved at every level, and culture spreads now even to the Devil,"
—Goethe, Faust Part One

Martin Finch came home one evening to find the Devil in his living room. The Devil was not exactly what Martin had expected the Prince of Darkness to look like, but then again, he had never given the subject too much thought. The Devil wore a suit with wide lapels, shimmering with layers of gold sequins. The fitted suit jacket rested over a red silk shirt with a ruffled collar and sleeves. The shirt was accented by a gold tie, the knot fashionably loosened, with a tie pin set in the center. The pin was obsidian with two little red horns of ruby and (what appeared to be) platinum sunglasses set over an unsmiling face with a lit cigarette etched next to the mouth.

The Devil's own face was immeasurably pale, although he had striking, high cheekbones, accented with a bit of blush, not unlike a drag queen might. His pupils were large and black, surrounded by very bloodshot white. His hair was slicked back with what appeared to be styling gel or oil so that his horns were prominent. The horns themselves were unquestionably authentic. They were a deep red, layered and cracked, just as an animal's might be. But they were also cared for, bearing the high gloss of a recent polishing and fresh, clear shellac.

Gold beams of light stabbed out into the room from his sequined jacket and matching cowboy boots, much like the light might reflect off a disco ball at a club. The room was thick with the

221

smell of sulfur. It was not from the source Martin would have imagined. But before we go any further, we must explain about Martin and his evening, pre-Prince of Darkness.

♣

Martin Finch was a wealthy hedge fund manager. His father had been a wealthy hedge fund manager, and *his* father had been a wealthy hedge fund manager. Martin was thinking about his accomplished genealogy that night as he drove home in his Alfa Romeo. Martin Finch had reached a comfortable plateau of wealth and luxury that was now, for the most part, permanent. He had too many aggressive investments to count, the security of a number of low-risk funds that continued to accumulate, and a quite sizable nest egg that was diversified, sheltered, and only promised to grow. Then he had his equity, not to mention cash savings, the interest able to support him.

If he had chosen to be content. But he was not that sort of man. Why settle when he could have more, he always said.

His suit was Brioni, one of only one hundred handmade each year from a blend of some of the rarest fibers in the world, such as qiviuk, vicuna, and pashmina. The stitching was made with white gold. His watch was a Rolex GMT Master, a nice classic look he liked; his tie Turnbull and Asser; his shirt a Charvet; shoes, Lingwood Russian calf; his belt and wallet both Salvatore Ferragamo, python leather editions; tie clip, cufflinks, and belt buckle today were twenty-four carat gold, but for tomorrow he was already leaning towards the platinum set with the diamonds.

He knew he was not the most handsome man. His shoulders were narrow, but at fifty, he was still slim, and with his goatee his weak chin looked a bit more masculine.

But it was his money and power that made him irresistible to the opposite sex.

His house was sleek, modern, and refined. He had practiced restraint in the decorating process. He thought so, at least, having kept the budget under a million. The garage door closed quietly as he stepped out of the car. Martin was accustomed to getting out of the car and smelling whatever dinner his maid, Agathe, a grandmotherly Greek woman, was preparing. But tonight, only the off gasses of the cement floor, rubber, and a faint whiff of engine exhaust greeted him. He felt his mood move into someplace between impatience and annoyance. For what he was paying the old woman, it was not unreasonable to expect dinner to be on time.

He was debating how stern he would be upon greeting her. Would he ask her directly why dinner was late—which would elicit a stuttering response from her—or better yet, he would say nothing, not even "good evening," until she apologized and realized why she was getting the silent treatment. This would drive her into nervous fits of earnest work, which in the end would be more productive. Mr. Finch had hired her because he had decided a paid maid would be more reliable, and ultimately less expensive, than marrying again. Marriages produced children and divorces. He had already had two of each, and they were a drain on money and time.

All these things were playing in his mind when Agathe burst into the garage. She was a fright. Her mascara was running down from her eyes, her hair was disheveled, and her apron tangled all about her. She ran up to Mr. Finch. She almost hugged him, but then she checked her advance. In one hand she shook an empty saucepan, with the other she repeatedly crossed herself.

"Mr. Finch. Mr. Finch! Oh, it is terrible, terrible. I am so afraid!"

"My God, woman, get a hold of yourself."

She was panting as if she had just run a marathon, but she made no effort to catch her breath. Maybe she couldn't. He realized a heart attack would delay his dinner further, so he told her to calm down and breathe. She took a few gulps of air before spitting out, "He is in the house. In your living room, and he won't leave. I called a priest. I'm terribly sorry. I hope you don't mind. But I was so afraid of him, and I didn't know what to do. He was giving away these," she thrust a fistful of gift certificates to various fast food restaurants in Martin's face. When Martin refused to take them, she dropped them to the floor, as if they were covered in spiders. She was shaking. "Orlando is in there with him."

Orlando, Martin's Haitian groundskeeper. Perhaps he might provide some answers to whatever mess this was turning into.

Martin decided he would have to see the visitor, intruder, whatever, for himself. He walked inside and set his briefcase on the kitchen table. Orlando began calling to him in his nearly incomprehensible English once he heard Martin enter the house. "Orlando" was not his real name. His real name was something in Creole that was impossible to pronounce. Orlando had chosen the name Orlando when he had first moved to Florida. Martin suspected Orlando had chosen the name because it was the same city Disney World was in; however, Martin had never asked for clarification, reluctant to have his hunch validated and Orlando's poor taste confirmed.

Mr. Finch sighed and walked into the living room, his phone in his hand, ready to call the police. Orlando was at the doorway, standing with a pitchfork aimed directly at the intruder, whose appearance has already been described. But in addition to his clothing, there were other items the Devil had brought with him. A McDonald's Happy Meal sat unopened on the coffee table. Long strings of sulfur fumes hung in the air from his cigarettes. Mr. Finch noticed that the Devil need not light these; he simply brought them to his blood red lips, and they lit the moment he inhaled. The sulfur smell produced by these cigarettes brought Mr. Finch back to memories of his childhood, to the time he had found rotten Easter eggs in his refrigerator, or when he'd set off a stink bomb in the school restroom.

The Devil slouched, as if the tonnage of millennia weighed heavily upon his back. His movements were slow but deliberate. His voice was tired and old, somewhere between a drunk David Attenborough and Katherine Hepburn. But there was definitely a flair in his expression, a confidence to the point of swagger.

"Good evening, Mr. Finch. It is a pleasure," he reached towards his Happy Meal. His fingernails were cherry red. Orlando, still in his work boots and khaki coveralls, jerked the pitchfork at him. The Devil was smiling, giving a dismissive wave at the pitchfork with his cigarette hand and opening the Happy Meal with the other.

"I'm the Devil, Orlando. Do you think I am going to be afraid of a pitchfork?"
Orlando's eyes darted to Martin. Martin could read the terror and panic in his face. The groundskeeper ducked towards the fireplace, where he swiped up a stick of kindling, then held it horizontally against the vertical pitchfork to make a cross.

"Ooooohhh, much better. A pitchfork and firewood. That always does the trick." The Devil turned on the television with the clicker, which he had grabbed while Orlando had been distracted. When he realized his improvised cross was not having the desired effect, Orlando backed towards Martin.

"Mr. Finch, what should we do?

Finch didn't know. He was, frankly, awed by the whole situation. Satan was in his living room. What does one do when the Prince of Darkness is in one's house? Offer him a cocktail?

The Devil flicked through the channels and stopped on the Home Shopping network. He smiled, settled back into the leather sofa, and began eating. He left the burger alone and concentrated on a container of fries. Martin felt like he needed to take charge of the situation, so he stepped past Orlando and approached the Devil.

"Can I help you? If you really are who you say you are, what do you want?"

"Shush, shush." The Devil waved his middle finger—the rest were clutching a bunch of fries. He craned his neck to see around Martin, who was blocking his view of the television. "This is my favorite part."

Martin did not move. Instead he opened his mouth to tell the Devil he was calling the police. The Devil seemed to sense this and preempted him with a shake of his finger. Suddenly, as if he had been there the whole time, Martin was sitting on the couch.

The sudden teleportation caused Orlando to scream out. Satan rolled his eyes and turned up the television. Orlando started a series of Hail Mary's, his voice growing loud with panic. Finally the Devil sighed, reached into his pocket, and produced six paper tickets, which he then threw at Orlando.

"Here, go to Disney World. There's a ticket for you, your wife, and three kids. The other one is for your seventeen-year-old mistress. It should be fun to have her along too. Oh, don't look surprised; your wife already knows."

Orlando jumped as the tickets landed at his feet. They might as well have been snakes. The Devil freed his hand by stuffing his fries into his mouth then pulled the Happy Meal toy out of the box. It was wrapped in a plastic bag with "Choking Hazard. For Children Three and Up Only," written across it. He looked over to Orlando, who held his ground, although his cross had lowered, his arms growing tired. Or perhaps he was distracted by the tickets at his feet. They were for premium access. Orlando inched away from them, his eyes darting from the Devil to the tickets and back. The Devil threw the toy at him and said, "Boo."

This was all Orlando needed. He dropped the pitchfork and kindling on the ground to turn and sprint into the kitchen. The door to the garage slammed, then opened and slammed again. Mr. Finch heard Orlando's steps returning.

His mouth full of fries, the Devil said, "Haforgaffhifftikiks."

Sure enough, a wide-eyed Orlando appeared again in the doorway, leaning over to pick up the tickets. His hand stopped just short of them as he looked to Martin, as if beseeching him for permission. Mr. Finch found this quite out of place. After all, he had not given them to Orlando, but perhaps Orlando wanted to know if Martin would give him the time off. Martin sighed loudly and nodded, more to get Orlando out of the house than anything else. Orlando snatched the tickets up in his fist, pulled them to his chest, and vanished through the kitchen.

"That's going to be an interesting family vacation," the Devil said, unwrapping his cheeseburger.

Martin was tired of sitting. He stood up and walked towards his liquor cabinet.

"Can I get you something?" he asked, pressing his thumb to the Bioscan pad to open the cabinet.

"No, thank you. I don't drink on the job," the Devil said, then took a long drink from a supersized soft drink that he had bought with his Happy Meal.

Mr. Finch took a shot of Jack Daniel's blue label and then another. He looked over at the Devil, who was now watching a news network. He took another shot, then he poured himself a single malt scotch on the rocks and went back to the couch. The Devil was finished with his cheeseburger. He had wrapped up the trash in the grease-spotted paper that had contained the burger. With a touch of his finger, all the trash vaporized in a flash of flame.

"All that grease is quite an accelerant. Alas, I do miss those Styrofoam containers with the CFCs."

The Devil pulled out another cigarette.

"You smoke but don't drink on the job? What kind of king of vice are you?"

The Devil sighed. "There are some companies that need my patronage more than others. The poor tobacco companies and soda makers are having a hard time right now, so I do what I can to help out. But humanity is never going to give up alcohol," he said, swinging his cigarette hand towards the open liquor cabinet. "The less I take, the more for you."

"How gracious."

The Devil nodded and smiled. "Trust me, I have only top shelf stuff at the den at home."

For a moment Martin found himself contemplating which brands the Devil would have in his den, liquor down to furniture. Were the floors stone, hardwood, or plush . . . .

The Devil surfed the channels. He stopped on a station where an old-style televangelist, Oral William, was beseeching funds, his hands clasped as if he were praying to the camera. Behind him were rows and rows of young girls, old ladies, and a few men, answering telephones, the old fashion kind that rang with bells to give the impression that people were calling and calling, giving and giving . . . . The Devil pulled out a phone in a red case that matched his nails, dialed, then raised the phone to his ear. Martin noticed it was pierced with six silver hoops.

"Gahangas. Beelzebub here. How are Oral Bill's ratings . . . Hmm . . . I see. . . ." He took a meditative drag of his cigarette. "Well, let's give him a bump. Pledge a hundred thousand. The number is on the speed dial."

He hung up the phone and replaced it in his jacket pocket. He turned to Martin as if to explain. "Oral Bill masturbates to kiddy porn, at least when he's not banging that fine young brunette who is about to answer my phone call." He gestured to a young, chaste-looking girl answering phone calls in the back. Thick brunette braids rested on her shoulders. She wore a blue shirt that buttoned to her neck. No flesh was revealed, but one would have to be blind to miss her firm, ripe breasts.

The unattainable breasts of a Christian woman are such a beautiful thing, Finch reflected.

"They're silicone and very attainable," the Devil said, reading his mind. "Oral Bill bought them for her."

"Really?" Mr. Finch responded, not particularly surprised at the Devil's powers of telepathy. It figured.

The Devil shook his head.

"That's nothing. The woman sitting in the second row, the one with the big crucifix around her neck, she's carrying Oral Bill's child. And that obese woman in the fourth row, Bill couldn't get himself to actually have intercourse with her, so they sixty-nined. The same with the man in the first row."

"My goodness."

"Yep, good old Bill plays for the home *and* away teams. He's mostly a bottom when the need arises. Who would have guessed? Wait, hold on," The Devil said, leaning forward. He snuffed his cigarette on the coffee table and flung it on the carpet.

"I have ashtrays you know." Mr. Finch stood up to pick up the cigarette.

"The world is my ashtray. Now watch the girl."

Mr. Finch turned to the television. The girl with the braids and the breasts was talking on one of the phones. Her blue eyes became enormous, and her lips mouthed the figure one hundred thousand in disbelief. She was so young and innocent-looking; Finch could hardly imagine her having sex with Oral William. He wondered if The Devil was putting him on. The girl looked up to Oral William and called his name. He turned away from the camera.

"Reverend, a Mr. Robert Love has just pledged a hundred thousand dollars to the cause."

The Devil brought his hand to his heart and fluttered his eyelashes in mock abashment.

"Let me talk to our brother," Oral William said. The Devil continued his surprise, pulling out his phone and turning it on as Oral William took the phone from the girl. Finch noticed how their hands lingered as they made contact. *I'll be damned,* he thought. *The Devil is right.*

"Robert. Robert. I am so glad you have found your path to the LORD. Your contribution will go to help so many," Oral William said into the phone while the camera zoomed in close to him.

"I am so moved, Bill," Satan responded on the couch next to Martin. "You have made me see the way. Don't worry, I know that about $80,000 will go in your pocket, $10,000 of which you will spend on whores in the next year, $20,000 towards your gambling habit. The rest you'll embezzle to invest. Wise move. It's good to think about the future."

Oral William's face was pale. He realized he was still on the air with a sort of start. He flashed his practiced smile and said, "Amen, brother." *His act was good,* Martin thought. Of course, no one watching the television, and no one on the set, could hear what the Devil was saying to Oral William. The girl still beamed as if there were nothing wrong.

"You have truly helped me to see how God works in my life, and that is why I have just sent you my son's college fund," the Devil continued.

"There is a great place reserved for you in heaven, Brother Robert." Oral William continued to smile broadly at the camera and all his loyal watchers, his eye betraying a twitch.

"Yesss, yesss. Keep up the good work, Bill. And by the way, you might want to have the chick in the second row take a pregnancy test. Just a hunch." The Devil hung up. Oral William gave a frantic glance towards the woman in the second row.

"Amen, Brother. Yes, God has truly touched you," he said into the dead phone, a pearl of sweat beading on his temple. "And may his light continue to shine down upon you while you journey towards the Promised Land. God bless you." He hung up the phone and dabbed at his brow with a handkerchief. "Mr. Love's contribution is such a blessing; I think we all should take a moment to kneel down and thank Go—"

The Devil changed the channel back to news. Pictures of cold, forlorn-looking children flashed across the screen as a concerned anchorman's voice narrated about ongoing sectarian strife in some failed Asian state: ". . . fighting has lessened in past weeks, but that has done nothing to aid relief workers in reaching these innocent victims of war. Government forces are still barring UN inspectors from the town where refugees reported the use of chemical weapons on civilians in an attack that is estimated to have caused over two hundred deaths, mostly women and children . . ."

"Blah, blah, blah. Yesss, yesss, the poor women and children. No clothes, no food. Things we take for granted. But look at all the airtime they get—and they sure take *that* for granted. There are kids here in the States that would sell their bodies to get on television. And trust me, many do." He flipped to a reality TV program. "See what I mean?"

Martin sat back on the sofa. Besides the smell of sulfur, which would take weeks to get out of the upholstery, and the fact that he could not use the remote control—the Devil was a bit of a remote hog—it was actually fairly interesting talking with his houseguest. The Devil reached into his pocket and produced a small plastic keychain shaped like a gun, from which dangled an electronic security fob.

"This," the Devil said with pride, "is the reason I love America."

"What is it?" Finch asked.

The Devil took the gun-shaped keychain in his hand and pulled the miniature trigger. A small plastic disc shot out and landed near Martin's single malt. The Devil shot a half dozen more, until the gun was empty.

"Isn't that fantastic!" the Devil said.

"That I now have miniature Frisbees floating in my drink?"

"Martin, you're so small brained. These little contraptions are mass produced. Not only do they promote gun culture, but they make about a hundred thousand of these things every three months. That is about five tons of plastic. *One* ton of that plastic would be enough to make water filters for twenty impoverished African villages, not to mention contraceptive devices, mosquito netting, or those little single-use syringes for vaccination. But does any of that plastic get used there? Absolutely not. Instead it goes into these inane little toys which get broken and thrown away in about a week."

"Very interesting. What is the fob for?"

"The gates of hell."

"The gates of hell are operated by an electronic fob?"

"Essentially, yes."

"I mean, shouldn't you have some gothic-looking key?"

"Oh, my daughter used to stand there with one, but she's too busy recruiting young ingénues for jobs in the porn industry. So, we decided to go remote."

"How efficient."

"Thank you."

"Isn't there supposed to be a dog of some sort too? With three heads, if I remember correctly."

"He's too busy now with his consulting business—private security—drug lords, arms dealers, and dictators mostly."

"Oh."

A commercial came on, urging watchers to buy their products before Christmas, which was a month away.

"Christmas must be a slow time of year for you," Martin said.

"You kidding? It's my busiest."

"Oh, of course," he said, unsure of as to why though. "When do you take a vacation then?"

"Halloween is always nice. I usually go down to Georgetown in DC, where they filmed the Exorcist. It's very sentimental for me."

"I imagine."

The news anchor was introducing a story about a cell of domestic terrorists who had been arrested for bombing an Apple store. They were a self-described anti-corporate, anti-technology socialist group, dedicated to the cause of sustainable living and ecological responsibility. Their bombing had killed six staff members, fourteen customers, and injured dozens more.

"Now there are some young people I'm sure you can get behind," Martin said.

The Devil sneered. "I applaud their methodology. Bad message though."

"They're against technology and industry. They're socialists."

"Exactly. I have a lot invested in those things and capitalism in general."

"Actual cash investments?" Martin asked, wondering what the Devil would be like as a customer.

"Think bigger, you hairless primate. What's the first commandment?"

Martin did his best to rewind back to Sunday school. But he had only gone once, and he didn't think they talked about the commandments that day.

"It's been a long time."

"Thou shalt not have any other gods before me."

"How does that apply?"

"False gods, Martin. Idols. The world is full of them. Take television—every one kneeling down on the living room rug before that iridescent idol, beamed to you by satellites, those orbiting angels of dark technology. And with the internet, what variety!" He took a long meditative drag off his cigarette, exhaling clouds of yellow smoke. "I used to have to settle for pathetic little sculptures of Baal or Golden Calves. Back in the dark ages, the false god was religion, of all things—eight crusades ain't bad. Then in the nineteen-thirties it was all nationalism, racial identity, and co-opted mythology."

Martin furrowed his brow, having lost the thread, but the Devil raised his arm out in a salute from the Third Reich and Martin understood. "But TV is so much more interesting, and the internet has even more possibilities," the Devil concluded.

Martin sat back. This was all very interesting to him, but why was the Devil visiting him? He opened him mouth, but Satan had read his mind again.

"You're wondering why I'm here. Yessss. Yessss. I knew we would have to get down to business eventually." He picked up another cigarette and set it smoldering to life with a touch of his lips, tossing the butt of the prior one onto the carpet once more. "We're here to talk about your soul, Martin."

"Oh, how archaic."

"I think cliché is the word you are looking for."

"That too."

The Devil ignored him and reached into his jacket for a small six-sided box. It was made of woven bamboo fibers, stained dark blue, almost black. He set it on the table.

"What is this?"

"It's the box I've been keeping your soul in for the past fifty or so odd years," the Devil said.

"Wait a minute, when did I sell you my soul?"

"You didn't. Your father did when you were little. Just as his father did with his soul. See, shrewd investors know that you have to invest early."

Martin picked up the box. The material was light but sturdy. The paint was still shiny. The bamboo fibers caught the light and gave it a layered, iridescent quality. The bottom was unpainted balsa wood. Green letters beside Chinese characters read: "Made in China."

"Where did you get this?"

"Your father gave it to me. It's a valuable family heirloom," he said with respect. "Your great-great-grandfather was an English sailor. His wife, Louise, put one of her rings in that box—which her grandmother got from China—and stowed it away in her husband's luggage for him to find when he was at sea. The box and its contents were very precious to him on those long lonely nights without a woman next to him in bed. While in a Spanish port, he bought a silver bracelet for her, which he also kept in there. Louise was pregnant, and your great-great-grandfather was supposed to return before the baby was due, but he was delayed by a storm. Unfortunately, as that soft portal in Louise opened up and the embryonic fluids and blood drained out of her, so did her life. Her baby could only be suckled by a corpse."

"You have a flair for the poetic."

The Devil grunted before he continued. "Gramps returned with the bracelet, ring, and box, only to find his wife dead. So he took his infant daughter to America. The only thing he took with him to remind him of his old life was that box and the two pieces of jewelry inside it.

"In America, they made the cross-country journey to the Northwest Territories. Along the way they had to sell the bracelet to pay for supplies. Eventually Gramps became a logger. He finally parted with his wife's ring when he sold it to pay for his daughter's schooling. But he never gave up the box. At one point he risked his life to run into a burning house to save it. It was all he had left of his wife. When he died at ninety-three, he was clutching it in his arms. His daughter treasured it simply because it was the only thing her father treasured. Her son inherited it and saved it because she told him to. *His* son, *your* grandfather, saved it simply because it was old.

"When I appeared to your father, he had it sitting on a bookcase holding paper clips—when I appear to people in desperate need and offer them what they seek for their soul, we usually use the nearest receptacle. You would not believe how many souls I have tied off in condoms. Anyway, this box was the nearest thing, and your father, in his irreverence, or insolence, or both, gave it to me."

"So why are you giving it back?"

"Well, we're changing our storage methods. We're going digital now. Everything is binary and digitized, magnetized and harmonized." He broke into a jingle from an old electronics company: *"Click it, press it, tune it, flick it, tune it on and turn it on, this is what you watch it on."* The Devil's singing voice was low and exhausted, as if all the sorrows and pain from his realm sounded in it all at once.

"So, what do I do with it?" Finch asked.

"Keep your soul in it or paper clips, for all I care. I only had a fifty-year lease on it, so it's yours again. Unless . . . ."

The doorbell rang. Finch started up, but when he turned the corner of the hallway, he saw that the Devil had disappeared from the couch and reappeared in the front hallway before him. Teleportation had to be an exhilarating power, Martin reflected. Then again, telepathy and pyrokinesis would have to be fairly intoxicating as well. His mind wandered again, wondering which he might chose if faced with picking just one.

He snapped to as the Prince of Darkness opened the door for whatever delivery man or neighbor had been so unfortunate as to call on Martin just then. This, of course, led to another brief reverie in which he considered the possibility of having the Devil over as the guest of honor for a dinner party. It would be hard to imagine a guest of higher status or better name recognition. Already Martin was certain the conversation would be lively. Religion, politics . . . nothing would be off limits.

The Devil walked over the marble floor of the foyer, his boots clacking like hooves on the stone. He opened the door to reveal a priest, alternately crossing the house and himself while mumbling prayers out of a little black book. He was a shortish man, with thick glasses and a small balding head. Agathe was behind him. She had covered her head with a blue scarf and was frantically praying a rosary. Neither of them would look directly at Satan. The Devil turned back to Mr. Finch.

"Oh, look Martin, it's Father O'Leary. What a pleasant surprise."

The Devil stepped across the threshold, putting his arm around the priest's shoulders and guiding him into the house. He slammed the door in Agathe's face, rolling his eyes as if to say to Martin, *would you get a load of her?*

Father O'Leary's voice rose to a crescendo while he read out a series of verses in Latin.

The Devil moved past Martin saying, "Oh look, Father O'Leary is trying to exorcise me. I appreciate the thought, Father, but I'm already fit as a fiddle." He laughed at his pun. Martin followed. The Devil called out behind him, "Martin, get Father O'Leary a drink. Bushmills, neat."

Father O'Leary produced a small flask of holy water and began to flick it on the Devil's lapels. The water sizzled but didn't do much else. The Devil ignored it, bringing Father O'Leary into the living room and sitting him down like a gracious host.

"Now Mr. Finch, let me introduce you to Father O'Leary."

The little Irish priest shot Martin a most disapproving stare. Martin was a bit embarrassed about the clutter: the pitchfork, the stick of kindling, not to mention the ashes from the Happy Meal and the scattering of cigarette butts and little plastic discs. The room was quite a fright really, even without the Prince of Darkness standing in the center of it. It was a situation that was not easily explained.

"Father O'Leary is a priest," The Devil continued. "That's someone who thinks he is very holy, if you forgot, Martin."

"I know that much."

"Well, you can't take anything for granted. Come, sit down. Help make Father O'Leary—Father Sean, can I call you Sean? I know, of course I can—comfortable."

Martin sat down on the couch on the other side of Father Sean O'Leary.

"Now Martin, let me explain. I'm actually a big fan of the clergy," Satan said.

"Really? Now that surprises me. Tell me more," Martin said, crossing his legs and looking across Father Sean.

"Well, didn't Dante say the hypocrites have their very own ring in hell?"

"I suppose he did."

"Who am I to argue?" the Devil said. "But in addition to squelching women's rights, trying to control their bodies, discriminating against people because of their sexual orientation, and let's not forget molesting children, covering it up, and harassing the victims, Father Sean here gave a sermon this past Sunday wherein he called homosexuality an 'abomination, a sickening offense to God.' Now that's all old hat really, for him, but what he didn't know is that young Patrick Evans, in his congregation, a well-meaning Catholic boy of just fifteen with the unfortunate luck of having been born gay, heard Father Sean that Sunday, and in a fit of guilt for his 'sinful' nature, hung himself in his parent's basement."

"That's terrible," Martin said.

"I know!" the Devil said, slapping the priest on the back. "Spreading hate, alienation, and suicidal self-loathing. It's some of their best work since the Inquisition or the Crusades. Now Martin, pour him a drink."

Mr. Finch went over to the liquor cabinet, a little reluctantly, if he was honest with himself. He had gay friends, after all. But he was host, so he poured a glass of Bushmills neat, the way the Devil had said the priest liked it.

Father Sean O'Leary's hands were shaking. Martin took one and curled it around the glass. Father O'Leary mumbled to himself: "Though you stand before the gates of Hell and Death is at your side, be not afraid . . . ."

"I know Death!" the Devil said.

"Do you really?" Mr. Finch was interested again. "Does he work for you? I've always wondered about that."

"No. We're both independent enterprises, but we collaborate. We have professional courtesy for one another. He's terribly unfashionable though. The phantom has got no style. Still wears that Charon robe and carries that grim scythe that he's been hauling around since . . . God knows when."

The snippet of a classic Led Zeppelin song blared from the television. The Devil smiled, cupping his hand to his ear to better hear the song.

"One of my favorite bands," he said.

Martin sensed the setup. "I'll bite. Why them?"

"Consummate rip-off artists, along with that king bubba, Elvis."

"Rip-offs?"

"You are clearly not a music man, Martin."

"No, not really."

"Well, I have a reputation to uphold. It's good to know what the kids are listening to. But I'm a big fan of misappropriation without proper attribution. Page, Plant, Presley; they were thieves you know, stealing from other artists—mostly artists of color. A good bit of racism and cultural exploitation gets the old heart racing," the Devil said, patting his chest. "Right, Father? You Christians did it, stealing the dates of festivals from pagans, Druids, and Celts, you sneaky boys you."

The Devil pinched the priest's cheek. Mr. Finch hoped that Father O'Leary was not too uncomfortable. The priest had grown quiet but was sweating now through his shirt. He noticed that the priest had drunk his entire shot of whiskey while they were not looking.

The Devil smiled, patting the priest on the knee. "That's a good little whiskey priest. Martin, get him another. Make it a double."

Martin did. But when he returned to the couch and handed the drink to the priest, who drank it in one eager gulp, his eyes bulging, the Devil stood up, stretched to his full height, and straightened his jacket. He pulled his spent cigarette from his mouth and aimed to flick it towards the kitchen doorway, but the pitchfork and Happy Meal toy were already left there. So he spun around on his heel and fired the butt into an empty corner.

"The time is coming for me to depart."

"So soon?" Martin asked.

"I will leave you with some parting wisdom." The Devil bent down so that he was eye to eye with Father O'Leary, his crimson lips moving so close to the priest's face that, at first, Martin thought he would kiss him. But instead he spoke in a soft, tender voice. "Yes Father, there was a time when man lived on bread alone, when he had not yet invented his companions: society, capitalism, consumption, marketing, and style. These were the horsemen who cried out 'You are lacking, primate. *Spend* and you will be saved.'"

The Devil turned to address them both. "Can you imagine what it was like without the little products that sit in your bathroom? There are still people who don't use these things. Their complexions are greasy, their hair oily and flaky, and their breath goes unchecked. The horror. Thank goodness deodorant keeps us from being too human!"

He turned once more to Father Sean O'Leary, a warm smile across his face. He gave the priest a light punch in the shoulder. "Keep up the good work, old chap. You all never cease to be entertaining. I mean, have you ever stopped to consider the orientation of a God of Love, transformed into a man, who hung out with a bunch of other men, traveling, eating, sleeping, even kissing them? I mean, we all know how effectively you all excised his marriage to Mary Magdalene from scripture—nice job, by the way— but really, when your deity is a God of Love, you have *got* to realize that he swung both ways, right?"

"Blasphemer, may you burn in the fires of Hell!" Father O'Leary stammered.

"Don't threaten me with a good time." The Devil shrugged before making his way to the front door. "I must be going now, Martin. At exactly eleven twenty-three Eastern Standard Time, Alphonso Rodrigues will be driving by this house in his taxi cab, after taking Mrs. Henderson of 6 Oliver Lane home from the airport.

He just overcharged her five dollars. He makes about forty dollars a night in overcharging riders. But not tonight."

"Because you are hitching a ride with him?" Martin asked, aroused by his proximity to prophecy.

"No, no. I'd let him overcharge me. Remember the JD, corrupter of mankind and all. No, I'm afraid that at eleven twenty-five, a deer will jump out in front of the cab, startling Mr. Rodrigues, causing him to swerve, then overcompensate, crash, and subsequently die. Death called me this morning and told me this one would be mine. There seems to be an unresolved issue of a hit-and-run involving a three-year-old girl in the projects, which occurred one night when the 'Fonz' had partaken a little too liberally in the juice of joy, the blow of bliss, and the love of whores. So now he will be spending some time with me . . . actually . . . *all* time."

The Devil let out a weary laugh at his own joke. He opened the door, revealing Agathe, who was sprawled across the front stoop. "You'll want to call the coroner for her. Heart attack, brought on by stress and trauma," he said, stepping over the body.

"She's dead?" Martin asked, coming outside.

"As a door nail. She's not one of mine though."

"Tragic."

"I know. I could have done great things to her, but she was a virtuous woman."

"Oh, no. I meant tragic that she passed. She had family," Martin said. This also meant he would have to find a new maid. The Devil was already halfway down the sidewalk. Martin cleared his throat, suddenly remembering, "What about the box?"

"What about it?" the Devil asked, without checking his stride.

"Well, what do I do with it? My soul, I mean. What about this whole wealth and material gain stuff. You know, the Dr. Faustus thing? What's in it for me? Accrued rewards over time, investment risks, you know, the usual."

The Devil stopped, turned on his heel, and his lips formed a long and sinister smile. His eyes were dark and laughing pearls as he stalked back up the sidewalk. When he was close enough that the smell of sulfur once again permeated Martin's lungs, Satan took Martin by the head, his thumb pressing, warm and abrasive, above his eyes.

"Oh, Martin, I'm not worried about you."

He took a drag off his cigarette and exhaled a cloud of yellow smoke. It curled and swam about his shoulders as he turned one last time. Martin Finch stood there watching Satan walk down his driveway, the gold sequins on his boots throwing off sparks and beams into the cloud following him, as he croaked out a few bars of Led Zeppelin's *Stairway to Heaven*. At that moment, he more resembled an old Vegas lounge singer than fallen angel or the Prince of Darkness, corrupter of hearts.

Then he was gone. Martin took a deep breath of the air. The sulfur had dissipated.

Well, if that was not interesting . . . .

He stepped over Agathe's body. He would have to make sure his story was straight before he called the police. Maybe he should call his lawyer first. He needed another drink. He returned to the living room to find the priest and the bottle of Bushmills missing. He poured himself one more single malt. Before he drank it, he froze.

The box. The little blue-black box was waiting on the coffee table.

Martin set down his drink, crossed the room, and reached for it, his hands trembling—more from exhilaration than fear. He picked up the box. It was light and sturdy. He was still impressed with how the bamboo material gave off such an elegant sheen, even in the dim light of his living room. *It had to be expensive, priceless perhaps,* he thought. *Where was Antiques Roadshow when you needed them?* With one of his manicured nails, he worked the top loose. The inside lip and edge were covered with black velvet that hissed as he opened it. He gazed into its interior, his heart leaping with expectation, before it was replaced with a suffocating heaviness. It weighed down his chest, sinking into his innards like a coffin into a swamp. He tossed the lid to the table, turned over the box and shook it over his hand before slapping it on the bottom like a bottle of ketchup.

Nothing was produced. It was empty.

18.

Frontiersmen

It was the Fourth of July. It was hot. Definitely hot enough to fry an egg on the sidewalk. We had actually fried several out behind the store. It was a slow day, and we had time for that. See, I'm a refrigerator repair man. In hot weather, we always have to be on standby; the heat puts a lot of strain on those old fridges. But since it was the Fourth of July, no one was actually coming into the store—it was a holiday; people were barbecuing, pool partying. I was waiting for calls at the store with Ray, a kid we hired that summer. Funny enough, no one had called that day, not a one. Either someone else was getting our business, like that new store at the strip mall down the street, or no one's fridges were breaking.

It was close to dinner time. I got in the car and drove over to 7-11. I got a Slurpee—red, white, and blue of course, a pack of Marlboro lights, and four hot dogs for me and Ray. They had some red, white, and blue licorice on sale at the counter. I decided it might be fun to try, so I bought some. On the way back, I drove down the street to look at the new appliance store, to see how they were doing. It was a sleek new store, attached to a custom-made furniture store. Inside they had salesmen in white shirts and ties standing beside their newest models. I saw a salesman inside, but no customers. The person at the counter was on the phone. Maybe they were getting our repair calls.

When I drove back to the shop, Ray was outside. He walked up to the van.

"Got a call from a lady in Covenant Hills. Says her fridge has been broken for two days now."

"Why didn't she call before?"

He rolled his shoulders. "Beats me. You got the food?"

"Yeah."

I handed him the hot dogs and his soda. I had finished my dogs on the drive over. He walked back to the store with his hands full. He left the address of the woman on the seat of the car. He also left the passenger-side door open.

"Ray, close the door."

But he was already in the shop. I think he heard me as the shop door was closing behind him, but he pretended not to. I pulled out from the curb and slammed on the brakes. I hoped that would cause the door to shake and close. It wobbled but stayed open. I tried it again, a lot harder. Things fell down in the back, but the door didn't close.

"Son of a bitch."

So I tried it going backwards. My Slurpee fell over, but fortunately I had drunk most of it already. The sheet of paper with the address dangled close to the edge of the seat—if it flew out I would be really mad, because I'd have to get out and get it. I lurched the car forward then stopped again. The door almost closed. I tried going backwards and turning the car—even closer, but not quite. Then I realized there was a line of cars behind me, waiting to pass to get out of the parking lot. There were quite a few, but no one had thought to honk. I pulled aside, leaned over, and yanked the door close.

♠

Covenant Hills was one of the older neighborhoods, houses built in the nineteen fifties; one levels, split levels, but not too many two-story jobs—those were mainly in the newer neighborhoods, which were farther out, where all the houses had been super-sized in the nineties. Most of my jobs were in older places like Covenant Hills. Old houses, old fridges. In the newer neighborhoods, people had the state-of-the-art fridges that never broke, and when they did, they just bought new ones. The customer I was going to, Mrs. Giles, lived at 165 Ridgemont Drive. While I was searching the neighborhood, I had the craving for something sweet. I looked around for the red, white, and blue licorice, but I couldn't find it anywhere. I stopped the van. I figured it wouldn't hurt to stop, after all, the side was plastered with the name of the store: *Daniel Boone's Appliance Repair*, with Daniel Boone there on the side with his coonskin cap and a wrench in place of a rifle. Parking was free advertising. The company was partly mine; my father and some of his friends had founded it. I don't know why they picked the name they did. None of the guys were named Daniel or Boone. My father's name wasn't Dan, and neither was mine. I couldn't find the licorice and realized I must have accidentally given it to Ray.

Greedy weasel.

I drove around again for fifteen minutes but couldn't find the house. Ridgemont Drive wasn't a problem to find; I had already found it. It was the house number I couldn't find. The highest number so far was 96. My GPS was no help. According to it, I had already arrived at my destination. I decided to ask for directions. I picked 65 Ridgemont; I had a feeling about them, maybe because they had two of the three numbers I was looking for.

My coveralls were navy blue, so you can imagine they soaked up the sun's rays like a solar panel. I couldn't wait for the sun to go down. The residents at 65 Ridgemont obviously had children; their toys were scattered all over the yard. I stepped on a plastic shovel by accident and pretty well broke it. What do you expect? It was left on the sidewalk. They could afford a new one by the looks of it anyway. There was a broken robot by the door and a tank with the turret missing in the bushes. These kids were ungrateful for their toys. I knocked on the screen door. I could see into the house. Looked like they were having a cookout on the back deck. I wondered if anyone heard me. I knocked again.

"Coming."

A short woman, thirty-ish, came to the door. She didn't open it.

"I didn't call a repairman."

"No, you didn't, ma'am." I tipped the bill of my baseball cap. I could feel it moving smoothly over the sweat on my forehead. "But someone on 165 Ridgemont did, and I just can't find that part of the street. I was wondering if you knew where to point me."

"Hmmm." She put her hands on her hips. She had long fingernails, painted red, white, and blue with silvery stars in the spirit of the holiday. "Let me ask my husband."

"Much obliged."

She disappeared from the door. I heard a sliding glass door open, then another set of footsteps. A man in white shorts appeared.

"You looking for 165 Ridgemont?"

"Yes, sir."

"Just go down to the end of that street where it terminates on Loyalty Heights. Turn left, then take the first right, and that will turn into the rest of Ridgemont. It's like a little hidden section of road where it extends. Don't know why they made it that way."

"Thank you, sir, you have a good fourth."

"You too," he said.

He never opened the screen door.

♠

When I pulled up at Mrs. Giles's house, I was so hot and tired I felt like I had already worked on a fridge. By the amount of sweat on the back of my suit and under my arms, you wouldn't think otherwise. I knew I had the right house, so I went to the back of the van and grabbed the tool kit. It felt extra heavy, and the shiny metal blinded my eyes. I wiped my forehead with a rag, and stuck it in my pocket. The house was a split level, with forest green siding, pea green trim, and turquoise shutters. There was an '83 duster in the driveway. The garage was open, and I could see it was too full of stuff—chairs, drawers, old lawnmowers—to accommodate the car. I walked to the door and knocked.

Mrs. Giles answered in a pink nightgown. There was what looked like a coffee stain on the part that bulged out right under her belt and above her crotch. She had a leathery brown face, probably from sun and smoking. Her hair was dyed black. There was a half inch of gray at the roots.

"Come in and have a look at the patient," she said, unlatching the door.

"Happy fourth," I said.

"Oh yeah, happy holiday. I'm glad you guys were still open."

"Twenty-four-hour emergency service, ma'am, three hundred and sixty-five days a year."

She grunted and walked into the kitchen. On the kitchen table a TV was playing, surrounded by empty coffee mugs with stained bottoms. There was a plate with eggs and ketchup hardening. The fork was in a coffee cup. There was a man on the TV describing a Fourth of July parade. I walked to the fridge.

"Hasn't been cold for two days," she said.

I took off the grate, pulled out a rag to wipe away dust, and peered under with the flashlight. Probably a busted compressor. It was an old model, about twenty years old. I was surprised it had lasted that long. It had to be the compressor. Compressors are the first to go on those old models.

"My husband used to fix all these things around the house."

"Really?" I said.

249

"He was handy. I guess that made him good for one thing. He's long gone now."

"Is that a good thing?"

She laughed, "You're telling me."

I had to look at the back. I stood up and rocked the fridge forward. I heard things moving inside, but Mrs. Giles didn't seem too worried about spills. I got my flashlight and looked in back. That's when you get into people's private lives, looking behind their fridge—seeing places where they don't clean, where things get lost and hidden. It's getting to the bottom of things. The linoleum was gray with dust in the back. I was right. The compressor was shot to hell.

"Compressor is broken."

"Well, can you fix it?"

"Yeah. I've got some replacement parts in the truck; I'll get them."

♠

I turned the fridge completely around and spread my tools all about the kitchen floor. People like to see that, lots of tools; they think work is being done. She leaned against the countertop in her bathrobe and watched me.

"Must be hot in that suit."

"It is. Real hot."

"I can't imagine working on the Fourth of July."

"Well, the holiday pay is good."

"That's consolation."

"You doing anything special?"

She grunted while she lit a cigarette.

"Haven't had plans on the fourth for years. That's the way I like it, though. Too old for all that crazy whistling and screaming explosive shit. Once you've seen a few, you've seen them all. I remember one year a house down the street caught on fire from some fireworks. The fire department had to come and everything. That was something."

"Some of those rockets do get noisy."

"That they do. I can just sit here and watch the show at DC on the television. It's always so pretty there, alongside all those monuments. I don't know which ones are which though."

"Well, the tall one's the Washington Monument," I said.

"I knew that," she said.

"The others, your guess is as good as mine."

"Is the one real near the Washington Monument, the one that's supposed to look like a Greek temple, is that the Lincoln?"

"I think so. But they all sort of look like Greek temples to me," I said.

"There is one for Benjamin Franklin that looks like a temple, I think. They took up all that space for those big ones and only had enough room left for one wall for the Vietnam memorial. But I guess that is what they do for wars we didn't win—because they sure made a big memorial there for World War II. I think maybe they should reassign which ones are which. You know? Lincoln's been dead a long time; they should use that spot for another memorial."

"Mind if I get a glass of water?"

"Sure. You should take that suit off. You're going to die in it."

"I just might." I drank the water. "You must be hot in that robe."

"Nah, I got nothing on underneath. That's no come on, you hear? See, when I get too hot, I just go lie down in the little pool I have out back."

"You've got a pool?"

"Just a little plastic one. It's left over from when my daughter's kids were little."

251

"Ah, okay. So, you just skinny dip for all the neighbors to see?" I said with a chuckle.

"Are you crazy? I've got a fence. I keep all those people out of my business. Live and let live, I say. It's the American way."

"Oh, right."

♠

I went back to the fridge: wrenching, screwing, socketing. Mrs. Giles flipped through the channels, not staying longer than a second or two on any one channel, except for when she landed on an old John Wayne western. She stayed on that a while, finally saying, "John Wayne, now that is when men were men."

"So how many grandkids do you have?" I asked, trying to make conversation.

"Three. Three that I know of. Just my daughter has children; my son's too young yet. Well, not too young. He just can't seem to get his act together."

"He'll straighten out."

"He's not a bad kid, just doesn't use his head. For instance, he studied art when he was at junior college. He's got talent but no common sense. He and a girl friend of his from art school—I don't know if she is a girlfriend or a just a friend, but if they are screwing, I sure hope he is using protection. He is not ready to be a dad. I'd probably end up taking care of the little brat—but they were walking by that bowling alley on Guinea Road . . . you know which one I'm talking about?"

"Yeah."

"Well, the side by the railroad tracks, you can't see it from the road, but it's all spray-painted. Now he and his friend thought that since the wall was already covered, they could go and paint it too. So they took some paint brushes and paint and went down there.

Thought of it as a community beautification project." She rolled her eyes and crushed out a cigarette. "The thing is, they did this at three in the afternoon. The owner came out—he was this Korean man— and just went crazy and called the police. My son and the girl were arrested. This wasn't good for my son, because he was already on probation."

I started to loosen the bolts around the old compressor.

"Probation for what?"

"Oh, this is a good one too. He got stopped for speeding. The officer asked if he could search his backpack. He said 'sure,' and the cop found his switchblade."

"What's he got a switchblade for?"

"His father gave it to him. I don't know how long he's had it—*years*, just carries it around like a keepsake or something. I don't know. So he got busted for carrying a concealed illegal weapon. We talked to a lawyer about it, but he said there was nothing we could do since he gave the cop permission. We might have a case if he had said no, but then the cop could have said he had probable cause and searched him anyway. They get you if they want to. You know how cops are."

"Yep, they really sock it to you."

"Thing is, he had weed in the backpack too, but the officer just ignored that." She lit another cigarette and blew a stream of smoke up at the ceiling.

I had the old compressor detached now. It was caked with dust. Its parts were long past salvageable. I pulled the new one out of its box and put the old one in the empty box.

♠

"It's so nice that you speak English," she said to me. "So many of the repairmen now, the delivery boys, the plumbers, don't speak the language any more. You got to be fluent in Spanish, or Korean, or something nowadays."

"Well . . . ."

"It's fine that they come over here; it's just that they should learn the language. I don't mean this to be racist at all, but let's be frank, it's really people like us that understand each other better."

She said it as if there was no arguing, and I guess there really wasn't.

♠

I put together the new compressor and had another drink of water. Mrs. Giles didn't have air conditioning. I wished she did. My clothes were so wet now—like I had worn them in the shower. They were sticking to my body. The washers would have to be replaced before I installed the new compressor. I went to the van to get some. On the way back inside, I saw Mrs. Giles go out into the backyard. I guess she was going to cool off. I wiped my hands clean and pulled out my phone to call Ray. He said no one else had called, so I took my time with the rest of the repairs. I heard a high-pitched sound from the wall. It was the outside spigot. Mrs. Giles was pouring fresh water into her pool. The TV was still on, so I stood in front of it while I polished some bolts. I hummed along with a commercial jingle I liked.

"What did your daddy do?" she asked when she came back inside. Her hair was wet and dripping on the shoulders of her bathrobe, but she didn't seem to mind. She looked as if she felt cool and refreshed.

"He was a refrigerator repair man too."

"Hmmm," she said. "It's always interesting to me how sons follow in their daddies' footsteps."

"He had more work back then, of course. Refrigerators broke down more then. Now they hardly ever do."

"Just my dumb luck then," she said.

"Well, this is an older model," I said. "My dad's dad was a repair man too, plumbing mainly, and his father was an immigrant."

"From where?"

"Eastern Europe. I don't know which country— Prussia, Poland, Austria, one of those. Do all those countries even exist anymore? Seems like they're always redrawing borders over there. I know they came through Ellis Island, though."

"Must have been some Irish in your family. You look like a good Irish boy."

"Possibly," I said and wiped some rust away from a bolt. "They all came over here looking for something better."

She moved the coffee cup to one side of the table and turned the TV so she could see John Wayne shoot a couple Indians, Mexicans, or both.

"A lot of people dying this weekend," she said.

"How's that?"

"Famous people. They just said on the radio this morning. Last night, that the guy who used to read the news died last, and then right after that, they said how this big movie director had died and also this aging Broadway star."

"Hmmm. They must not have liked the summer heat," I said.

"Pretty unpatriotic to die on a day like today."

"My friend's granddad died two days ago."

"They having the funeral next week cause of the holiday?"

"No, had it today."

"You didn't go?"

"No, I'm working," I said.

"Your friend go?"

"He's not really my friend, just a guy I work with, Ray."

"Oh, but did he go?"

"No, had work to do," I said, if getting paid time and half to eat hotdogs and my stolen licorice could be called "work."

The compressor was in and humming away. The fridge would be cold soon.

"You know. You got some rubber hoses back here that are about to go. I'm going to replace them."

"How much?"

"No charge."

"That's mighty nice of you."

"No worries," I said. *No worries,* I think that's what Australians would say.

"I have some beers in the neighbor's fridge next door. I'm going to get them," she said, shuffling across the kitchen in her slippers.

"Sure."

I heard the front screen door slam shut. I yanked the old hoses out, threw them in the trash, then went out to the van. The sun was down, but the air would be hot all night. So hot it made me weak. I sat down in the back of the van before walking back. I found a water bottle in the back. The water inside was so warm, it was undrinkable. I poured it into my hat and dumped it on my head instead. It felt nice. My suit was already so hot and heavy from the moisture, more water didn't make a difference. I saw Mrs. Giles return with the beers, so I got up, wiped off my face, and went in with the hoses.

Mrs. Giles watched me from the table with her beer while I hooked up the hoses, the TV still playing behind her. I could see John Wayne just over her shoulder. He was poised there the way angels or devils are sometimes in the cartoons, whispering in the ears of the characters. I wondered if John Wayne would be an angel or a devil. Mrs. Giles had got real quiet, and I wondered if she was sad. When she saw that I was done, she offered me a beer.

"No, sorry, I'm on the job."

"Come on, it's a holiday."

"Let me finish cleaning up first."

I put away my tools, wiped my forehead, face, and neck again. I picked up my trash, wiped the floor, and took another drink of water. I calculated the bill, writing extra hard on the sheet to press though on the carbon paper. My hands left wet prints on the paper. Sweat, of course. I showed it to Mrs. Giles. She noted the amount, folded it up, and slipped in into the pocket of her robe.

"I'll write you a check."

"Sure," I said.

"You want that beer?"

"Let me think about it."

I went to the van and put away the tools. Went back for one last look. I saw she had left the check for me on the table. The fridge was a bit off center. I knew she wouldn't mind if I left it that way, but I centered it anyway. Mrs. Giles was setting up the TV to watch the DC fireworks. I called Ray. It rang five times. Mrs. Giles settled on a station she liked and tilted her head back to drink another beer. Ray's phone rang five more times. I tapped my foot on the floor. I guessed Ray was watching the fireworks too. I leaned on the counter. Mrs. Giles smiled.

"Look at you, you're soaked with sweat. Go take that horrid suit off and soak your feet in the pool."

Why not? I thought. Why not?

"All right." I went out back, took off my boots, and stuffed my socks in them. I took off the suit and folded it up beside the boots. I was in my boxers and T-shirt now. My whole body was moist and smooth with perspiration. I glistened like I was covered in Vaseline. The backyard grass was yellow and drying. Its brittle blades crunched and occasionally hurt my feet as I walked over them. The pool was little, pink, and plastic. There were pale, sand-colored fish painted on the bottom. I imagined that they were bright yellow before the sun got to them. The hose was by the pool. I stood in the water and sprayed myself. There was a pop in the distance, then a bigger one. I heard the crackle of sparklers and voices over the fences.

"Whooowiiiieee," I said, getting into the spirit of things.

I came back inside. Mrs. Giles had a cold beer for me. Fireworks were exploding on the TV.

"You want to stay and watch the fireworks? I ain't got nothing to eat here, but I've got beer here, and liquor for later. What do you think? You're such a nice boy."

I stood staring at the beer. My boiler suit was in my hand, and I dried myself with it. *Stars and Stripes Forever* was playing on the television. There was an announcer describing the fireworks.

"Why not," I said. "Why not."

There was nowhere else left to go.

19.

Grocery Cart

My son found a grocery cart in the creek today. He plays in the woods and the creek behind our house a lot. The first time we came to see our house, as it was being built, he was only an infant. I carried him down the hill to the creek in the baby-pack on my back. I remember standing there and thinking, "Nick, you'll have a lot of fun down here."

His fingers were so small then. There are a lot of things to marvel at about a baby, but it was his fingers that amazed me the most. They were so small, not even bony then. Now that he's nine, his fingers are much more like my own, longer and skinny. He even has dirty fingernails like I did at that age. I remember the first time he got a cut on his finger; he was two. His mother wasn't home, and he made me feel strong and useful as I swept him up onto the counter, put a Band-Aid on the cut with a kiss, and gave him M&Ms.

I follow Nick and his friend Gi down to the creek where they had found the grocery cart. I like Gi. Nick met him in *Tae Kwon Do* class. The first time I saw Gi was at their test for their green belts. I watched as Gi put his fist right through a board with this bloodcurdling scream. It was like a Bruce Lee movie, if Bruce Lee was an eight-year-old. I could hardly believe it. Nick broke a board that day too, but I could tell he felt more confident after seeing Gi do it first. They were good friends like that.

The grocery cart is upside down and in one of the deeper parts of the creek—deep for this creek is three feet or so. The wheels stick up in the air and look a little ridiculous. The seat and the handle of the cart are submerged, but I can recognize the name of the grocery store where we shop stamped on them. We go up there every weekend.

"Bad teenagers probably did this," my son says.

In my son's world, it's teenagers who are always misbehaving. I find his moralizing a little amusing, but if it keeps him from getting into the trouble I did as a teenager, I don't mind.

"Vandals," Gi echoes.

I'm glad they have consciences. They are good kids, the best. Better than I was. I watch them move around the banks, assessing the situation. Nick, in his bright red windbreaker, looks a little out of place among the softer earth tones of the woods.

"What are you guys going to do?" I ask.

Nick looks at Gi, and then he says, "Let's take it out!"

"Yeah!" Gi says.

"That might take some work. It's really wedged in there, boys."

"We can do it," Nick continues. "We've got all day, and we know the creek. Maybe they'll give us a reward if we give it back."

"Maybe we can make it into a go-cart," Gi said.

"No, Gi," Nick says. "We should return it to its rightful owners. It's the right thing to do."

Who am I to argue with that?

"Good luck boys. Call me if you need any help."

♠

Back at the house, I help my wife, Elaine, with her own Saturday morning project. She is putting lining onto the pantry shelves, so she's pulled everything out of the pantry and set it on the kitchen table. Canned soups, beans, sweet potatoes, bags of corn chips, crackers, and peanut butter sit on the table before me. White potatoes, garlic, and onions are on the chair across from me, beside the roll of plastic lining and scissors Elaine is using. Breakfast cereals rise from the counter like a city skyline. The dog walks by, sniffs the detergents and toilet cleaners on the floor, then moves on. Nothing interesting there. His treats are out of his reach on the counter.

Elaine is placing the lining on the shelves and smoothing out the bumps with her hand. She is crouched, balanced on her tip toes with her knees bent. She looks like a dancer about to take a leap. The position opens a gap in her clothing at the small of her back. Her hair is in a ponytail. She isn't wearing makeup and is in just shorts and an old T-shirt. She'd never go out in public like this, but strangely, I find her beautiful as is. Maybe it's because she wouldn't let anyone else see her like this. I guess there is some security and intimacy in these domestic chores.

We met at my first office job. I was selling equipment to restaurants. I grew up working in my parent's café after Dad got sober, left his corporate job, and opened it up with my mother. I used that job to pay for college and had worked in the front and back of restaurants since. We met when I was just a young, funny-looking guy with an eye patch, trying to make the shift from a blue collar to a white collar job. I'm glad she met me then and not before. We actually attended the same university during overlapping years. But our lives then were not overlapping. She was living in dorms and doing work-study in the library. Me, I was in cramped off-campus housing, living among empty cases of beer and cigarettes, fighting with frat boys, and studying between deliveries in the back of my parents' café.

Compared to this one, I was living in a horrid world at the time: binge drinking, promiscuous sex, drugs, drunken fights, all the things you try to protect your child from. How parents can send their kids to college is a mystery to me. I take comfort in the idea that it is years away for Nick.

I hear the kids rummaging around in the garage. I go outside and see that they are looking for ropes. They find some jump ropes that they decide will suit their purpose and then go back to the creek. I change my clothes, gas up the mower, and mow the lawn. It takes an hour. Afterwards, I use the trimmer to trim the edges of the yard along the sidewalk. I am afraid I'm not quite as good at it as some of my neighbors, whose yards look more like carpets than lawns, but I'm not sure I care enough to put the time and energy into it. I'd rather help Elaine.

Elaine sets up a card table, and we have lunch outside on the back porch, since the kitchen table is still covered with the debris of her pantry operation. We have turkey and cheese sandwiches, with apples and oranges. I call the boys, who return without the cart. I see their shoes and pant cuffs are muddy.

"How's the salvage operation going, boys?"

"It's a lot tougher than we thought. There's a tree fallen across the creek that's really in the way," Nick reports.

"It's really heavy too," Gi says around a bite of his sandwich.

"You guys look like you're getting pretty muddy," Elaine says. The boys are not sure how to react. They can sense her disapproval, but as far as they see it, they are still doing the right thing in salvaging the grocery cart.

"We can't help it," Nick says. Gi becomes quiet, as most kids do when their friends parents are not happy with them.

"Hey, it's not the end of the world. Just wrap some trash bags around your legs and feet, like waders. Then you can walk right into the water," I say.

"Yeah, that's a radical idea!" Nick says. I chuckle under my breath at the fact that the word 'radical' is making a comeback. But Elaine looks at me as if I've just suggested that they parachute from the roof with bed sheets.

"Sidney . . . ."

"It's okay, I used to do it all the time when I was a kid. It works fine. If it doesn't, I'll do all their laundry," I say.

Elaine shakes her head, but she's smiling so I know she's decided to trust me. She says to the boys, "Make sure you have some fruit too."

They tear into their oranges and talk to each other about all the new parts of the creek they can reach, now that they have discovered a way to walk through the water using the trash bag trick.

After lunch, I show the boys how to secure the tops of the bags underneath their knees with rubber bands from the newspaper. I offer to help them with the cart, but Nick says,

"It's alright, Dad. I think we've got it now."

I help Elaine finish the shelves and then go back outside to haul some dead branches out of the woods that will make good firewood in the winter. By the time I have a sizable pile, it's late afternoon, and I go out onto the deck to start a fire for the grill. Afternoons are my favorite time of day on the weekend. There's a feeling of fullness after a hard day of work and the promise of an evening, perhaps lovemaking, and soon another day.

I work on the grill and find myself thinking of a man with a blind son I once saw on the subway. I'm not sure why they popped into my head then, but they just did. I remember that it had been interesting to watch them. The son seemed happy and comfortable, despite his white eyes rolling this way and that in his sockets. The father, he seemed stern. Maybe it was out of self-consciousness, or even shame—which would be sort of sad, I reflect. When the son stepped too close to the edge of the subway platform, the father scolded him. He guided his son's hand, which was holding a white cane, so that the end of the cane moved over the bumps at the edge of the platform. I had never realized until then that those bumps were signals to blind people that they were nearing the ledge.

263

Would I be able to reprimand a blind child, I wonder? That father didn't seem too sympathetic to his son at the time, but maybe familiarity eliminates sympathy. Maybe it was just tough love. Someday the father would be gone, and his son would have to navigate the subways alone. The reprimand came from a place of love, even a fear of loss. I feel a pit in my stomach at the thought, just then, and suddenly feel like I have some insight into the dad. The blind boy never stopped smiling though. That was important. The father was doing something right. I watch the charcoal catch fire and turn red.

Shortly before dinner, I hear the unmistakable rattle of a grocery cart rolling along the sidewalk. I go out front to take in the boys and their victory march. They wave at me, triumphant, from behind the cart, their heads just as high as the handle. One of the wheels can't turn because of mud caked on it. Algae hangs in green strands all over the cage, yet the steel glints in the afternoon sun like a prize trophy. The boys allow me to hose it down for them. Gi goes home for dinner. Elaine and I listen to Nick's account of the rescue operation all through dinner.

"When I get home from work Monday, we'll take it up to the grocery store in the car."

"With Gi, right?" Nick asks.

"Of course, you all are a team."

Nick asks to be excused, so he can go try to get one of the wheels unjammed from the mud. That night, after a bath, he sleeps like a log wrapped in blankets, dreaming of creeks, jump ropes, trash bag waders, and grocery carts.

♠

Monday, I get home at a quarter to six. I drive up to the house, listening to my books on tape, to find Nick sitting by the cart in the driveway. He must be excited to return it and collect a reward. I take off my suit jacket, roll up my sleeves, and lift the cart into the trunk. I use some bungee cords to close the trunk lid down on it and secure it. We pick up Gi at his house and drive to the grocery store. In the backseat, the boys speculate about what kind of reward they might get. I pull up in the loading lane and lift out the cart. The boys take over from there and push the cart inside. They say they want to do it themselves; I tell them that is great and to just ask for the manager when the find an employee.

No one else is pulling up to the loading lane, so I lean up against the car, cross my arms, and watch the boys through the windows. I see the boys walk up to a woman behind a cash register and ask her for the manager. She picks up a phone next to her station and pages her boss on the overhead speakers.

The boys wait beside the cart. Gi has his hands in his pockets. Nick has his on the cart. A tall, balding man in about his fifties in blue pants and striped shirt wearing a keycard on his belt comes up to them. His face is lined, and he does not get that smile that some adults wear when talking to kids. I feel a knot in my stomach for the boys. The manager gives off a grumpy vibe. I can tell Nick picks up on it. But Nick perseveres. I can't hear what he is saying, but he gestures to Gi and the cart, recounting how they had found it. The man listens without saying anything. He looks serious, like he is mediating a disagreement between feuding employees or something. I wonder if he doesn't believe the boys or something. He asks them where their parents are. I can lip read that much. Nick points to me, and the man glances my way.

For a moment, I can see what he sees, as my reflection is staring back at me in the window: a dad in a collared shirt, his tie loosened, his sleeves rolled up, his hair with flecks of premature gray, and an eye patch. Who knew what the manager thinks of that, but hopefully I give the kids' story some credibility as a responsible-looking guardian. But I don't want to intervene. Nick is feeling out his autonomy. I respect that.

The manager reaches into his pocket and pulls out a bunch of keys that he spins around his fingers, like a nervous tick, then shoves them back in his pocket. The motion reminds me of a gunslinger twirling his gun, for some reason. It was an empty gesture though, done out of habit, without much thought or meaning, I realize. He shakes hands with Nick and Gi, then walks away, pushing the cart into a line of other identical ones. Nick and Gi sense that they had been dismissed, their orphaned cart returned to its herd. They trudge out to the car and get in the backseat without saying a word.

I start the car and wait until they are belted in.

"Did he give you a reward?" I ask.

"No," Nick says.

"He didn't walk back to the office to get you something?"

"He said, 'thank you very much' and that he hoped it wasn't too much trouble. Then he said to have a nice day."

"Like the teacher does when you go home for the day," Gi says.

"It was just like that," Nick says.

"He was grumpy."

"He was," Nick agrees.

I can tell they are both disappointed. If I had been that manager, I would have just pulled out a fiver and given it to the kids for their honesty.

"We should have made it into a go-cart," Gi says.

"No, we did the right thing. We returned it to its owner," Nick says like a little sage, like he is trying to convince himself.

♠

We drop off Gi. As we drive down our block, I say, "Well, I think you and Gi deserve a reward, Nick. What you did was really good, and I'm proud of you."

"Why didn't he give us a reward though?"

How do you tell your son that the world isn't fair, that sometimes you do the right thing, and that's its own reward?

"We'll get ice cream this weekend," I say, to buy myself some time, but it doesn't matter to him. Things that far away don't, to kids

"He didn't even seem to care," Nick says.

"I know. I know. But I do. Your mom and I do. We're real proud of you."

He smiles a bit after that. I still want to take him for ice cream though. He deserves it.

♠

Nick is quiet at dinner, like he is trying to process his afternoon. Afterwards, I do dishes and talk to Elaine about how hard it is for kids to be good in today's world. Elaine listens and drinks some lemon ginger tea before she kisses me and heads upstairs to put Nick to sleep. I follow her up when I am finished. She is getting ready for bed herself. I go to check on Nick. He is sound asleep, but his face looks different from the night before. It looks as if he has worn his disappointment to bed. It was his first great hurt from a world that will just keep hurting him. I know then that my words can only ameliorate it so much.

I'm sorry Nick, I'm sorry. I wish I could protect you, your heart, your idealism, from it all—keep you precious and innocent. I wish I could give everyone who ever disappointed you and *will* ever disappoint you a beat down. Bad teenagers, vandals, grumpy managers, even me.

You're better than me. You're better than us all.

267

Made in the USA
Columbia, SC
17 November 2017